ENTERPRISE

STAR TREK®

MY BROTHER'S KEEPER

BOOK THREE OF THREE

ENTERPRISE

MICHAEL
JAN
FRIEDMAN

POCKET BOOKS
New York London Toronto Sydney Tokyo Singapore

An *Original* Publication of POCKET BOOKS

POCKET BOOKS, a division of Simon & Schuster Inc.
1230 Avenue of the Americas, New York, NY 10020

This book is published by Pocket Books, a division of Simon & Schuster Inc., under exclusive license from Paramount Pictures.

ISBN: 0-671-01920-1

First Pocket Books printing January 1999

10 9 8 7 6 5 4 3 2 1

Printed in the U.S.A.

For the New York Yankees,
the best team in baseball

ENTERPRISE

Chapter One

ENSCONCED IN his center seat, Captain James T. Kirk readjusted the cast on his left hand and regarded his bridge's forward viewscreen, where the planet of his birth was depicted in all its deep blue, cloud-swaddled glory. At any other time in his life, the captain would have looked on the sight with gladness and anticipation.

Gladness, because there was something in every man that responded warmly to the sight of the familiar and the traditional. Anticipation, because there were people who loved him on Earth, people whose embrace Kirk would have sought out at his earliest opportunity.

But this time, there was no gladness in his heart, no warmth, no anticipation. There would be no fond reunions with relatives and old cronies lasting long into the night.

After all, the captain was still reflecting on the death of a friend. And not just any friend.

He and Gary Mitchell had been buddies almost since their first encounter at Starfleet Academy fifteen years earlier. They had served on three different ships together, rescuing each other from deadly peril more times than either of them had cared to count.

Then that string of rescues had ended. A peril had come along that was so staggering, so unimaginable, that Kirk hadn't been able to save his pal's life. On the contrary . . .

He was the one who had taken it.

Sometime later, in the irony to end all ironies, Gary's parents had informed the captain that they wanted him to speak at their son's funeral service. In fact, they wanted him to deliver the eulogy, since he was both Gary's commanding officer and his closest friend.

Under other circumstances, it would have been an honor for Kirk, albeit a sad one. It would have been an opportunity to pay tribute to his friend's memory. But under these circumstances, it was a nightmare.

How could he stand up at Gary's funeral and speak of his death as if it were someone else's doing? How could he say such a thing or even imply it, when he knew it was he who had pressed the phaser trigger and sent his friend to an early grave?

The captain sighed. "Establish synchronous orbit," he told Lieutenant Sulu, until recently his astrophysics chief and now his primary helmsman.

"Synchronous orbit," the lieutenant repeated,

making the necessary adjustments on his instrument panel.

"Captain Kirk," said Dezago, the communications officer. "They're ready for you in the transporter room."

Kirk swung around in his chair. "Thank you, Lieutenant," he told Dezago. "Tell them I'll be down there in a minute."

The communications officer nodded. "Aye, sir."

The captain turned to Spock, his Vulcan first officer. "You have the conn," he said.

Spock, who was seated at the science station as usual, inclined his head ever so slightly. "Acknowledged," he said.

It was comforting to know he could count on someone with the Vulcan's intelligence and efficiency. In fact, Kirk would have felt comfortable leaving Spock in command even in the middle of an enemy attack.

As it was, they were in orbit around the planet where Federation headquarters was located, arguably the most secure location in the galaxy. The captain didn't anticipate trouble of any kind.

At least, not up there.

With that thought in mind, Kirk got up and headed for the turbolift. As the doors opened with a whisper of air, he entered the compartment and used his good hand to press the control stud indicating the transporter deck. The doors slid shut and he was on his way.

Less than a minute later, the lift deposited the captain at his destination. The transporter room was only a few meters away, down the corridor to the right. Still, when Kirk reached its double doors, he couldn't help hesitating for a moment.

Beyond these doors, he told himself, was change—and quite possibly a great deal of it. When he came back the next day, his sojourn on Earth complete, things would be different.

There would be personnel alterations at the very least. New faces coming, familiar ones going. But it was the face of the man sitting in the captain's chair that he was most concerned about at the moment.

What kind of person would he be when he returned to the *Enterprise?* One who had come through his ordeal with his self-respect intact—or one who had compromised himself for the sake of his duty to the point where he could no longer look at himself in the mirror?

Only time would tell.

Taking a deep breath, Kirk moved forward and saw the red orange doors part at his approach. There were four people waiting for him inside the room—Lieutenant Kyle, who was standing behind the control console, and the three crewmen gathered on the round, slightly elevated transporter pad.

One of them was Mark Piper, who had served as chief medical officer on the *Enterprise* since the captain assumed command of the vessel a year earlier. The doctor was retiring from the fleet after a long and prestigious career to spend more time with his children and grandchildren.

On Piper's right was Daniel Alden, the *Enterprise*'s primary communications officer. Alden's fiancée had gotten a job as administrator of a

Federation colony and he was leaving the ship to be with her.

Yeoman Barbara Smith stood on Piper's left. An attractive woman with an efficient, thorough manner, she had somehow never clicked with Kirk. However, he knew that was his fault as much as hers, considering he had only recently managed to recall her name with any consistency.

"Captain," said Piper, as Kirk approached the platform.

"Doctor," the captain replied. Then he glanced at the others. "Alden," he said. "Smith."

"I guess this is it," said the communications officer.

The captain smiled—first at Alden, and then at the others as well. "I guess it is," he replied. "But before you go, I want to thank you for all the good work you've done on this ship. Those you leave behind will always be in your debt."

The yeoman smiled back at him. "It's nice of you to say so, sir."

"I'd be remiss if I said anything else," Kirk told her.

"Captain," said Kyle, "they're ready to receive our friends here down at Starfleet Headquarters."

The captain nodded to show he had heard. "Thank you once again," he told the trio on the transporter pad. Then he glanced at the transporter technician and said, "Energize, Mr. Kyle."

A moment later, the air around Piper, Alden, and Smith began to shimmer with an iridescent light. Then they and the light faded to nothingness as their molecules were absorbed into the transporter's pattern buffer and sent streaming down to Earth along an annular confinement beam.

Kirk sighed and wondered if he would ever see any of them again. At the rate the Federation was growing, it seemed unlikely. But then, one never knew.

"How long before we greet our new arrivals?" he asked Kyle.

The technician consulted his instrument panel. "Not long," he told the captain. "In fact, sir, any moment now."

Right on cue, three separate forms began to take shape on the Enterprise's transporter platform. One of them was male, the other two female. Very female, Kirk couldn't help but notice, even before the newcomers completed the materialization process.

Under happier circumstances, he might have studied the women a little more closely. As it was, all he could think about was the friend he had left behind on Delta Vega.

"Welcome to the *Enterprise,*" he told the newcomers, knowing how flat his voice must sound to them.

The male figure, a rawboned, boyish-looking specimen, descended from the platform and held out his hand. "Pleased to meet you, Captain. Lieutenant David Bailey reporting for duty."

Despite the cast he was wearing, Kirk took the man's hand. Bailey's grip was strong and enthusiastic—and if he hadn't held back because of the captain's injury, it might have been even more so.

Somehow, Kirk thought, frowning, David Bailey hadn't looked quite so baby faced in his Starfleet file photo. If he had, the captain might have thought twice about making the man his primary navigator.

Then again, he reminded himself, Bailey had impressed the staff of the *Carolina* with his charting abilities and his command potential. *I probably shouldn't be judging a book by its cover,* he mused.

"At ease," Kirk told the lieutenant.

Bailey smiled. "Thank you, sir."

By then, the two women had stepped down from the transporter platform as well. They flowed around Bailey as a river might flow around an especially obtrusive hunk of rock.

"Lieutenant Uhura," said one of them, a dark-skinned beauty with long lashes and prominent cheekbones. "Communications," she added.

Alden's replacement, the captain remarked inwardly. He shook her hand as well—not very warmly, he was afraid. "Uhura."

The other woman, who had flaxen hair and sparkling blue eyes, introduced herself as Janice Rand. "Yeoman," she explained, as if her uniform weren't explicit enough on that point.

"Yeoman," said Kirk.

He scrutinized the newcomers for a moment, finding intelligence and an abiding curiosity in their faces. They all seemed capable, responsible, eager. No doubt they were among the finest the fleet had to offer.

But the captain couldn't give them any guarantee they wouldn't wind up as Gary had. As Kelso had. He couldn't assure them their lives wouldn't be cut short before their curiosities were satisfied.

"Again," he said, "welcome aboard. Mr. Kyle here

will be happy to direct you to your quarters, where you'll find your duty schedules posted." He frowned. "At some point, I would like to speak with each of you individually. But right now, other matters require my attention."

"Of course, sir," Bailey replied.

"Acknowledged," Uhura responded.

Kirk looked at them a moment longer, trying to see people standing there in front of him and not prospective casualties. It wasn't easy, he thought, sighing again.

Finally, he said, "Dismissed."

The newcomers moved aside for him and the captain ascended to the transporter platform. Then he turned to his transporter chief and said a single word: "Energize."

Uhura watched the transporter effect surround Kirk with its undulating brilliance. A moment later, he was gone.

She made her way across the room to the transporter control console. The transporter technician, a tall man with blond hair and a narrow face, was still gazing at the empty platform.

"Is he always like that?" she asked.

The blond man turned to her. "Beg your pardon?" he asked with a distinct English accent.

"The captain," she said. "Is he always so solemn?"

The transporter operator smiled a little sadly at her. "No," he told her. "Not always, Lieutenant."

Uhura glanced at the empty platform, as if something of Kirk remained there that might give her a clue about his demeanor. "He looked as if he had lost his best friend."

The blond man frowned at the remark.

"What did I say?" the communications officer asked, realizing she had hit some kind of nerve.

"As a matter of fact," the transporter operator explained solemnly, "the captain did lose his best friend."

By then, the yeoman and Lieutenant Bailey had joined Uhura at the control console. "Under what circumstances?" asked Bailey.

The blond man looked uncomfortable. "To tell you the truth, sir, I'm not really sure about that. No one is—it's classified information. And the captain hasn't made any effort to fill us in. All he's said is that Lieutenant Mitchell died in the line of duty."

"In the line of duty," Rand echoed appraisingly. "I guess that's the way I'd want to go." She glanced at Uhura, then Bailey, and reddened a little. "I mean, if I had to go at all."

"One never knows when one's time is up," Bailey remarked soberly.

"That's true," the yeoman responded in the same theatrical tone of voice. "One never does."

But as she said it, she turned to Uhura and rolled her eyes. The communications officer had to suppress a laugh.

Well, she thought, more than a little relieved, *at least one person on this ship has a sense of humor.*

One moment, Kirk was standing on the *Enterprise*'s transporter platform, gazing at Kyle and the three newcomers he had just greeted—if it rightfully could have been called a greeting given the lack of warmth and enthusiasm he had demonstrated.

The next moment, the captain found himself on a considerably more spacious platform in the transporter room at Starfleet Headquarters. And it wasn't Kyle or Uhura or Rand or Bailey he was looking at. It was Leonard McCoy, hotshot research biologist at Starfleet Medical and, more importantly, one of Kirk's best friends.

"Jim," said McCoy, obviously torn between his happiness at seeing the captain and his sadness at the reason for it.

"Bones," Kirk replied, stepping down off the platform.

McCoy put a hand on the captain's shoulder and squeezed it affectionately. Then he glanced at Kirk's cast. "What happened to you?"

The captain shrugged. "I'll explain later."

His friend accepted the answer. "Come on," he said. "Let's get out of here, shall we?"

Kirk couldn't have been more surprised. "Get out . . . ? But aren't you on duty?" he asked.

"To hell with duty," the doctor responded. Then he took his friend's arm and led him in the direction of the exit.

"To hell with duty?" Kirk echoed. He took a closer look at his friend's face, but the biologist didn't seem particularly upset by anything. "That doesn't sound like the Bones McCoy I knew on the *Constitution.* That Bones McCoy couldn't have been dragged out of his lab by a team of muscle-bound security officers."

The biologist harrumphed. "Well," he said, "maybe I've learned a few things since I was that Bones McCoy."

"Such as?" the captain asked as they emerged from the transporter room and made their way down the corridor, passing headquarters personnel going in the other direction.

His friend shrugged. "Such as . . . you take from life what you can get, whenever you can get it. Because when it's over, it's over, and there are no second chances."

Kirk made another attempt to read the man's profile—to no avail. "And . . . you came to that conclusion when your father died?" he guessed.

McCoy shook his head from side to side. "I came to it when you sent me the message about Gary. My father was an old man, at least, god rest his soul. He'd had a chance to live. By comparison, Gary was only a baby."

A baby who had seen the stars, the captain thought. But that didn't mean he didn't see the sense in what his friend was saying.

"So where are we going?" he asked, as they made a left turn down another corridor.

A smile tugged at the corners of McCoy's mouth. "A little hole in the wall I found after I moved back here. You're going to love it. It's called Velluto's and they make the best—"

"Veal saltimboca?" Kirk ventured.

The biologist shot him a searching look. "I was going to mention their seafood fra diavolo . . . but, yes, they make a great veal saltimboca, too." His eyes narrowed. "I guess you know the place."

The captain grunted. "Are you kidding? My senior year, I ate there every Sunday night. I guess I never mentioned it."

McCoy grunted, too. "Or maybe you did. I probably had my nose in a medscanner at the time. Anyway, Sal's expecting us."

Kirk nodded, allowing the years to fall away as he remembered. "Sal . . . my god, Bones. I wonder if he ever married that woman who used to sit at the corner table."

"By the big, ol' mural of Positano?"

The captain smiled. "That's right. You've seen her?"

The doctor chuckled as they stopped at a turbolift. "Damned right I have. And let me tell you, the woman still sits there a lot. But that's only because she wants to keep an eye on her husband."

Kirk was delighted that Sal had gotten his heart's desire. "Good for him," he replied. "Gary always said she'd—"

He tried to finish his sentence, but he couldn't. His mouth had suddenly gone dry. The smile must have vanished from his face because McCoy's vanished as well.

"You all right?" the biologist asked.

The captain nodded. "Fine," he said, readjusting his cast.

But he was anything but fine. The tragedy of his friend's death was weighing him down again, crushing him the way he had tried to crush Gary with that rock on Delta Vega.

For a moment, Kirk had forgotten what had happened to his friend. For a moment, he had begun to smile again. But it was only for a moment.

"Listen, Jim," said McCoy, his expression a sympathetic one, "if you'd rather we didn't—"

The captain held up his good hand. "No. I want to go." He took a deep breath and watched a couple of officers walk by. "I want to see Sal again. After all, I have to congratulate him."

His friend seemed to sift through the statement, analyzing it for its truth content. The researcher in McCoy must have been satisfied with the results, because he said, "Yes, you do. And I imagine Sal will be glad to see you too, after all these years."

Kirk had an idea. "Just one request," he told McCoy.

"What's that?" the biologist asked.

"Let's walk there," the captain suggested.

McCoy smiled a little uncomfortably. After all, the restaurant was a mile away up a pretty steep hill, and Kirk knew his friend had never been one for pursuing an exercise regimen.

But McCoy didn't argue with him. All he said was, "Suit yourself."

Chapter Two

ON THE WAY to Velluto's, which was nestled among hundred-year-old, white towers on the old, patrician incline of Nob Hill, Kirk and his friend the research biologist spoke of many things.

First, they spoke of McCoy's daughter. Joanna McCoy had gone on a ski trip to Wyoming and broken her leg crashing into a tree. Of course, the doctor said, the injury had occurred on the last day of the excursion, after the girl had sent him a message telling him what a good time she was having.

Apparently, the injury wouldn't have taken place at all if Joanna hadn't been horsing around with a boy who had caught her eye. The boy in question broke an arm on a neighboring tree.

"Teenagers," McCoy muttered, as an old-fashioned cable car slid up the street beside them on electromagnetic rail tractors. "You can't live with them and you can't place them in stasis chambers until they've attained some modicum of sanity."

The captain and his friend also spoke of the *Constitution* and the officers under whom they had served there. Captain Augenthaler, First Officer Hirota, and Chief Medical Officer Velasquez had remained on the vessel, Kirk had heard. However, Communications Officer Borrik, a Dedderac, had returned to his homeworld to assume the leadership of his clan.

"What about Gaynor?" asked the biologist.

Several weeks before McCoy's arrival on the *Constitution,* Kirk had thrown security chief Jack Gaynor in the brig for insubordination. But by the time the doctor came aboard to work under Velasquez, Kirk had forgiven Gaynor—and vice versa.

"He transferred to the *Potemkin,*" the captain said. "Left a couple of months after you did, in fact."

"I thought you and he had made your peace," McCoy suggested.

Kirk shrugged. "We did. In fact, I'd filed several commendations for him, as you know. But a second officer's slot had opened up on the *Potemkin* and Gaynor jumped at the opportunity."

The biologist grunted. "So he finally got what he wanted."

"I guess so," the captain returned.

The two of them climbed the hill for a while in silence, the sky a deep blue canopy arching over them, the waterfront sprawling below them in all its alabaster glory.

Finally, they spoke of Gary Mitchell.

"You didn't get along with him when you first met," McCoy commented. "I remember you telling me that."

"We were different," Kirk noted. "He was irresponsible. I was a stickler for doing the right thing."

His friend chuckled. "Seems to me you must have rubbed off a little on each other. By the time I met Gary, he was anything but irresponsible. And you . . . well, you scared me sometimes."

The captain was surprised. "I scared you?"

McCoy nodded. "You seemed so eager to take risks. You were like a kid with a new toy."

Kirk had never thought of himself that way before.

"It's funny," the biologist continued. "Unlike you, I got along with Gary pretty much right off the bat. But then, I never ended up getting as close with him as you did."

The captain looked at him. "What was it you called him that time?"

McCoy thought about it for a moment, squinting in the bright sunlight. "When he was trying to get Carvajal to switch shifts with Barton?"

Kirk nodded, picturing the scene in his mind. He could see his two best friends, Gary and McCoy, squaring off in the rec lounge—not angry, exactly, but pretty close to it.

"I said he was manipulative," the biologist recalled.

"That's right," the captain said. "Manipulative."

"He just went too far sometimes," McCoy remarked. "There was a certain arrogance about him, as if he didn't just think he was right—he *knew* it."

He frowned. "But I have to say, even when he was playing god, his heart was always in the right place."

Playing god? Despite the warmth of the day, Kirk felt a chill in the small of his back. Had Gary been doing that all the way back on the *Constitution?* Had he been treating people as if they were pawns on a giant chessboard?

Then the captain remembered their days at the Academy together—how Gary had tried to mold him into what he thought a commanding officer should be, how he had even tried to orchestrate his friend's romances. Maybe he *had* played god, long before he ever gained the power to become one.

But there was a difference. Until his transformation began, Gary had never manipulated anyone or anything for his own benefit. He had always performed his machinations with others in mind.

Suddenly, McCoy stopped and drew a deep breath. "All right, Jim. Do me a favor. Tell me you didn't want to do this just for the exercise."

Kirk looked at him, caught off-guard. "I beg your pardon?"

"To be honest," said the biologist, "my feet are killing me . . ." He held his thumb and forefinger about a millimeter apart. ". . . and I'm about this close to jumping on the next cable car. So if there's something you want to talk to me about that you can't say in a restaurant, I wish you'd let me know what the hell it is already."

Kirk gave in. "All right, Bones. I'll tell you what it is."

As luck would have it, a park was looming on their right—a plot of grass and shrubs surrounding a marble spire dedicated to those who had perished in the Battle of Donatu V. There were several benches made of the same marble positioned along the perimeter of the greensward.

They looked too comfortable to pass up. "Let's sit," said the captain, "shall we?"

The two of them sat on a west-facing bench and Kirk felt the sea breeze wash over him, full of brine and bluster. Beside him, McCoy waited with uncharacteristic patience.

"Where to begin," said Kirk.

"Always a problem," his companion conceded.

The captain sighed and picked a place. "Some weeks ago, I received orders from Starfleet Command. Classified orders, mind you. The kind that I wasn't supposed to discuss with anyone."

"Not even an old friend at Starfleet Command?"

"Not even him," Kirk confirmed.

"Or it would cost you your career?"

"Something like that."

McCoy nodded. "I hear you. Go on."

The captain frowned as he reconstructed the briefing in his mind. He could see Admiral Saylor's face on the monitor screen in his quarters as he outlined the mission's parameters.

"They wanted the *Enterprise* to go out to the edge of the galaxy, Bones. They wanted me to map what I found out there."

His friend's eyebrows shot up. "The edge of the galaxy, eh? You must have been excited."

"To say the least," Kirk replied. "No Federation vessel had ever probed that far. It was going to be a groundbreaking voyage—and Starfleet Command had selected the *Enterprise* to carry it out. I was proud of that, I don't mind telling you. Damned proud."

He glanced at the base of the memorial spire, where the names of the Klingons' victims were inscribed. They hadn't been the first to die in space, he thought, nor would they be the last.

But some deaths are better than others, the captain told himself. Not only for the deceased, but for those who remain behind. Some deaths are clean, straightforward. And others . . .

"So you went," McCoy prodded him.

Kirk nodded. "And the trip was relatively uneventful. The most remarkable thing we encountered was an asteroid belt. Then, shortly before we arrived at the prescribed coordinates, we discovered something unusual after all—an old disaster recorder."

His friend tilted his head. "A what?"

"A disaster recorder," the captain repeated. "They were launched by spacegoing vessels in the twenty-first century whenever things looked bleak. That way, if the situation continued to go downhill, there would at least be a warning posted so other ships wouldn't make the same mistake."

McCoy regarded him incredulously. "This thing was two hundred years old? Are you pulling my leg?"

"Not in the least. What's more," said Kirk, "it was still functioning. Mr. Spock analyzed its memory banks and found out it was launched by a ship called the *Valiant,* which had set out from Earth nearly a hundred years before the dawn of the Federation."

His friend whistled. "And it was out there, near the galaxy's edge? Two hundred years ago?"

"Not just near the edge," the captain replied. "It went *past* it. But in the process, it seemed to have run afoul of some unknown force—something that battered the *Valiant* and claimed the lives of six of her crewmen."

"Sounds ominous," said McCoy, his expression clouding a bit.

"I thought so too, at the time," Kirk recalled with a shiver. "And the behavior of her captain sounded even more ominous. Not long after the *Valiant*'s encounter with that unknown force, he began searching the ship's data files for information on ESP."

"Extrasensory perception?" the biologist asked wonderingly. He shook his head. "What the devil for?"

A cable car bell rang in the distance. The air seemed to vibrate with the sound.

"Our question too," said the captain. "Unfortunately, the man in charge of the *Valiant* didn't tender an answer. Then, after a while, he stopped searching for data—and started thinking about destroying his ship."

McCoy's eyes narrowed. "That's horrible. But . . . did he say why? Did he give a reason?"

Kirk shook his head. "No. He just went through with it. At least, that's what the evidence suggests."

His companion mulled that last part over. "So, essentially, he was telling everyone to turn back—to avoid whatever fate he fell victim to."

"I suspect he was," the captain agreed.

"But knowing you," McCoy continued, "you didn't do that."

"No," Kirk admitted softly, as the cable car bell rang again. "I didn't. If anything, I thought the warning made it more important that I investigate. After all, I told myself, other Federation ships would come that way eventually—and when they did, they had to know what they were up against."

The biologist chuckled humorlessly. "I know you like a book."

"Maybe so," the captain allowed. "In any case, I went on. And I hoped our twenty-third-century technology would enable the *Enterprise* to survive whatever had doomed the *Valiant.*"

He was wrong, it would turn out. Terribly wrong. But he didn't want to get ahead of himself.

"Before long," he said, "we came to the edge of the galaxy—or at least, what we in the Federation have come to think of as the edge of the galaxy. That's when we found what the *Valiant* had found—some kind of undulating, naturally occurring energy field. We could see its glare, measure the force it exerted against the deflector shields . . . but external sensors couldn't seem to get a coherent fix on it.

"Nonetheless," Kirk went on, "we stuck with our mission and went in for a closer look." He could feel the muscles in his stomach tighten. "That's when everything started to fall apart."

McCoy was interested—intensely interested. "In what way?"

The captain told him how the *Enterprise* was tossed about like a leaf in a tornado. The captain told him about the disabling of the ship's warp drive and the casualties the crew suffered.

And he told him what happened to Gary Mitchell.

"Lit up?" the biologist echoed.

Kirk nodded. "As if he were an old-fashioned light bulb and someone had just given him a jolt of electric current. And he wasn't the only one. There was a young psychiatrist on the ship, a woman named Elizabeth Dehner. The same thing happened to her."

McCoy screwed up his features in an expression of sympathy. "Is that how Gary died, Jim?"

Kirk shook his head. "No. Gary didn't die. He just . . ." How could he put it? ". . . underwent some significant changes."

The biologist looked at him, almost as annoyed as he was fascinated. "Now, what the blazes does that mean?"

The captain adjusted his cast again. Here and now, overlooking the ocean and a pristine array of upland buildings under a bright blue sky, it was difficult to imagine that any of it had happened. Gary's transformation and death . . . it all seemed so impossibly far away.

But back then, on the dark and lonely edge of the galaxy, it had been as real as the matter-antimatter reaction that gave the ship the power to traverse the stars, or the blood pumping through Kirk's veins. It had been as real as life itself.

"His eyes were the first indication of it," the captain remembered. "As soon as I picked him up off the deck, I saw them glowing at me."

"Glowing?" McCoy blurted.

Kirk nodded. "Hard to imagine, I know. They stayed that way, too, even though the rest of him appeared to return to normal." He swallowed. "But he wasn't normal, Bones. He was already starting to become something inhuman. Something strange and powerful."

McCoy scowled. "You're scaring me, Jim."

"No more than Gary's transformation scared me, Bones."

"When you say strange and powerful . . ." The biologist struggled with the concept. "What do you mean, exactly?"

The captain shrugged. "He began reading at speeds even Spock could barely believe. And when Dr. Dehner was in his room, he shut down his vital signs. Frightened her half to death, it seems."

McCoy was at a loss for words. No doubt he was pondering what he had been told, trying to wrap his mind around it.

"Then," said Kirk, "he graduated to fiddling with the *Enterprise*'s critical systems—taking them over, if you can imagine that—and all from the comfort of his biobed."

His friend stared at him, his face having lost some of its color. "That's powerful, all right."

Birds cried out in the distance, as if echoing the sentiment.

"About that time," the captain told him, "Mark Piper discovered something. Apparently, Gary, Dr. Dehner, and the nine crewmen who had perished had something in common."

McCoy looked puzzled for a moment. Then, gradually, his eyes lit up, as he began to put two and two together. "Don't tell me," he said. "A talent for extrasensory perception."

"Exactly right," Kirk confirmed, impressed with his friend's insightfulness. "Suddenly, the *Valiant*'s logs took on a whole new sense of immediacy for us. Had there been someone like Gary on the *Valiant?* we wondered . . . someone who had begun to evolve into something superhuman? And had the *Valiant*'s captain feared him enough to destroy his vessel rather than bring that individual back to Earth?"

McCoy sighed. "So what did you do?"

What indeed? the captain thought. "Nothing, at first. After all, I had always trusted Gary implicitly, no matter what was at stake. Sure, there was something in his attitude . . . an arrogance, a disdain for those around him . . . that put me on my guard a bit. But I couldn't bring myself to believe he was a threat to my ship and crew."

"And Dehner?" asked the biologist. "She was a psychiatrist, wasn't she? What did she say?"

"She believed it even less," Kirk replied. "But then, she was young, and she may have had some feelings for Gary."

He shook his head as he recalled how Dehner had argued on Gary's behalf in the *Enterprise*'s briefing room. At the time, she had made sense. In retrospect, he wasn't so sure.

"We were fools, as it turned out. Both of us," he said.

McCoy regarded him. "And what changed your mind?"

The captain frowned. "I have Mr. Spock to thank for that—Spock, with his dispassionate, characteristically Vulcan view of the situation. He set me straight about Gary. Then he told me I had two choices—I could kill my friend or I could abandon him on a barren, unpopulated world called Delta Vega, the site of a lithium cracking station."

"My god," said McCoy.

Across the street, two people walked by—two ordinary people who had never heard of Gary Mitchell. They would never know how narrowly they had escaped his godlike attentions.

"At first," Kirk told him, "I rejected both those options. Spock told me that was probably what the captain of the *Valiant* had said at first. As you can imagine, that put things in perspective for me. Reluctantly, I had Kelso chart a course for Delta Vega.

"But when we got there," the captain went on, "Gary knew what we were up to. By then, he was able to read people's minds almost effortlessly. Still, we got him to drop his guard long enough for us to sedate him, then beam him down to the planet."

"And you left him there?" asked the biologist, understandably horrified by the prospect.

Kirk shook his head. "Don't forget, our warp drive was in need of repair. We imprisoned Gary behind a forcefield while we cannibalized some of the station's hardware to fix the drive." He swallowed. "It turned out to be a mistake. We shouldn't have lingered there, no matter what."

"Something went wrong," McCoy divined.

"Very wrong," the captain admitted. "We—or rather, I—misjudged the rate at which Gary's power was growing. As we were getting ready to leave, he reached out with his mind and strangled Kelso with a power cable. Then he burst free of the prison we'd made for him, knocked us unconscious and took Dehner with him."

"Poor girl," said his friend, perhaps thinking of his daughter.

"That's what I thought," Kirk recalled, "when I woke up some time later. And I couldn't help thinking it was my fault Gary had taken her, my fault he had gotten so far."

He looked down and saw that his fingers had curled into fists. With a conscious effort, he relaxed them.

"I left orders for Spock," the captain said. "If I didn't contact the ship in the next twelve hours, he was to take the *Enterprise* out of orbit—and then irradiate Delta Vega with full-intensity neutron beams. Then I picked up a phaser rifle Spock had brought down with him and went after Gary . . . as if I were some kind of big game hunter."

"You were taking quite a chance," McCoy observed.

"I thought I had to," Kirk told him. "He had Dehner at his mercy—or so I believed. As it happened, I was wrong again."

"How's that?" asked his companion.

Kirk sighed. He told McCoy how he had heard Gary's voice in his head, assuring him that he would find his friend if he took the right path—and how, a moment later, he had turned around and seen Dehner standing there.

"She had changed, too, Bones," he related. "Her eyes . . . they were glowing just like Gary's."

McCoy muttered a curse. It drifted away on the warm air.

"Pretty soon, I realized, Dehner would be just as powerful as he was, just as evolved. And I wouldn't have a chance against two of them. Hell, I might not have a chance against *one.*"

"What did you do?" asked his friend.

The captain shrugged. "I tried to enlist her help—tried to appeal to her humanity. It wasn't easy. She was already thinking like Gary, already talking like him. But I played on her fear of him, and then on her pride in her abilities as a psychiatrist, and little by little I started to get somewhere. I started to wear her down.

"But before I could get her to help me," he said, "Gary himself showed up. He had changed even in the short time since I had seen him last. His hair was graying at the temples and his eyes seemed dreamier, somehow, more alien even than before. He scrutinized me as if I were some kind of insect, barely worth his notice."

McCoy shook his head, but he didn't say anything. He seemed to have his hands full just taking it all in.

"I fired at him," Kirk remembered, "for all the good it did. As far as I could tell, Gary didn't even feel it. With a gesture, he disarmed me. Then he dug me a grave."

"Dug . . . ?" said his friend.

"With a blast of his power," the captain explained. "He even made me a headstone with *James R. Kirk* inscribed on it."

"But your middle name is—"

"Tiberius," Kirk acknowledged. "It was a joke

between Gary and me. He never forgot it—not even when he was about to kill me."

"But he *didn't* kill you," McCoy pointed out. "Or we wouldn't be sitting here having this conversation."

"He didn't," the captain agreed, "but only because Dehner saw what was happening. She saw that Gary was becoming colder and crueler with each passing moment, just as I had told her he would. So, before he could put the finishing touches on my demise, she sent him staggering backward with a bolt of pure white energy."

"One titan attacking the other," the biologist breathed, his eyes losing their focus as he tried to picture the majesty of it.

"It was something to see, all right," Kirk conceded. "A battle for the ages. Either one of them was powerful enough to rip a hole in a starship, if he or she wanted to. But for the moment, thankfully, all they wanted to do was rip holes in each other.

"Back and forth they went, sending bolt after bolt at each other, weakening each other more and more. Dehner, unfortunately, hadn't evolved as quickly as Gary had. In the end, she couldn't stand up to him. The last blow she took was a mortal one.

"But she hadn't given her life in vain," the captain said. "Gary was drained by the exchange, exhausted—so much so that the light had gone out of his eyes. I knew it was the last chance I would have to stop him . . . and I took advantage of it."

McCoy's Adam's apple climbed his throat. "You tried to kill him."

Kirk nodded grimly. "I did. But I had no choice, Bones. He wasn't Gary anymore. He was something so monstrous, so dangerous—"

The other man waved away the explanation. "You don't have to excuse what you did, Jim. At least, not to me. I know you would never have hurt Gary if there were any other way."

"Never," the captain responded. "That's the truth. But there *was* no other way. So, while he was weakened, vulnerable, I battered him with my fists as hard as I could. Eventually, I knocked him off his feet. I straddled him, found a boulder . . . and raised it over my head."

Even now, light-years removed from the experience, Kirk could feel his heart race. Even in this beautiful city by the bay, he could feel the soreness of his limbs and the lethal weight of the boulder in his hands.

"Then he looked up at me," he said, "and I hesitated. After all, it wasn't a monster I was looking at. For a moment, at least, it was Gary again, dazed and innocent looking—and there was at least a possibility that his power had abandoned him for good."

The captain frowned. "So I hesitated . . . and it was almost the end of me. Gary's power returned and he flung me away, almost breaking my neck in the process.

"I tried to grapple with him some more," he said, "but I knew I didn't really have a chance. I was just hanging in there as long as I could, hoping against hope that another opportunity would present itself. And to my amazement, it did.

"Gary picked up a boulder about as tall as he was and prepared to crush me with it. But he underestimated how much steam I had left. I moved quickly enough to tackle him around the knees and send us tumbling into the grave he had dug for me.

"Certainly," said Kirk, "Gary was much more powerful than before. His strength was immense, greater than anything I had ever seen. But he wasn't any quicker than the average human being. I, on the other hand, was propelled by fear—not only for myself, but for the four hundred men and women orbiting the planet above us, and beyond that, for the rest of the galaxy.

"With the help of that fear, I climbed out of the grave first and spotted my phaser rifle. It was only a few meters away at the bottom of a rocky slope. I slid down the incline as quickly as I could, grabbed the thing and whipped it around. And as Gary began climbing out of the grave after me, I tried to think of a way to beat him.

"I knew it wouldn't help to hit him with a barrage," the captain recalled, adjusting his cast again. "He'd already shrugged off my phaser beam. Then I caught sight of a huge hunk of rock in the cliff face above him—a hunk of rock he had begun to loosen a few moments earlier.

"Taking aim, I fired at it. It fell on Gary, appearing to crush him, driving him into the grave meant for me." The captain took a breath, let it out. "I waited, half expecting him to obliterate the rock and come climbing out of the grave again. But he didn't.

"Unbelievably," said Kirk, "my friend Gary was dead. And against all odds, I had survived."

McCoy swore beneath his breath. "It's unbelievable, all right."

The captain searched his friend's face. "You mean what Gary became? Or the fact that I killed him?"

The biologist shrugged. "Both, I suppose." He glanced at Kirk's wrist. "And that's how you hurt yourself? Tussling with Gary?"

"With what he'd become," the captain insisted.

High overhead, a hovercar skimmed the tops of the buildings, twisting in the bright sunlight. Somewhere down the hill, beyond the Academy, the surf pounded the Pacific shore.

"So . . . are you all right with all this?" McCoy asked finally.

Kirk made a bitter sound deep in his throat. "Sometimes it doesn't seem real, you know? Those are the good times, the times when I can go about my business. Then I remember the way Gary looked up at me when I was holding that boulder over him, as if he couldn't believe I would have the heart to do him in. I guess you'd say those are the bad times."

A couple of birds alighted on the neatly cut grass in front of them and began pecking for worms. Somewhere in the distance, someone was playing the upbeat music of an ancient orchestra.

"Come on," said McCoy. "Sal's expecting us."

The captain nodded. "It'll be good to see him," he replied, though he had a feeling he had mentioned that already.

Then the two of them got up from their marble benches, took a last look at the spire dedicated to those who had died fighting the Klingons, and resumed their trek up the hill.

Chapter Three

KIRK WAS GLAD he had told his friend about Gary's death before they got to the restaurant. It enabled them to leave the horror of what happened to Gary outside the place—to cleanse themselves, in a way, before they sat down at their table.

Besides, Velluto's wasn't a place where one went to mourn. It was a place where one went to celebrate life.

It made that statement with its light and airy Mediterranean decor, with its immense skylights, with colorful pottery and paintings scattered about the place with apparent abandon. It made that statement with its menu, a wild collection of dishes that mixed the daring with the traditional.

But most of all, it made that statement through its host, the effervescent and omnipresent Sal, who hadn't changed one iota since the captain frequented Velluto's a decade earlier. The man was as energetic as ever behind his thick, dark mustache, moving from table to table to make sure his guests were all being taken care of.

When the restaurant owner set his eyes on Kirk, they crinkled at the corners for a moment. Then recognition seemed to set in and a smile spread across his face.

"Jim!" he said, grabbing the captain's hand and squeezing it with unexpected strength. "Jim Kirk! How long's it been?"

"Ten years," the captain estimated, smiling back despite his somber mood. "Maybe as many as eleven."

"And look how you've come up in the world!" Sal exclaimed, stepping back to admire Kirk's uniform and the bars on his sleeve. "I guess you've got your own ship now, eh?"

The captain nodded. "The *Enterprise.* Constitution-class."

The man's eyes widened. "The *Enterprise* . . . that's you? I've heard a lot about that ship."

Kirk shrugged. "Nothing bad, I hope."

"Bad?" Sal echoed incredulously. "She's the pride of the fleet. If I'd known, I would've sent you some tiramisu to congratulate you. You always liked my tiramisu, eh, Jim?"

"Yes," the captain conceded. "I did, indeed."

The restaurant owner turned to McCoy. "And you . . . how do you know this guy? You serve on a ship together or something?"

"That's it, exactly," said the biologist. "On the *Constitution.*"

Sal nodded. "I've heard of that ship, too. It's not a bad one, either, from what I understand." He glanced slyly at Kirk. "Of course, it's no *Enterprise,* but it's not bad."

The captain couldn't help chuckling a little. "You're too kind," he told the restaurateur.

"No," Sal told him, "I'm just kind enough." The skin around his eyes crinkled again. "And your friend," he said, "the one who used to win all those drinks at my bar . . . what was his name again?"

The captain felt a cold shadow fall over him, even in the midst of all that filtered sunlight. "You mean Gary," he answered, adjusting his cast again. "Gary Mitchell."

The restaurateur laughed. "Gary . . . yes, of course. How is he, anyway, bless his thieving heart?"

Kirk frowned. "Sal, he—"

Suddenly, the proprietor's eyes brightened and he held up a forefinger, cutting the captain off. Reaching over to the next table, he secured a cloth napkin and brought it over. Then he wrapped the thing around the top of Kirk's slender water glass.

Using the napkin like an old-fashioned measuring tape, Sal touched its corner to its hem to mark the length of the glass's circumference. Then, grasping that same spot on the hem between thumb and forefinger, he let the rest of the napkin dangle.

The restaurant owner looked up at them, an antic expression on his face. "Your friend Gary, he would ask people which was greater, the height of their glass or the measurement around it. And they would look at him like he was crazy. After all, with a tall, thin glass in front of them, everyone figures it's going to be the height, right?

"But he would say no," Sal went on. "The measurement around, he would say, is greater. And he would bet them a drink that he could prove it."

The restaurateur lowered the napkin next to Kirk's glass until its corner was just brushing the table. Of course, the spot between his thumb and his forefinger was higher than the glass's lip.

The captain wasn't surprised. Like Sal, he had seen Gary perform the same trick a hundred times.

"Then," said their host, "he would show them he was right. The way around really *was* greater. And they would curse themselves for being so stupid and buy him a drink."

Sal shook his head and stuck the napkin in his pocket. "Those were the days," he chuckled, "eh, Jim?"

"They were," Kirk agreed.

"So where is he?" asked the restaurateur. "Gary, I mean? What's he doing these days?"

The captain sighed. "I hate to be the one to tell you this," he replied, "but Gary died recently."

The color drained from Sal's face. "No . . . you're kidding me, right? You're pulling my leg?"

Kirk shook his head. "Believe me, I wish I were. He was killed on a world called Delta Vega just a few days ago."

"My god," said the restaurant owner, "I'm so sorry." Suddenly, it all came together for him. "That's why you're here on Earth . . . isn't it? For your friend's funeral?"

The captain nodded. "That's right." Apparently, he wasn't the first Starfleet officer who had passed through San Francisco on his way to a colleague's memorial service.

Sal regarded the two of them for a moment. "I'll tell you what," he said. "I'm going to send a bottle of wine over to your table. On the house, of course. So you can toast your friend Gary's memory."

"That's very kind of you," said McCoy, "but—"

The restaurant owner held up his hand. "I insist, Doctor. A toast to Gary Mitchell. It's the least I can do."

Kirk smiled. "Thank you, Sal."

The man dismissed the idea with a wave of his hand. "As I said," he replied, "it's the least I can do. Bon appetit, gentlemen."

As Sal withdrew, McCoy chuckled softly. "I think you caught him off-guard, Jim. Did you see the look on his face?"

"I tried not to embarrass him," the captain noted. "Unfortunately, he walked right into it."

"Unfortunately." The biologist leaned back in his chair. "So, you haven't told me . . . when and where?"

Kirk looked at him for a second, wondering what he meant. Then it hit him. "The funeral, you mean. It's tomorrow, in New York."

"I'm going with you, of course," said his friend.

The captain smiled. "I figured you would want to."

He paused for a moment, asking himself if this was the best time to ask McCoy what he needed to ask. In the end, he decided it was probably as good a time as any.

"Bones," Kirk began, "I've got a bit of a problem. I believe you can solve it for me."

The biologist eyed him suspiciously. "A problem? You mean, beyond what happened to Gary?"

"That's right."

McCoy shrugged. "Tell me about it and I'll see what I can do."

"All right," said the captain. "You know Mark Piper, don't you? The CMO on the *Enterprise?"*

"Not well," said his friend, "but I know him by reputation. An old buddy of mine has spoken rather highly of him."

Kirk understood the reference. "I guess I have, at that. But then, the man has served me well for the last year or more. The problem is Piper's leaving. Retiring from Starfleet."

McCoy grunted. "Good for him. He's earned it." Then he added, "Who have you gotten to replace him?"

The captain looked at him. "I haven't gotten anyone yet, Bones. But I have my eye on a pretty talented candidate. Someone I've worked with before, as a matter of fact."

For a fraction of a second, the biologist seemed intent on figuring out whom Kirk was talking about. Then realization dawned.

"You're not referring to me, are you?" he asked.

"Why wouldn't I?" the captain returned. "I've seen you in action, Bones. They don't come any better."

"But . . . that was years ago," McCoy sputtered. "Dammit, Jim, I'm a research biologist, not a doctor."

"And a pretty good research biologist from what I understand. But I saw the kind of work you did on the *Constitution,* remember? If you performed half as well on the *Enterprise* I'd be getting my money's worth."

The other man shook his head, his forehead creased with thought. "I don't know. I mean, I just finished a tour of duty on Capella Four. It wasn't exactly what I'd call satisfying."

"Well," said Kirk, "I've never had the pleasure of visiting Capella Four, Dr. McCoy. But I've been to Kratosian Prime and Bender's Planet and Pareil Seven, and I've seen you save lives in those places that no one else could have saved."

"My work here saves lives too," the biologist argued.

But the captain could tell by the sound of his friend's voice that he wasn't arguing from his heart—not really. He was putting up barriers in the hope that Kirk could knock them down.

"No offense to Starfleet Medical," said the captain, "but there are dozens of people qualified to do what you do. But how many doctors have the wisdom and the toughness to serve as the chief medical officer of a starship?"

McCoy didn't answer him. Not right away, at least.

"All right," he said at last. "I see your point. But I'll need some time to think about it. After all, it's a pretty big decision I'll be—" Suddenly, his expression changed to one of annoyance. "Aw, who am I kidding? I haven't been happy at Starfleet Medical for some time now. You want a chief medical officer? By god, you've got one!"

Kirk smiled. "Welcome aboard, Doctor."

His friend nodded. "It's good to be aboard . . . Captain."

Just then, their waiter arrived at the table with a bottle of dark red wine in hand. "Chateau Picard," he said, "one of the few French varieties Sal carries. I believe you'll enjoy the vintage."

The captain looked at the label. The bottle was nearly twenty years old. "I believe we will," he agreed.

The waiter extracted the cork from the wine bottle and offered it to Kirk. Sniffing its aroma, the captain nodded to show that he approved of it. Then he watched as the waiter poured a little into his glass.

"I'm sure it's fine," he said, declining the traditional sip.

"As you wish," the waiter replied. Then he poured for both Kirk and McCoy, set the wine bottle down on the table and left the two Starfleet officers to their own devices.

The biologist picked up his glass and swirled the contents around. "It's not Saurian brandy," he remarked, "but it'll have to do."

"To Gary," said the captain, raising his glass with his good hand.

"To Gary," McCoy echoed, clinking his glass against his friend's.

Kirk sipped his wine. It was full-bodied, flavorful. He might even have enjoyed it if the circumstances were a little different—if he didn't have so much on his mind.

His friend looked at him askance. "Let it go, Jim. Just try to relax for a little while."

The captain shook his head. "There's more to it, Bones."

"More to it?"

Kirk nodded and stared into his wine. "Gary's parents have asked me to deliver the eulogy at his funeral service."

McCoy regarded him for a moment, absorbing the import of the remark. Then he said, "You lied to me, didn't you?"

Kirk looked at him, perplexed. "Lied about what?"

"You said you had just one problem," the doctor replied. "Sounds to me like you've got at least two."

The captain nodded again. "I've got to get up in front of his friends and family, Bones, and tell them a story about how he died. Can you imagine if I told them the truth? Gary was a great friend and a terrific colleague, folks. Oh, and by the way, I'm the one who killed him."

McCoy leaned back in his chair and folded his arms across his chest. "I hear what you're saying. It's a dilemma, all right." He paused. "On the other hand, maybe it's not such a bad idea."

Kirk looked at him. "What isn't?"

The doctor looked back. "Telling them the truth," he said.

The captain recoiled at the very thought of it. "Are you out of your mind?" he asked.

McCoy shrugged. "Maybe so. But wouldn't it make you feel better if you *could* tell them the truth—the same way you told me?"

Kirk shook his head. "Why even consider it? I can't do it. Not at Gary's funeral service. Not when we're supposed to be mourning him."

"You can't tell everyone," his friend agreed. "But you can tell some of them. The ones who matter."

The captain didn't know what McCoy meant, at first. But after a moment, he began to figure it out.

"You're talking about Gary's parents," he concluded. "You think I should tell them how Gary really died."

His friend leaned forward. "I'm no psychiatrist, Jim, but I can see how this is eating at you. I think it would eat at you a damned sight less if you told the Mitchells the truth."

Kirk swallowed. Even if he could work up the courage, he thought, even if he could find the words . . .

"What if they hate you for it?" McCoy asked, posing the question the captain would have posed to himself.

Kirk nodded. "What then?"

The other man appeared to weigh the possibility. "Then you'll have to live with it."

The captain made a derisive sound in his throat. "Not much of an improvement, I'm afraid."

"I'm not saying it'll be easy," McCoy told him. "But at least you'll have given them their due. For godsake, if you were in their place, isn't that what you would want? To know the truth?"

Kirk considered it. It didn't take him long to come to the conclusion that his friend was right. *I would want to know the truth,* he told himself, readjusting his cast on his wrist.

No matter how badly it reflected on the messenger.

Chapter Four

THE MITCHELLS LIVED on Manhattan Island, a continent away from Velluto's and Starfleet Headquarters, in a sleek, well-lit forty-story edifice overlooking the dark flux of the East River.

Thanks to the Starfleet transporter facility in Battery Park, the captain had been able to leave San Francisco and cross the continent almost instantaneously. And the officer on duty had been kind enough to have a hover taxi waiting for him at the curb.

Kirk wrapped his coat around himself against the autumn chill and shouldered his way into the weather. Sensing his approach, the door panel slid open. He got in.

"Where to?" the vehicle's computer voice inquired in the vernacular of the old-time cabbies who used to ply Manhattan's thoroughfares.

"Uptown," he replied. "Three Twenty East Fifty-third Street."

"Gotcha," said the computer as the taxi began to ascend. "Sit back and enjoy the ride."

A moment later, he was speeding through the city's deep canyons, her pedestrian walkways a good thirty meters below him. Other vehicles zipped by at various heights and velocities and in different directions, all of them coordinated by a network of traffic computers.

The captain had forgotten how gaudy Manhattan could seem to an occasional visitor, from its white-crowned skyscrapers to its green-glowing street-lamps to the red, blue, or purple signs announcing its restaurants, night spots, and never-closing coffee bars. With the rain sheeting hard against the cab's windows, it seemed even more exotic, more alien.

Then the Mitchells' building separated itself from the other behemoths, and Kirk felt a little more at home. In fact, he might have smiled at the sight except for the icy coldness in the pit of his belly.

Suddenly, the vehicle dropped to street level and made a loop to stop in front of the captain's destination. He breathed a sigh of relief. Somehow, he felt more comfortable in a starship careening through space at warp six than a New York taxi weaving its way through traffic.

Tapping his personal commerce code into the wafer-thin pad on the surface in front of him, Kirk watched the readout reflect the transaction. Then he touched the control stud next to him and saw the door open.

As he got out, cold, heavy drops pelted his head

and the back of his neck, the sidewalk around him hissing with their concerted assault. Pulling the collar of his coat up higher, the captain made his way through the front door of the building into the cavernous, imitation-stone lobby.

It was much quieter inside. And when the door slid closed behind him, it was quieter still. He ran his fingers through his hair, shedding raindrops on the orange ceramic floor.

"Please identify yourself to the party you wish to see," said an artificial female voice. "The communications panel is on your left."

Kirk hadn't needed to be told. He recalled the place well enough from all the visits he had made here in previous years. Crossing to the comm panel, he entered the number of the Mitchells' apartment.

It took only a few seconds for a response to manifest itself on the panel's readout. *Entry authorized,* it said.

The elevator that served the west side of the building was just a few paces away. The captain pushed the button on the wall beside it and the doors whispered open. Then he got in, saw the door panels close again and heard the mechanism begin to hum.

It was a short ride—less than thirty seconds to ascend to the thirty-fifth floor. From Kirk's perspective, it was *too* short. He reached his destination before he was ready for it.

But then, he wondered, how could one ever be ready for something like this? How could one prepare for the hardest thing he had ever done?

When the lift doors opened, the captain stepped

out and looked around. It was just the way he remembered it. A foyer with four black doors, the gaps between them illuminated by narrow, vertical lighting strips. The first door on the left was the one he wanted.

He drew a breath, touched the pad beside the door and waited. It would take a few moments, he estimated, before Gary's parents could stop what they were doing and react to the chime. He steeled himself.

Then, with breathtaking suddenness, the door in front of him slid aside with a rush of air. And there they were—Mr. and Mrs. Mitchell. The parents of the man Kirk had killed on Delta Vega.

Thomas Mitchell was a sturdy, broad-shouldered man with thinning hair and dark, inquisitive eyes. His wife was small and slim by comparison, an attractive brunette with high cheekbones and blunt but expressive features.

It had been a long time since the captain had seen them in person. More than a few years, in fact. Perhaps that was why Gary's parents looked so much older than he remembered—older and grayer and more beaten down.

Or maybe it was something else. Something other than just the advance of the years.

Losing your only son can do that to you, he found himself thinking. *It can whittle you out, leaving your skin too big for your bones and your eyes too big for their sockets.*

"Jim," said Mrs. Mitchell. She pulled him in and hugged him earnestly, as if he were her own son. "It's good to see you."

"I wish I could've come sooner," Kirk told the woman as she eased her embrace, "but I was called to a starbase first to—"

"Don't apologize," Gary's father interrupted. "We understand. You're the captain of a starship. Your life's not your own, right?" He clapped the captain's shoulder and reached for his hand—until he saw the cast on Kirk's wrist. "Little gymnastics injury?"

The captain didn't tell him that he didn't do much in the way of gymnastics anymore, because that would have begged the question as to how the injury had really occurred. "Something like that," he said instead.

"Give me your coat," said Mrs. Mitchell, tugging at a wet sleeve even before the captain could divest himself of the garment. "Can you believe this weather? It's like a monsoon out there."

Gary's father grunted. "I'm sure the boy's seen worse, Dana. He's probably been on planets where it *never* stops raining."

As he turned his coat over to Gary's mother, Kirk nodded. "That's the truth," he replied politely. "Quite a few, in fact."

Mr. Mitchell ushered him into the living room, where two comfortable-looking black couches faced each other across the expanse of a transparent, free-form table. The walls were decorated with colorful oil renditions of Paris, London, and Rome.

The captain hadn't recognized the locales the first time he set foot in Gary's parents' apartment some fourteen years earlier. Back then, he hadn't seen enough of Earth to distinguish Boston from Barcelona, much less one planet from another.

It was Gary who had taken the time to identify the subject of each painting for him. Unlike his friend, Gary had been around the block a few times. As he had once gibed, he was the city mouse to Kirk's country mouse.

And now he was dead. Here more than other places, it was a difficult thing to believe. The captain half expected Gary to come walking into the room as he had so many times in the past, a couple of cold ales in his hands and a jest on his lips.

Rain stitched and sloshed its way across the only window in the room, a large, rectangular pane that stood perpendicular to both couches. Through the darkness and the downpour, Kirk could see the distant, distorted glows of penthouse lights on the neighboring apartment buildings.

"I'm glad we had a chance to get together before the funeral service," said Mr. Mitchell. He tilted his head to indicate the kitchen. "Can I get you something? Some wine, maybe?"

The captain shook his head. "Thanks, but no. Actually, I just wanted to talk to you for a moment."

Gary's father turned to his mother, who had hung up Kirk's coat and was joining them in the living room. "Something for *you,* dear?"

Mrs. Mitchell thought for a moment. "Maybe some tea. But I'll make it." She glanced at the captain. "Tom brews it so strong I can't drink it. You'd think after all these years, he would have learned."

As his wife left the room, Gary's father shrugged.

"She's right. A simple thing like making tea . . ." His voice trailed off as he contemplated the phenomenon, probably not for the first time. Then, as if remembering that there was someone else in the room, he looked up and blushed. "I've been doing that a lot the last few days," he said.

"Doing what?" asked Kirk.

The man smiled self-consciously. "Getting all wrapped up in little things. Forgetting where I am and who I'm with."

The captain's heart went out to him. "It's not very difficult to understand," he said.

"You mean under the circumstances," said Mr. Mitchell.

Kirk nodded. "Exactly."

Gary's father grunted. "You'd be surprised how many times I've run into that phrase since we learned of Gary's death. 'Under the circumstances, Mr. Mitchell.'" He shook his head helplessly. "I'll be glad not to hear it anymore, I can tell you that."

The captain didn't know what to say to that. Fortunately, Gary's mother chose that moment to return to them. She held a tray with a gray, ceramic teapot and three matching cups.

"I know you said you didn't want any," she told Kirk, "but . . . well, I brought a cup for you anyway. I know how shy you can be about taking food from people—even people who are like family."

Like family. The words echoed in the captain's mind as he adjusted his cast for the twentieth time that day. He wished Gary's mother hadn't used them. Hell, he wished a lot of things.

"Now that you mention it," Kirk said, "maybe I

will have a cup." After all, he didn't want to disappoint the woman.

Mrs. Mitchell smiled knowingly and poured the tea. She gave the captain the first cup and her husband the second. Only when they had been served did she pour a cup for herself.

"So," she said at last, sitting down next to Mr. Mitchell, "you said you wanted to talk about something."

Kirk's heart began thudding in his chest. "That's right," he told Gary's mother, "I did, didn't I?"

The Mitchells sat there on the other side of the transparent table, looking at him expectantly. The rain pattered a little harder against the windows, but only the captain seemed to notice.

"There's no easy way to say this," he started out.

His voice must have sounded grave because it made Gary's mother put down her teacup. "What is it, Jim?" asked Mr. Mitchell.

What indeed, Kirk thought.

He tried to give the man an answer, but his mouth suddenly became a senseless, clumsy mess of flesh, unwilling to do his bidding. Refusing to stop now, he pressed it into service as best he could.

"I . . ." he began.

Gary's parents continued to regard him. Their concern was evident in their faces, though they didn't know yet what they were concerned about.

The captain tried again. "I . . ."

I killed your son, he thought.

But he couldn't seem to make himself say it out loud. Maybe, he told himself, because speaking the words would change his entire world—and once they were out there, they couldn't be taken back.

The Mitchells leaned forward, something deeper than concern etched in their faces now. "Go ahead and take your time," Gary's father advised him, managing a smile. "We're not going anywhere, y'know."

Kirk knew that expression, that tone of voice. They were the same ones Gary had often used when he was hurt or scared about something. And with their help, the navigator had fooled people. He had made them think he was doing fine when he wasn't doing fine at all.

The captain recalled the last time Gary had done that. And as he did, the memory seemed to stick in his brain. Suddenly, he couldn't think about anything else—including the two people sitting opposite from him, waiting for him to go on with his confession.

There had to be a reason the memory wouldn't let him go, Kirk told himself—and he had a feeling he knew what it was. After all, he had believed once before that he was the cause of his friend's death.

It had begun on a planet called Dimorus . . .

Chapter Five

THE NAVIGATOR LAY pale and motionless on his biobed, the dark circles under his eyes making the sockets look disturbingly hollow. If not for the persistent throbbing of the life-signs monitor above the bed, the captain would have been convinced that Gary Mitchell was a goner.

Out of the corner of his eye, he saw Dr. Piper and Nurse Hinch enter the pastel-pink enclosure. Kirk acknowledged their presence with a glance.

"How's our patient?" asked the chief medical officer.

The captain managed a smile, albeit a weak one. "I thought *you* were going to tell *me*, Doctor."

Piper studied Gary's monitor for a moment, then shrugged. "Well enough not to need sedation, I'd say."

He asked his nurse for a hypospray full of something. Hinch, a squarish woman with a perpetual scowl, went over to a drawer and followed the doctor's instructions, then delivered the hypo.

"Thank you," said Piper and held the device to his patient's neck. He glanced at Kirk. "Just try not to get him too excited, all right? I'd hate to have to put him under again."

"I promise," said the captain.

He heard a low hiss as the doctor emptied the contents of his hypo into Gary's system. A moment later, his friend's eyes fluttered open. Gary looked around, orienting himself. Then he realized that Kirk was standing there and he grinned.

"Miss me?" he asked over the hum of the engines.

"Did you go somewhere?" the captain quipped back.

"The way I feel," said the navigator, "it must have been all the way to hell and back. I haven't been this fatigued since I spent a weekend with the Renault triplets."

"I remember the Renault triplets," Kirk returned. "And I doubt even they could have laid you out this way."

His friend smiled and heaved a sigh. "I guess you don't remember them the way *I* remember them."

The captain turned to his chief medical officer. "Is the poison going to have any lasting effects, Doctor?"

"Yeah," Gary asked Piper with feigned seriousness, "am I going to get varicose veins or something?"

Kirk had to smile. His friend's sense of humor was returning. Clearly, that was a good sign.

The doctor eyed his patient soberly, then shook his head. "No, Captain, no lasting effects as far as I can tell. It'll take a couple of days, but Mr. Mitchell should be fine. Of course, if he had received the antidote just a few minutes later . . ."

"It would've all been over for me," Gary interjected, completing the older man's thought. "Go ahead and say it, Doc. That way, it'll make a better story when I tell it in the rec lounge."

Piper frowned. "All right, Commander. If we hadn't gotten the antidote to you as quickly as we did, your exposure to the alien poison would have likely proved fatal. Satisfied?"

Gary leaned back in his bed. "It would've been better if I'd saved a beautiful woman like Nurse Hinch here instead of some wet-nosed captain . . . but I think I can make it work."

Hinch scowled at the mention of her name. But then, not everyone was a fan of the navigator's womanizing remarks.

The doctor turned to Kirk. "You've got two minutes, Captain. Then your friend here needs to get some rest."

"You're the boss," Kirk assured Piper.

As the doctor and Nurse Hinch left the enclosure to see to some of their other duties, the captain regarded Gary. "You know," he said, "you gave us quite a scare there for a moment."

The navigator grunted. "I gave *you* a scare? How do you think I felt when I saw that rat-faced Dimoran setting his sights on you? You know how embarrassing it can be to come home without your commanding officer?"

The captain did know, of course. Several years earlier, he had come home without his commanding officer on the *Farragut*—a memory that still twisted in his gut from time to time. But in his weakened state, Gary seemed to have forgotten about that.

"Anyway," said Kirk, "I'm glad you're going to be okay. Is there anything I can get you while you're convalescing? Something to read, maybe?"

His friend chuckled. "You mean that long-haired stuff you inflicted on us back at the Academy? Not on your life, old buddy. I'd rather mix it up with the Dimorans again."

The captain shrugged. "Have it your way."

Gary looked up at him, waxing serious for a moment. "Actually," he told Kirk, "there is one thing you can get me."

"And what's that?"

The commander's sober expression gave way to a grin. "They say a bottle of Saurian brandy can do wonders in poison cases."

"Right," said the captain. "I'll smuggle some Saurian brandy into sickbay—and afterwards, you can visit me at the penal colony on Tantalus Five. I'll tell you what, Mitch . . . you get yourself a clean bill of health from Dr. Piper. *Then* we'll talk about that bottle of Saurian brandy."

Gary shrugged. "Fair enough."

"I guess I should go," Kirk told him. "The doctor says you need your rest, and he ought to know."

"Go on," said the commander. "Get out of here."

The captain started to leave. But he hadn't gotten halfway to the exit before Gary called his name and made him turn around.

"What now?" Kirk wondered, feigning impatience.

"For the sake of those busybodies in the rec lounge," said the navigator, "how about we say it was *three* darts?"

"It'll make for a better story?" the captain asked.

"Infinitely better."

"In that case," said Kirk, "why not?"

"Thanks," said Gary. "You're a pal."

Piper stuck his head into the room. "Time's up, Captain. You'll have to come back later."

"I hear you, Doctor," Kirk replied.

With a last comradely glance at his friend, he left and returned to the bridge.

As Piper rejoined his nurse in the softly lit, pink corridor that connected Mitchell's patient care unit with all the others, he saw that Hinch was frowning even more deeply than usual. "Something troubling you?" he asked.

"I don't like that man," the nurse told him.

"No?" said the doctor, as he began to make his way down the corridor.

"Not at all," Hinch insisted, as she fell in line alongside him.

"Because he doesn't treat you with respect?" Piper asked.

"Because he doesn't treat *anyone* with respect. Not even the captain," the nurse pointed out. "Did you see the way Mitchell spoke to him? As if Captain Kirk were his lackey, not the other way around."

The doctor grunted. "I wouldn't exactly call the commander a lackey."

"You know what I mean," Hinch said. "He shouldn't be speaking that way to his commanding officer. I mean, can you imagine if anyone else spoke to Captain Kirk that way? He'd find himself charged with insubordination faster than you can say 'court martial.'"

"You know," Piper reminded her, "the captain and Mitchell are old friends. They served at the Academy together."

The nurse glanced sharply at him. "And you think that gives the commander the right to mock him? In public, especially?"

The physician shrugged. "I don't particularly approve of it, no. But it's not my place to judge. It's the captain's—and if it doesn't bother him, I don't suppose it bothers me, either."

Hinch harrumphed. "Well," she said, "it bothers *me.* And from what I understand, it bothered Captain Augenthaler as well."

Piper looked at her. "Augenthaler? On the *Constitution?*"

"That's right. I have a friend who works in the science section who knew Commander Mitchell when he was posted there. She told me the commander didn't treat Captain Augenthaler any more respectfully than he treats Captain Kirk."

"Is that so?" the doctor asked.

"It's so, all right—and Mitchell and Augenthaler were most definitely not Academy buddies. In fact, I wouldn't be surprised if Commander Mitchell wound up on the *Enterprise* because no one else would take him."

Piper stopped in front of the doors to another

patient care unit and frowned. "As I understand it, the captain and the commander came over from the *Constitution* together. You don't think Augenthaler rejected both of them, do you?" he asked half-seriously.

The nurse pondered the idea for a moment as if it were a real possibility. Then she shook her head. "No. I think it's what I said before. Captain Kirk brought Mitchell over because no one else would have him."

The doctor sighed. Hinch's mother must have been bitten by a bulldog, he decided. Once the woman had embarked on a train of thought, she wouldn't allow herself to be deterred for anything.

"In that case," Piper told her with just a hint of sarcasm in his voice, "it's lucky for Mitchell he's got a friend in Captain Kirk. Otherwise, he wouldn't have anyone for whom to risk his life on a regular basis."

Hinch started to nod . . . then stopped herself. "Was that a joke?" she asked the chief medical officer, her tone a bit suspicious.

Maintaining a deadpan expression, Piper shook his head. "I'm a doctor, Nurse Hinch. I don't have time for jokes."

Then he advanced on the doors, watched them open for him, and went to see to his next patient.

Captain's log, supplemental.

We have completed our survey of Dimorus, our landing parties having managed to avoid further contact with the planet's lone sentient species. Commander Mitchell—who sustained serious injuries protecting his commanding officer from the above mentioned species—has recovered from his wound and returned to duty. We are now proceeding to the Muhlari system to chart the changes that have taken place there since the Federation's last visit more than thirteen years ago.

Gary Mitchell leaned across the rec lounge table and lowered his voice, though there were only the four of them in the room. "You guys hear the one about the Klingon prison camp?"

Scotty, who was seated on the other side of the table between Kelso and Sulu, looked askance at the navigator. "I cannae say I have," he replied, his voice echoing.

"Me, either," said Kelso.

"But I bet you're going to tell us about it," Sulu chuckled.

The navigator took that as an invitation. "Well," he said, "as it happens, an Earthman is captured by the Klingons during a skirmish out near the neutral zone. They bring the poor bastard to a prison camp in some steamy, smelly jungle, where he meets the commandant of the place."

"Sounds lovely," Scotty commented.

"Naturally," Gary went on, "he's expecting all manner of horrors at this place. But the commandant tells him it's not as bad as he thinks. After all, Klingons are a lot more sensitive than other species give them credit for. The prisoner says he doubts that."

"I'm with him," Kelso interjected, drawing a

laugh from his companions—the navigator included.

"Anyway," Gary said, "to prove his people aren't as vicious as they're made out to be, the commandant goes on to outline the prison camp's schedule of events. 'Tell me,' he says, 'do you like good food?' The guy says, 'Of course I do.' And the commandant says, 'Well, you're going to like Mondays. Every Monday, we have a picnic on the grounds of the prison, and we serve all kinds of Klingon delicacies. But because we're sensitive to the needs of other races, we also serve Vulcan mollusks, Terran hot dogs, Orion wing slugs and Romulan ale.' "

"Doesn't sound half-bad," Sulu remarked.

"That's what our friend the prisoner is thinking," the navigator noted. "Then the commandant asks him, 'Do you like listening to music?' The Terran says, 'Sure, I guess so.' And the Klingon tells him, 'Then you're going to like Tuesdays. Every Tuesday, we perform a Klingon opera for all the prisoners. But because we know tastes can vary from planet to planet, we also bring in musicians from Earth and Vulcan and other Federation worlds to display their talents.' The prisoner says, 'You're kidding me.' And the commandant says, 'I wouldn't kid about something like that. We Klingons take our music very seriously.'

"Then the commandant asks the guy, 'Do you like women?' And the guy says, 'Very much so.' And the Klingon says, 'Then you're going to like Wednesdays. You see, we know how lonely prison life can be, so every Wednesday we bring in a ship full of women from one of our other prison camps . . .

women of every species, I might add, so each prisoner can find his or her own soul mate to help pass the time.' "

"Where do I sign up?" asked Kelso.

Gary grinned. "The Terran can't believe all this. He asks the Klingon if it's all true, and the Klingon swears by his first ancestor that everything's just as he says it is. And the prisoner is beginning to think he's not going to have such a bad time at this place after all.

"Then the commandant claps him on the shoulder and says, 'Tell me, my friend . . . do you like being in an arena with a dozen strapping warriors, carving each other to pieces with razor-sharp blades until only one of you is left standing to bellow the praises of the Empire?'

"The Terran looks at him, horrified. 'Uh . . . no,' he says, 'I don't think I'd like that at all.' And the Klingon says, in a sympathetic voice, 'In that case, you're not going to like Thursdays.' "

Scotty laughed his heartiest laugh. Sulu chortled as well. But Kelso was so amused he could barely contain himself. In fact, he threw his head back so hard his chair tipped and he went sprawling backward onto the floor.

That made Gary laugh too. And when they saw him laugh, his friends laughed that much harder. Before the navigator knew it, there were tears standing out in his eyes.

Still lying on his back, Kelso shook his head as if he were being tortured. "You're not going to . . . to . . ."

"You're nae goin' t' like Thursdays!" Scotty blurted out, red faced with honest mirth.

Sulu shook his head. "That's a good one," he gasped.

"Oh, man," Kelso moaned, holding his stomach. "Oh, man . . . for godsakes, Gary, you're going to be the death of me."

"Mr. Mitchell," said a voice that rang authoritatively through the rec lounge, "whatever you've been doing to my helmsman, I suggest you desist . . . before you disable the man permanently."

The navigator glanced over his shoulder and saw the figure of Jim Kirk standing inside the open doorway. As the doors whispered closed behind the captain, Gary turned all the way around and got to his feet.

"Begging your pardon, sir," he said, doing his best to contain his merriment, "but whatever damage I may have caused Mr. Kelso was entirely unintentional, I assure you."

"Acknowledged," Kirk replied, obviously resisting a smile. "I know how little you enjoyed being in sickbay yourself. I'm sure the last thing you would want to do is put your friend there."

By then, Scotty and Sulu were helping the helmsman to his feet. Kelso looked embarrassed but none the worse for wear, despite the captain's remarks to the contrary.

Gary took a breath to steady himself, then let it out. "So what can we do for you, sir? Engage a Klingon battle cruiser? Beam down to Rigel Ten to rescue some hardheaded ambassador?"

Kirk chuckled dryly. "Nothing quite so dramatic,

Mr. Mitchell. I just came to inform you gentlemen that I'll require your presence in the briefing room in ten minutes."

Scotty nodded briskly. "We'll be there, sir."

"Aye, Captain," said Sulu.

"Ten minutes, sir," Kelso confirmed.

The navigator shrugged. "Whatever you say, sir."

It wasn't a Starfleet response. But then, his friend wouldn't be expecting one. Not from him.

Kirk shook his head in mock disapproval. Then he turned to the lounge's exit again and the doors opened for him. A moment later, he was gone.

Sulu whistled. "I don't know how you do it, Mitchell."

Gary glanced at him. "Do what?"

"How you get away with it," Sulu explained. "If I said that to the captain, I'd find myself in the brig."

"You and me both," Kelso commented, picking his chair up off the floor. "But then, we didn't go to the Academy with Captain Kirk."

"Hey," said the navigator, grinning, "can I help it if I always seem to be in the right place at the right time?"

"Speakin' of that, we'd better get up t' the briefin' room," Scotty noted. "After all, the captain made a point of comin' down here t' tell us about the meetin' himself. The least we can do is be on time."

"Mr. Scott's right," Gary declared. "Let's get going."

As the other men filed past him on the way to the door, he put his arm around Kelso and said, "Tell me, Lieutenant. Do you like good food?"

Caught by surprise, the helmsman doubled over

with laughter and nearly slammed his shoulder into the bulkhead beside the door. Pulling him back on course, the navigator guided him out of the exit.

After all, he had promised his friend Jim he wouldn't do Kelso any permanent damage, and he was nothing if not a man of his word.

Kirk looked around at the officers who made up his command staff. There were six of them seated around the briefing room's sleek, oval table: Spock, Piper, Kelso, Scott, Sulu, and Alden.

And Gary. Of course, Gary.

"As you're no doubt aware," the captain said over the ever-present hum of the engines, "the Muhlari system contains a binary star pair in a potentially cataclysmic configuration, which is why the Federation is interested in the system in the first place."

Heads bobbed in agreement.

Kirk went on. "We know that such a configuration produces violent nova outbursts when one star comes into relatively close proximity to the other. As a result, we were prepared to turn our shield strength up a notch as we approached the system's coordinates."

"I sense a 'but,'" said Gary.

The captain nodded. "You sense correctly, Mr. Mitchell. A little while ago, long-range sensors turned up something we were *not* prepared for—namely, a series of subspace wormholes."

"A series?" Kelso repeated. "As in more than one?"

"More than one," Kirk confirmed. "They range from less than a hundred meters to two thousand meters in diameter. What's more, they seem to be appearing and disappearing without following any obvious pattern."

"Wormholes are by nature unpredictable," Spock pointed out.

"So I've heard," said the captain. "And if there were any inhabited planets in the system, we would certainly have cause for alarm. Fortunately, that's not the case. We have only ourselves to worry about."

"And you'd like to know what we have to do in order to worry a little less," Piper ventured.

"Exactly," said Kirk. "Suggestions?"

Alden frowned. "We'll have to see if there's any particle activity that precedes the appearance of one of the wormholes." He smiled at Spock. "Maybe we can learn to predict the unpredictable."

Poker faced as usual, the Vulcan shrugged. "We can certainly make the attempt," he said.

"We dinnae know if these wormholes have any pull t' them," Scotty noted thoughtfully, "but just in case, we'll divert as much power as possible t' the impulse engines."

"Good idea," said the captain.

He knew full well that he couldn't bring the *Enterprise*'s warp engines to bear anyway. Within the bounds of a solar system, especially one as complicated as Muhlari, a warp maneuver could wreak havoc.

"There's another problem," Sulu noted.

"What's that?" asked Kirk.

"Our sensors," the physicist replied, leaning forward in his chair. "With all the additional magnetic fields and x-ray emissions we're bound to encounter, we may end up getting in and out safely but never collecting the data we're after."

"He's right," said Scotty. "And what a pity it'd be. A cataclysmic star pair is rare enough. But one surrounded by wormholes . . ." He shook his head. "It may be a once-in-a-lifetime opportunity."

"We will need to recalibrate the sensors," Spock stated flatly. "By employing a wider spread of frequencies, we will increase our chances of gathering the data we require."

That seemed to make sense as far as the captain was concerned. Then he saw his friend Gary shake his head in disagreement.

"By taking that tack," the navigator said, "we'll also be limiting ourselves in terms of how much data we can collect. We're better off finding the *right* frequency and sticking with it."

The Vulcan raised an eyebrow. "A risky maneuver."

"Risk is our business," Gary told him. He turned to Kirk again. "That's my recommendation, sir."

The captain considered the two options. It didn't take him long to make his decision. "We'll see if we can't find the optimum frequency, as Mr. Mitchell suggests." He included everyone present in a single glance. "I'll need you to get to work immediately, gentlemen. We'll be at Muhlari's outer boundaries before we know it."

His announcement was met with a chorus of affirmatives. Everyone appeared eager to get on with the task ahead—or rather, everyone except his first officer. Spock seemed somewhat less than enthusiastic, his alien features utterly devoid of animation.

But then, he was a Vulcan, Kirk reflected. His people didn't exactly wear their hearts on their sleeves, now did they?

The captain rose from his seat. "Dismissed," he said.

His officers got up as well and filtered out of the briefing room. Spock was the last of them to approach the door. Kirk saw the Vulcan hesitate for a moment, as if he had determined that he wanted to say something else.

Then he made his exit, just like the others.

Chapter Six

HOURS AFTER the meeting in the briefing room was over, Spock still found himself mulling it over in his mind.

As a youth, he recalled as he negotiated the corridor that led to his quarters, he had been taught to avoid emotions like anger, jealousy, and resentment. He had aspired to be like Surak, the ancient Vulcan philosopher who taught that wisdom could only be achieved through the pursuit and application of logic.

Still, he thought, it was difficult not to feel dissatisfaction with a captain who had made what appeared to be the wrong choice. And it was even more difficult when that choice seemed to have been based on friendship rather than cold facts.

No, Spock told himself. *I will not allow my emotions to rule me. I will accept the decisions of my commanding officer as my duty demands, in accordance with the vows I have taken.*

Besides, it was possible that he was wrong—both about the sensor strategy and the extent of Mitchell's influence on Captain Kirk. It was possible that he was too close to the situation to be objective about it.

As Surak had taught, all perceptions were by their nature subjective—even those of a Vulcan Kolinahr master. All observations, Surak said, were colored by the observer's unique set of experiences and expectations.

To be fair, the captain had been nearly flawless in his short stint as the captain of the *Enterprise*—as flawless as Captain Pike before him. Considering that Kirk had overcome every obstacle the galaxy placed in his path, it seemed more than likely he would overcome the obstacles presented by the Muhlari system as well.

I will contend with my resentment, Spock told himself. *I will conquer my dissatisfaction. And by doing these things, I will demonstrate my devotion to the principles espoused by—*

"Listen," said a voice that came from around a bend in the corridor, "you know me. Normally, I mind my own business. But what I saw in that briefing room made it hard to do that."

"Was it really that blatant?" asked another voice—one too high-pitched to be anything but female.

"It seemed that way to me," said the first voice. "I mean, Spock's suggestion sounded like the way to go. But when Mitchell offered an alternative, the captain backed him up—the way he always does."

"I don't know," the second voice responded. "I don't see it the way—"

Suddenly, the voices' owners came around the bend in the corridor and the Vulcan was able to identify them. When the pair saw him, they stopped short, no doubt uncomfortable with the possibility that Spock might have overheard their conversation.

"Mr. Alden," said the first officer. Then he turned to Alden's companion. "Yeoman Smith."

"Mr. Spock," the communications officer responded. He smiled. "I . . . er, didn't hear you coming."

"Clearly," said the Vulcan. "Or you would have refrained from discussing the events of the meeting Captain Kirk conducted earlier."

"Mr. Spock," Alden began, "I hope you won't mention to the captain that I disagreed with his decision. It's just that—"

"I will not mention it," the first officer assured him.

Alden nodded. "Thank you, sir."

"There is no need to thank me," Spock told him. "I see nothing to be gained by quoting you."

The humans weren't sure of what to say about that. Finally, Alden said, "Well, thank you anyway."

And with that, they continued along the corridor. The first officer watched them go for a moment, absorbing what he had heard. Then, instead of proceeding to his quarters as he had originally intended, he headed instead for the nearest turbolift.

The captain stood in the middle of the *Enterprise*'s large, white-walled gymnasium and tried to imagine where he might fit a horizontal bar.

After all, he had been rather expert at the apparatus back in his Academy days. And though it had been a while since Kirk had tried any of his old maneuvers, he believed he could still execute a triple flip if his life depended on it.

As he chuckled at the thought, the doors to the gym hissed open and someone walked in. Glancing over his shoulder, the captain saw that it was his Vulcan first officer.

"Mr. Spock," he said, a bit surprised. "I didn't know you were in the habit of using the gymnasium."

"I am not," the Vulcan responded succinctly, his voice echoing from bulkhead to bulkhead. "As it happens, I came here to speak with you, sir."

"With me?" Kirk asked. "In that case, I hope you didn't have too much trouble finding me."

"It was not troublesome in the least," Spock told him. "I merely set out to do it and then did it."

The captain sighed. There were some things the Vulcan just didn't get. The concept of trouble was one of them apparently.

He held his hands out. "What can I do for you, Mr. Spock?"

Kirk's first officer didn't answer his question—not directly, anyway. Instead, he said, "In the meeting you called earlier today, you ignored my recommendation regarding the ship's sensors."

The captain considered the remark—and found himself disagreeing with it. "I don't believe I ignored it, Spock. I mulled it over as I would have any other recommendation. It just happened that, in the end, I decided to go with another option."

The Vulcan frowned ever so slightly. "It has been

standard practice for you to . . . go with another option, as you put it. And invariably, it is the option suggested by Mr. Mitchell that you decide to go with."

Kirk was more than a little taken aback by the comment. "I wasn't aware of that," he said honestly.

"You sound skeptical," Spock observed.

The captain shrugged. "I suppose I am."

"Then I advise you to check the record," said the Vulcan. "You will find it supports my contention."

Kirk smiled to indicate his good intentions. "Even if that turned out to be so, Mr. Spock, there's nothing personal in my decisions . . . nothing for you to be concerned about, certainly."

"I believe otherwise," the first officer responded. "When I agreed to remain on the *Enterprise* as first officer, it was my understanding that I would be treated with the respect due a first officer. At the present time, that does not appear to be the case."

The captain felt the sting of Spock's remark—as the Vulcan had no doubt intended he should. "I'm sorry you feel that way," he replied.

But Spock wasn't done yet, it seemed. Not by a long shot. "Might I suggest," he said, "that some other vessel might benefit more from my services at this time."

Kirk absorbed the comment. "You're requesting a transfer?"

"I am," the Vulcan confirmed dispassionately, his features devoid of anger or any other emotion.

The captain frowned, knowing there was little he could say in response to that. "I'll take it under consideration."

"Thank you, sir," Spock replied.

Having had his say, the Vulcan didn't linger. He left the way he had come. Kirk watched the gymnasium doors close with a whisper behind his first officer, then considered what the man had said.

It was true that the captain often felt more comfortable relying on Gary's input. But then, he had good reason to feel that way.

For one thing, he had known Gary a long time—practically all of his adult life. A good part of that time, the two of them had worked side by side on one ship or another. They had learned to trust each other and to value each other's advice—even when they declined to follow it.

Also, the first officer was a Vulcan—a member of an aloof and unemotional species. It was difficult for Kirk to place his faith in someone who thought strictly with his head and never with his heart.

In fact, when he took over the *Enterprise* from Christopher Pike, the captain hadn't even considered making Spock his first officer. Then Pike had made a personal request. He had asked that the captain promote Spock, who was only a science officer at that time, to the position of exec.

Kirk could still have done as he pleased. However, he wasn't about to ignore a recommendation from someone like Pike, who had blazed more trails and earned more honors than any captain before him.

So he had named the Vulcan his first officer, just as he had brought Gary aboard as his navigator, Piper as his CMO, and Kelso as his helmsman. Nor were any of them the slightest bit put off by the choice of an unheralded candidate like Spock.

And Gary was the least put off of all. After all, he

hadn't been bucking for a promotion. The only ambition to which he had ever confessed was a desire to see the stars, and he could do that as well from the *Enterprise*'s navigation console as anywhere else.

The only feelings the captain hadn't taken into account were those of the Vulcan himself. But he was so cold and distant, Kirk hadn't imagined he *had* any feelings—much less that he would object to the situation, no matter how it turned out.

And up until a few moments ago, he hadn't.

The captain looked at the doors again and heaved a sigh. Maybe Spock had a point. Maybe he was relying too heavily on his friend Gary for advice . . . at the expense of the Vulcan and maybe even some of his other senior officers.

He would have to give the matter some more thought, he decided. And it wasn't the only one he would have to ponder. After all, Spock had made a request of him, and he would expect an answer.

Do I give in to that request and let him walk? Kirk asked himself. *Even if it'll mean disappointing Chris Pike? Or do I try to hang on to Spock in the hope that I can still make this work?*

Unfortunately, he would have to put the question of where to place the horizontal bar on hold. All of a sudden, he had a couple of more nettlesome problems to worry about.

Every Thursday morning since they had left Earth's solar system, Gary Mitchell had had breakfast with his friend Jim in his captain's quarters. It was an event the navigator had come to anticipate eagerly.

It wasn't because Kirk's quarters were so much larger or more well-appointed than Mitchell's, or because the food was better there, because none of that was the case. It was much more a matter of the informality that marked these occasions.

After all, the captain and his navigator were limited in what they could say to each other in public—Kirk more so than Mitchell. But there in the privacy of the captain's quarters, they could say or do whatever they pleased and rest assured that no one would take them to task for it. They could bare their souls or act like giddy kids and know that it would never go any further than Kirk's front door.

On Thursday mornings, Mitchell reflected, Jim Kirk could be a human being, with all the fallibility that it implied. He could forget that he was the captain of a starship for a moment and just be himself.

"So how are you feeling?" Kirk asked him from the other side of a black foldaway table.

As he awaited an answer, the captain dipped his spoon into a bowl of cereal and milk—what the navigator liked to call Kirk's "farmboy breakfast."

"Any complaints?" the captain prodded.

Mitchell shrugged. "Plenty. But none of them have anything to do with that dart I took for you."

"Just checking," said the other man.

"And don't think I'm not appreciative," his friend told him. He sprinkled some maple syrup on his steaming, golden brown stack of pancakes, which were already streaming with rivulets of melted butter. "The way Nurse Hinch was looking at me, I figured she had brewed up a batch of her own poison in case the Dimoran stuff didn't do the trick."

Kirk rewarded him with a chuckle. "You think Nurse Hinch dislikes you enough to violate the oath she took?"

"I think she dislikes me enough to steal a phaser and cut me to ribbons," Mitchell gibed back. "I tell you, Jim, I got a chill every time the woman walked by my biobed."

The captain shrugged. "It didn't stop you from getting under her skin now and then."

"Hey," said the navigator, "I thought I could smoke her out—you know, get her to go after me with a chair or something."

Kirk smiled at that and shook his head. "Honestly, Mitch, I don't know why you pick on her so much. Nurse Hinch is a dedicated individual with a great deal to contribute."

Mitchell grunted. "That's what they said about Attila the Hun. It all depends on your perspective."

The captain sighed. "You're an evil man, Mitch. A very evil man."

The navigator smiled. "Flattery will get you nowhere."

After that, their conversation lapsed for a while, yielding to the necessary and not unenjoyable consumption of breakfast foods. The navigator ate his pancakes and his companion ate his cereal.

Nor did Mitchell feel at all uncomfortable with the silence. He knew Kirk too well to be uncomfortable with him in any circumstances. In the end, it was the captain who spoke up first.

"Incidentally," he said, "Mr. Spock came to see me."

The navigator looked up at him, intrigued by the comment. "Did he?"

Kirk nodded. "Tracked me down in the gym. Seems he wasn't exactly thrilled about what happened in that meeting yesterday."

Mitchell wasn't at all sure what the other man was talking about. "Something happened?" he asked.

"If you recall," said the captain, "Spock presented an alternative to your sensor frequency plan."

It took Mitchell a second or two to remember. "That's right. And you rejected it, as I recall."

"I did," Kirk agreed. "But in retrospect, I think I may not have given it the consideration it deserved."

The navigator tilted his head, wondering if he had heard his friend correctly. "Are you trying to tell me you've changed your mind?" he asked. "You, Captain Consistent?"

Kirk nodded again. "The more I think about it, the more I wonder if Spock may have had a point." He paused. "Also, there's something else I've got to take into account."

"What's that?" Mitchell asked, honestly curious.

The captain frowned, obviously trying to figure out the best way to say it. "Spock told me I lean on you too much. He said I always go with your suggestions over those of other people."

The navigator chuckled at the notion and stabbed another piece of pancake. "Maybe I've just got a knack for good suggestions," he offered.

"As a matter of fact," said Kirk, "I think you do.

But Spock's my first officer, Mitch. I can't have him thinking I prefer your advice to his—or to anyone else's, for that matter."

The captain leaned back in his chair. "If this expedition were a life-or-death matter, I suppose I'd be forced to go with whichever plan made the most sense to me—regardless of who came up with it. But considering this isn't life or death, I'm going to take this opportunity to show Spock that I value his opinion."

"Really," said the navigator.

Kirk nodded. "Really."

Mitchell thought about it for a moment . . . and realized he wasn't the least bit offended. And as for which sensor strategy they pursued . . . his friend was right, of course. It wasn't nearly a matter of life or death.

"All right," he said. "You're the boss." And he inserted the piece of pancake into his mouth.

The captain regarded him warily. "No hard feelings?"

The navigator chewed, swallowed and shrugged. "And if there were?"

"I've already changed my mind once," Kirk told him. "I'd have to say that's my limit."

Mitchell smiled at the remark. His friend's sense of humor had improved quite a bit since their days at the Academy.

"I'll tell you what," said the navigator. "If you want me to take a backseat to Mr. Spock, I'll do it. Just don't leave me alone with Nurse Hinch anymore and I'll do anything you want."

The captain nodded, looking more than a little grateful for his pal's understanding. "It's a deal," he said mock seriously.

But Mitchell wasn't done making his terms. "On the other hand," he added, pointing a finger at Kirk, "don't forget I'm around, okay? After all, I am your rabbit's foot."

Kirk looked at him. "My rabbit's foot?"

"Your lucky horseshoe," the navigator responded. "I mean, think about it. Where would you be without me? Lying in a street somewhere in Heir'at, the victim of scaly, orange dissidents? Or maybe part of a big, brown dragonhawk's nest on Kiticha'a Four?"

"I see your point," the captain told him.

"And more importantly," his friend went on, "I'm the only officer on board who won't hesitate to tell you when you're wrong. You may not admit it, Jim, but you need someone like that."

Kirk had to smile. "Sounds to me like you're indispensable."

"You don't know the half of it," Mitchell quipped.

"In that case," said the captain, "I'll have to remember not to give you any commendations that might draw attention. I wouldn't want any of my colleagues snatching you away to serve as their first officer."

The navigator made a derisive sound. "First officer?" he echoed. "Don't make me laugh. Why would I want all that paperwork and responsibility when I'm perfectly happy the way I am?"

Kirk grunted. "That's what you keep telling me."

Mitchell downed the rest of his orange juice, then

pulled his napkin off his lap and placed it on the table. "Enough of this. Some of us have got to do some work around this ship."

"Oh?" said the captain. "And you don't call what I do work?"

His friend looked at him askance. "Come on, now . . . be honest with me for a second. How hard is it to say 'Set a course for Rigel Seven'? Or 'Engage tractor beams, Mr. Kelso'? A monkey could do it."

Kirk's features hardened almost imperceptibly. "You're coming dangerously close to insubordination," he said. And then, in a slightly lighter tone, "I may have to keelhaul you, Commander."

Mitchell grinned. Yes, the man's sense of humor had definitely improved. And he was only too glad to take credit for it.

"Go ahead," he told the captain as he got up and brought his plate and glass to the food slot. "That is, if you can find a keel on the old girl—which I tend to doubt."

"Remind me to have one built for you," Kirk responded.

The navigator chuckled again and waved off the remark. "See you on the bridge," he told the captain.

"On the bridge," Kirk echoed.

And on that note, Mitchell left the captain's quarters.

Chapter Seven

KIRK WATCHED his door slide closed behind his friend with an exhalation of air, rather pleased at the way his day was starting out. After all, Gary could have made a fuss about his remarks, but he didn't. He took the change in sensor strategy in stride.

And that was a good thing. Because in a sense, Kirk mused, the navigator *had* been his rabbit's foot over the years—his ever-dependable good luck charm. With Gary's timely assistance, the captain had gotten out of one tight spot after another long before either he or the other man had ever heard of a planet called Dimorus.

Without question, Gary's presence over the years had been an asset, albeit sometimes in ways Kirk might not have expected. The man had proven his courage and resourcefulness time and again, and the rest of the captain's command staff knew that.

But Kirk didn't want to depend on his friend to the exclusion of his other officers. He didn't want to alienate any of them. That was why he was glad Gary hadn't objected to taking a "backseat" to Spock.

For a moment, he thought he might have had to choose between his friendship with Gary Mitchell and the exigencies of command. And that was a choice he hoped he would never have to make.

Abruptly, his thoughts were interrupted by the sound of Alden's voice over ship's intercom. "Captain," said the lieutenant, "I have a communication from Starfleet Command. It's for your eyes only, sir."

For your eyes only. Kirk hadn't often heard that designation. He couldn't help wondering what kind of situation had warranted it. Fortunately, he wouldn't have to wait long to find out.

"Put it through," he told Alden.

"Aye, sir," came the response.

The captain made his way to his workstation, which sat atop his desk in another part of the room. The monitor screen showed him a field of blue with the United Federation of Planets symbol emblazoned in gold.

A moment later, the image on the captain's monitor screen changed. Instead of the Starfleet insignia to which he had become accustomed, he was looking at a gray-haired woman in a rear admiral's uniform.

What's more, Kirk knew her, though she had changed a bit in the years since he had seen her last.

Her face, which he had once thought of as matronly looking, had grown sharper and sterner. Her hair, which she had pulled back into a bun, was even grayer than before. And her expression, friendly in times past, was more businesslike than ever.

"Captain Kirk," she said.

"Admiral Mangione," he responded, his pulse beginning to race.

The first time the captain had encountered the woman, fourteen years earlier, she was serving as the first officer of the *Republic*—a Constitution-class vessel often used for cadet training missions. He and his friend Gary happened to take part in one of those missions.

One night, as the *Republic* skimmed along the Federation side of the Klingon neutral zone, Mangione used the ship's intercom to confine Kirk and all his fellow cadets to their quarters. The order wasn't lifted until the following morning, and none of the cadets were told what had taken place in the intervening hours.

Having been named a full lieutenant by that time, Kirk did his best to put the matter out of his mind. Gary couldn't do that, however. He became obsessed with trying to figure out what the first officer was keeping from them.

In the end, he convinced Kirk to help him sneak into the *Republic*'s sensor control room and hack into the logs of the night in question, so they could get an inkling of what all the fuss had been about. But they found that the logs had been wiped clean—a security measure so extreme it could only have been contemplated at the highest levels of Starfleet Command.

They withdrew from the room as quickly as they could. Nonetheless, they were apprehended by a couple of command officers and brought to the *Republic*'s captain, a man named Bannock.

Gary was afraid that he had wrecked their chances of becoming Starfleet officers. However, they managed to get away with a slap on the wrist. The greater punishment was knowing they would probably never find out what had happened that night on the *Republic.*

Kirk had believed he would never hear anything about the incident again, much less have the mystery cleared up for him. Then, six or seven years later, he was serving as second officer on the *Constitution* when the ship received orders to follow a certain course—one which would eventually lead them to the Klingon neutral zone.

It was Gary, who was the ship's navigator, who recognized where they were going. It was the same part of space the *Republic* had been headed for when Mangione confined the cadets to their quarters.

Soon after, the *Constitution*'s captain, whose name was Augenthaler, received another message—this time, from an Admiral Ellen Mangione. She gave him the set of coordinates that would serve as their destination.

By then, of course, Kirk and Gary had put the coordinates together with the name Mangione. They began to wonder if their mission had something to do with what had happened on the *Republic,* and whether they might live to see the mystery of that night revealed to them after all.

But none of their speculation—Kirk's nor Gary's—prepared them for what they saw when they reached the location in question. Suddenly, their viewscreen was riveted on the image of a Klingon battle cruiser.

A Klingon ship . . . *in Federation space.*

But as Augenthaler girded the *Constitution* for battle and started to close with the enemy, Admiral Mangione's face filled his forward viewscreen. In no uncertain terms, she told the captain to power down his weapons and leave the vicinity immediately.

Augenthaler asked her if she knew there were Klingons in Federation space, but it didn't seem to make much difference to her. Mangione simply repeated her orders to power down and withdraw.

Then, to add insult to injury, she added that no one present on the bridge at that moment was to discuss what he had seen with anyone—ever. And without a single word of explanation, she signed off.

So, far from being solved, the mystery had deepened. And neither Kirk nor Gary had seen Admiral Mangione again.

Yet there she was on the captain's monitor screen. Again, he felt his curiosity coming back like a powerful liquor, setting every cell in his body ablaze. Every time he saw Mangione, he brushed against the dark, fluttering heart of one of Starfleet's most closely guarded secrets.

"It's good to see you again," the captain told her, trying to keep his voice calm and even.

"Likewise," she answered curtly.

"What can I do for you?" he asked Mangione.

Back on the *Republic,* the woman had seemed warm, understanding . . . almost a mother figure to the cadets who served under her. Somewhere along the line, she had become quite the opposite.

"I need a ride," the admiral told him. "Some other old friends of yours will be coming along as well."

"Coming along where?" Kirk inquired.

"I'm afraid that will have to remain classified for the time being," Mangione advised him. "All you need to know is that we'll be waiting for you at Starbase Thirty-one."

"I see," he said.

"When can we expect you?" she inquired.

Kirk performed a mental calculation. "At warp six, we can be there in less than a day."

"That will be perfect," the admiral told him. "I'll see you when you arrive. Mangione out."

As her image vanished from the screen, Kirk frowned. The woman was just as determined as ever to keep her secret, it seemed. However, he was determined as well.

After all, the captain had blown two chances to find out what had happened that night on the *Republic* fourteen years earlier. He would be damned if he was going to blow another one.

Gary Mitchell had already programmed the turbolift and was well on his way to the bridge when he heard his friend's voice come to him via the *Enterprise*'s intercom system.

"Commander Mitchell, this is the captain. I need to speak with you immediately. And I do mean *immediately.*"

Considering how recently he had seen Kirk—a few minutes ago, at most—Mitchell had no idea what the man wanted. *Maybe he's going to ask me what size keel to order,* the navigator mused.

Nonetheless, he punched in a command. A fraction of a second later, the compartment came to a halt, the whine of its motors diminishing sharply and then stopping altogether.

"Go ahead," he told Kirk. "I'm alone in here."

"Brace yourself," said the captain.

Mitchell wondered what his friend was up to. "For what?"

Kirk paused—for effect, it seemed. "I just spoke to Admiral Mangione," he informed the navigator.

Mitchell wouldn't have been more surprised if the floor dropped out from beneath him. "You didn't."

"I did," the captain insisted. "An eyes only communication, no less."

Eyes only, the navigator thought, his mind racing. But not classified. "So it's up to you how much of that communication you care to share with your intrepid command staff."

"That's correct," Kirk confirmed.

"And what did she want?" his friend asked.

"Get this," said the captain. "She wants us to pick her up at Starbase Thirty-one. And not just her, but what she described as some other 'old friends' of mine."

"Old friends?" Mitchell echoed, his curiosity reaching new heights.

"That's what she said."

"And why are we doing this, exactly?" the navigator wondered.

"Mangione told me *that* part was classified," Kirk replied. "But naturally, I couldn't help thinking—"

"That this has something to do with that night on

the *Republic,"* Mitchell blurted, finishing the thought for him.

Dammit, he thought. *What if it* does *have something to do with that? After all these years, is it possible we'll finally find out what that confinement-to-quarters business was all about?*

"Exactly," said the captain.

"When are we scheduled to arrive at Starbase Thirty-one?" the navigator inquired. Then he held up a hand, though Kirk couldn't see him. "No, no, don't tell me." He made some quick calculations in his head. "Twenty-two hours, more or less?"

"That was my estimate as well," his friend responded. "If you don't mind getting up at an ungodly hour of the morning, I'd like you to help me greet the admiral and her entourage—whoever they are. After all, if they're my old friends, they're likely yours as well."

Mitchell grunted. "Are you kidding? For something like this, I'd stay up all night. And it wouldn't be the first time the old girl cost me a night's sleep, now would it?"

"I guess not," said Kirk. "Anyway, you'd better get going. And remember—not a word about what happened on the *Republic* or the *Constitution* to anyone. We were sworn to secrecy."

"How can I forget?" asked the navigator.

"Good. I'll see you in a few minutes."

"Aye, sir," Mitchell answered dutifully.

As the captain signed off, the navigator punched in another command and sent the lift compartment moving again. Admiral Mangione, he thought, here on the *Enterprise.* And not just her, but some of her cronies.

Mitchell rubbed his hands together greedily as the turbolift's motors began to whine. This could be interesting, he told himself. It could be very interesting indeed.

Kirk stood between Spock and his friend Gary in front of the dark disc of the *Enterprise*'s transporter platform. The platform was empty, though the captain had been assured that wouldn't be the case for long.

"Old friends," the Vulcan mused.

"That's what the admiral said," Kirk returned.

"With whom you served on another vessel," the first officer noted.

"That's correct, Spock," said the captain.

With his friend on one side of him and Spock on the other, Kirk felt as if he were performing a balancing act. His first impulse had been to bring Gary alone to the transporter room, considering he was likely to know Mangione and her companions as well as Kirk did.

However, after his conversation with the Vulcan, the captain was leery of making it seem he was excluding Spock from anything at all. So, in the hope of keeping peace, he had asked his first officer to report here as well.

"It can't be Bannock," Gary said, and not for the first time. "Bannock's retired, right? And Gorfinkel too."

"We'll find out soon enough," said Kirk.

A moment later, as if to substantiate his prediction, the air in front of them rippled and shone with the transporter effect. Their visitors began to materialize—five of them in all.

Naturally, one of them was Admiral Mangione. She seemed to be a bit slimmer than the captain remembered, the effect no doubt enhanced by the tailored lines of her gold admiral's uniform.

Broad-shouldered Andreas Rodianos stood at Mangione's side. When Kirk first met him, the man had been the security chief on the *Republic*. In the fourteen years since, Rodianos had risen steadily through the ranks of Starfleet administration, though he didn't seem to have aged much. To Kirk's eye, he looked every bit as strong and fit as ever.

Miyko Tarsch, the Vobilite who had served as the *Republic*'s medical officer, was a different story. With his yellowing thicket of white scalp spines, the tusked, red-skinned doctor had seemed old to the captain a long time ago. Now he seemed positively ancient.

Hogan Brown was standing behind Tarsch. Like Rodianos, the former chief engineer of the *Republic* hadn't changed a great deal. Currently the chief engineer of another starship, he had a few gray hairs in his bushy black beard, but his smile was still dazzling.

It didn't surprise Kirk to see any of these people. After all, the mystery had begun with the *Republic*—it was only natural that her former officers would remain involved with it.

But the fifth member of Mangione's party was anything but expected. As the captain of the *Enter-*

prise gazed into her large, black eyes, a flood of memories came back to him.

Intimate memories, at that.

Phelana, he thought. Phelana Yudrin—the platinum-haired Andorian beauty with whom he had carried on a brief but ardent and finally disappointing love affair on the *Republic.*

Kirk had lost track of her after they graduated and went their separate ways. But judging by the uniform she was wearing and the gold bars on her sleeve, Phelana had done all right for herself.

Gary grunted and spoke under his breath. "Looks like it's old home week, all right."

"So it does," the captain whispered.

"Captain Kirk," said Mangione, stepping forward.

The captain regarded her and grasped the hand she held out to him. "Admiral," he replied. He turned to the Vulcan. "May I introduce Mr. Spock, my first officer?"

Mangione acknowledged him. "Mr. Spock."

"Admiral," said the Vulcan.

She gazed at Gary next. "And I already know Commander Mitchell. I was pleased to learn he was serving on the *Enterprise* as well."

Gary smiled. "It's been a long time, Admiral."

"So it seems," she said. Mangione gestured to indicate her companions. "You remember Dr. Tarsch, I trust?"

"Of course," Kirk replied. "How are you, Doctor?"

"Well enough," said Tarsch, his Vobilite tusks slurring his speech just the way the captain remembered.

"And Mr. Brown?" asked Mangione.

"Good to see you, sir," Kirk remarked warmly, though he had come to outrank the engineer.

"Same here," said Brown, grinning his patented wide grin.

Rodianos didn't wait for an introduction. He held his hands out to indicate the entirety of the ship. "You've come a long way from the helm of the *Constitution,* Mr. Kirk."

The captain smiled. "As have you, sir," he said.

Finally, he turned to Phelana. Her antennae bent forward, an Andorian demonstration of respect.

"Do you know Commander Yudrin?" the admiral asked Kirk and Gary. "As I recall, you were on the *Republic* at the same time she was."

"That's correct," the captain responded. "In fact, we were assigned to the same security location on Heir'tzan during the meeting of the telepaths in the world capital."

"Ah, yes," said Mangione, her eyes lighting up with the recollection. "Then I needn't make any introductions?"

"No, Admiral," Phelana assured her.

Mangione turned to Kirk again. "Thanks for being prompt, Captain. Now, if you have no objections, I'd like to retire to my quarters. I haven't gotten much sleep the last couple of days."

The captain nodded. "Of course. Mr. Spock will show you all to your quarters." He hesitated. "Did you have a particular course in mind at this time, Admiral?"

Mangione smiled a thin smile. "I think we both know what course I have in mind," she said.

Kirk could feel Gary's eyes burning a hole in his skull. What's more, he knew why.

"But that can wait until we're settled in," the admiral continued. She turned to the Vulcan. "Well, Mr. Spock?"

With a deferential glance at Kirk, the first officer led the way out of the transporter room. As the doors opened for him, the admiral, Rodianos, Brown, and Tarsch followed in his wake.

Only Phelana hesitated for a moment, as if she wanted to say something to the captain. Then she seemed to think better of it, because she fell in line with the others and departed.

Gary turned to him and spoke low enough so Kyle couldn't hear him at his transporter console. "She still wants you, Jim."

Kirk scowled, remembering the softness of her blue skin under his fingertips. "What happened between us . . . that was almost fifteen years ago, Mitch. I doubt I made that big of an impression on her."

"You don't give yourself enough credit," said his friend.

"And you give me too much," the captain responded. He glanced at the transporter technician. "Thank you, Mr. Kyle."

Kyle smiled. "You're welcome, sir."

With a gesture to Gary, Kirk headed for the doors. His navigator was right on his heels. But neither of them said another word until they emerged into the corridor.

"So, to recap," Gary said, "we've got four former officers from the *Republic,* where the mystery first started, and a former cadet who was there with us as well. And Admiral Mangione as much as admitted where we're going with that remark about your knowing what course she had in mind."

The captain nodded. "It sure looks that way."

"But that doesn't mean we'll be privy to what's going on," the navigator reminded him. "After all, Augenthaler was left in the dark. And maybe Bannock too, for all we know."

Kirk looked at him. "Maybe we'll get lucky this time."

"Men make their own luck," Gary pointed out. "We're not going to find out what's going on unless we—"

He stopped himself. A moment later, a couple of female ensigns came around a bend in the hallway up ahead. The captain and his friend nodded to them as they passed each other and the ensigns nodded back. Then the women continued on their way.

"—unless we take some action," the navigator finished, having made sure the ensigns were no longer in earshot.

Kirk frowned. "Where have I heard this advice before? And why do I feel a court-martial coming on?"

"I'm not talking about hacking into the sensor logs," Gary told him. "I'm talking about . . . well, maybe I don't know what I'm talking about. But this may be our last chance to get to the bottom of this."

The captain sighed. "I know. I thought the same thing myself." He glanced at his friend. "I'll see what I can do, all right?"

The navigator shrugged. "I guess it'll have to be."

Chapter Eight

KIRK HAD BARELY returned to the bridge when the admiral contacted him via the ship's intercom system.

"Captain Kirk," she said, "this is Admiral Mangione. I'd like to meet with you in your briefing room as soon as possible."

The captain didn't dare turn down the invitation—nor did he have any desire to do so. He was eager to learn whatever it was Mangione intended to impart to him.

"On my way," he responded.

Gary turned to look at Kirk over his shoulder. He seemed to be saying, *Give 'er hell, Jim.* The captain met his friend's gaze squarely, as if to say, *I'll do my best.*

Turning the bridge over to Spock, he made his way to the turbolift. At his approach, the doors whispered open to admit him. When they closed again, he programmed the lift to take him to the briefing room.

As he listened to the turbolift's increasingly high-pitched hum, Kirk couldn't help but tingle a little with anticipation. What if the admiral just flat out told him what he wanted to know, without his even asking? It was possible, wasn't it?

Sure, he thought. But then, it was also possible to break warp nine, though he didn't think anyone would be doing that anytime soon.

A moment later, the lift's hum decreased in pitch, the compartment stopped moving and the doors opened. Exiting, the captain turned left and headed down the corridor. The briefing room, he knew, was situated just a couple of meters before the next junction.

He was almost there when he saw Mangione approaching from the other direction. Right on time, Kirk thought.

"Captain," she said.

"Admiral," he replied.

The doors to the briefing room parted for her and she went inside. The captain followed. As the doors closed behind him, they took their seats and swiveled to face one another.

"I have a set of coordinates for you," Mangione said without preamble. Then she told him what they were.

Kirk recognized them immediately. After all, they were the same coordinates to which the *Constitution* had been dispatched seven years earlier—the location of a class-M planet in an unaligned sector of space.

But what attraction it held for Starfleet since his days as a cadet . . . that part had yet to be explained, the captain mused. And that was the part that interested him the most.

"We'll need to be there as soon as possible," the admiral noted. "I recommend warp six."

Kirk didn't like being told how to operate his ship. Still, he had to acknowledge it was Mangione's right to do so.

"Does this planet have a name?" he asked.

"Only a designation," she told him.

"And you'll be discharging some important duty when we get there," he speculated. "You and the personnel you brought with you."

"Clearly," the admiral responded.

The captain managed a smile. "But you're not going to tell me what it is you'll be doing."

"That's correct," Mangione confirmed.

Kirk leaned back in his chair and eyed her across the briefing room table. "This is my ship, Admiral. My crew. I think I have a right to know."

Mangione seemed intrigued by his declaration. "You know," she said, "it's funny. Captain Augenthaler thought he had a right to know also, as I recall."

The captain would have expected no less of the man.

"But in the end," the admiral continued, "he accepted the necessity of carrying out his mission *without* knowing." The wrinkled skin around her eyes seemed to go taut for a moment. "I wish I could share the details with you, Captain, just as I wished I could share them with Captain Augenthaler. Unfortunately, that's just not possible."

Kirk wasn't satisfied with the woman's response. "I don't like the idea of going into a situation with blinders on."

"Nor would I, in your place," the admiral conceded. "And as you know," Mangione went on, "I've been in your place. Nonetheless, that's the way it'll have to be."

The captain felt no animosity toward the woman; she was only following orders, after all. But he hated the idea of being manipulated, even when it was Starfleet who was doing the manipulating.

"What's more," she said, "I want you to swear your bridge crew to secrecy in this matter, the same way you were sworn to secrecy when you served on the *Constitution*. None of them is to speak of this mission or refer to it in any way . . . ever."

Kirk bit the inside of his cheek. He wanted to protest the admiral's stance. He wanted to demand an explanation from her. However, he was only a captain. He didn't have those options at his disposal.

"As you wish," he told Mangione stiffly.

The admiral nodded. "Thank you, Captain. And now, I'd like to return to my quarters. It's been a long day."

"Of course," said Kirk.

To all of it, unfortunately.

Gary Mitchell had never wanted to be a starship captain. His ambition had never gone further than the navigator's console.

But for once, he found himself wishing he were the commanding officer of the *Enterprise.* That way, he reflected as he ran a routine diagnostic at his navigation console, it would be him in that briefing room with Admiral Mangione instead of his friend.

Not that he didn't think Kirk would do his best to wring every last drop of information from the admiral. After all, the captain wanted to know what was going on every bit as much as the navigator did.

But Mitchell would have been less concerned about breaking the rules. He would have pressed Mangione a little harder perhaps, thrown caution to the proverbial winds . . .

The navigator stopped himself and sighed. *And that,* he mused, *is precisely why you'll never be in that briefing room. You take too many chances for anyone to put you in charge of four hundred sentient lives.*

Give your friend a chance, he told himself. *Let Jim do what he can in his own way. If it's possible to pry anything out of the admiral—*

Suddenly, his thoughts were interrupted by the whoosh of the turbolift doors sliding open. Swiveling in his chair, Mitchell saw Kirk emerge from the compartment and make his way down to his center seat.

The navigator continued to stare at the captain, knowing he would eventually catch his friend's eye. It took a while, but Kirk eventually met his gaze. For a moment, his face was a blank slate.

Come on, thought Mitchell, *what did you find out?*

The captain didn't say anything. He just frowned—an admission of failure, as clear to the navigator as any words Kirk might have said out loud.

Damn, thought Mitchell, his spirits sinking. *Even now, they're determined to keep us in the dark. Even now.*

Kirk had barely sat down in his center seat, his disappointment hovering over him like a dark cloud, when he saw his yeoman approach him with a padd in her hand.

"Captain," she said.

He nodded to her. "Jones."

The woman frowned. "Smith, sir."

The captain looked at her. "Smith?" he repeated, wondering what she meant by that.

"That's my name, sir," the yeoman explained with an air of resignation. "You called me Jones."

Kirk felt himself flush with embarrassment. Of course her name was Smith. And if he hadn't been so distracted by what Mangione had told him in the briefing room—or rather, what she had neglected to tell him—he would never have made so ridiculous a mistake.

He could see Spock studying him from the bridge's science station. Clearly, thought the captain, the Vulcan was less than impressed with his superior's mental capabilities. Kirk turned back to the yeoman.

"My apologies," he told her.

She smiled understandingly. "That's all right, sir."

But it wasn't all right and the captain knew it. He

resolved to remember Smith's name the next time he addressed her.

As he accepted the padd from the yeoman, he glanced at his friend Gary again. The navigator had turned around to face the viewscreen, but Kirk could feel the man's frustration. It radiated from him the way heat and light radiate from a sun.

The captain wished he could have brought back better news from his joust with the admiral—or at least have held out the hope of something promising on the horizon. However, he didn't believe Mangione would become any more forthcoming as they delved deeper into their mission. She had made it pretty clear that Kirk simply wasn't in the loop.

Sighing, he applied himself to the bureaucratic odds and ends with which his yeoman had presented him—fuel consumption reports, cargo manifests and the like. It took the captain the better part of half an hour to go over them, during which time he found his mind wandering over and over again—and always in the same direction.

He wished he had never met Mangione. He wished he had never been to the coordinates she had given him. And most of all, he wished he had never seen that Klingon ship in Federation space.

But he had done all those things. And having done them, it was difficult as hell to concentrate on anything else.

Finally, Kirk finished with the last item on the yeoman's padd. Turning to her, he handed the device back and smiled.

"Thanks for being patient," he told her.

Jones . . . no, Smith smiled back at him. "No

problem, sir." Then she left him and made her way to the turbolift.

Smith, the captain told himself. The woman's name is Smith. *Why am I having so much trouble with this?*

The rest of Kirk's morning passed slowly, laboriously. When his shift was finally over, he turned control of the bridge over to Spock again, entered the turbolift, and considered his destination.

Most days, the captain would have preferred to go to the rec lounge to share a meal with Scotty or Piper. This particular afternoon, he didn't imagine he would be very good company. He decided to eat his lunch in his quarters instead.

In less than a minute, the lift doors opened on the appropriate deck and Kirk stepped out. He was halfway down the corridor when he heard a feminine voice call out his name.

Turning, he saw who it was. She was standing there, illuminated by the passageway's overhead lighting, looking every bit as breathtaking as the first time the captain had seen her in the *Republic*'s lounge.

He could feel the pull of his old longing for her. With a considerable effort, he stifled it.

"Commander Yudrin," Kirk said.

The Andorian frowned at the use of her official title. "Do you have a moment?" she asked him.

The captain shrugged. "I was just about to have some lunch in my quarters. You're welcome to join me."

Phelana nodded. "I'd like that. It will give us a chance to talk."

He looked at her for a moment, wondering what it was she wanted to talk about. Then he gestured in the direction of his quarters.

"This way," he told her.

When they got to the door, Kirk tapped in his personal code and it slid aside. The Andorian peered at the place with her large, black eyes, scanning it for a moment—perhaps comparing it to whatever preconception she had held in her mind.

"Please," he said, "come in."

"Thank you," Phelana replied, her antennae lying back against her platinum-colored hair in an Andorian expression of gratitude. The door slid closed behind her with a whisper of air.

"Have a seat," the captain told her. Then he went to the food slot. "What can I get you?" he asked.

"I'm not very hungry," she said, her eyes big and black and just as appealing as ever. "Maybe just a bowl of urrl soup with kaizis sprouts. Oh, and some corn on the cob."

He glanced at her, feeling a rush of memory. "Corn?"

The commander smiled, momentarily transformed into the cadet he had known fourteen years earlier. "Remember how much I used to hate getting it stuck between my teeth?"

Kirk nodded. "Now that you mention it, yes." The first time he had offered her a cob, he had regretted it almost immediately.

She shrugged, the smile fading. "I guess I've gotten used to it."

"I guess you have," he said.

He programmed the food slot to deliver what

Phelana had asked for, along with a glass of tomato juice. After all, she had liked tomato juice a great deal when they were on the *Republic*.

Then he requested a chicken salad sandwich with some sliced pickles and a cup of black coffee for himself. It all came out on a tray complete with the appropriate silverware, which he brought to the black foldaway table in the center of his anteroom.

"Smells good," the Andorian said, closing her eyes and sampling the aroma of the urrl soup.

"I'll pass your compliments on to the chef," the captain jested.

She opened her eyes, but she didn't respond to his jest. She just removed her food and her accoutrements from the tray and began to eat.

For a minute or two, neither Kirk nor his guest said a word. Then the captain's curiosity got the better of him and he asked, "So how did you wind up working with Admiral Mangione?"

Phelana scooped out the last of the urrl soup and savored it. Then she pushed her empty bowl aside and looked up at her host.

"A couple of years ago," she said, "I was serving on the *Hood* as second officer. We docked at Starbase Twenty for some shore leave. But after a few hours, I was called back to the ship."

Her eyes seemed to glaze over for a moment. "When I entered the briefing room," the Andorian continued, "I found the admiral and Commander Rodianos waiting for me inside. They asked me if I was happy on the *Hood*. I told them I was. The admiral said that was a pity because I would be leaving the ship in just a few hours."

Kirk grunted. "Rather abrupt, wasn't it?"

"Very much so," the Andorian confirmed. "From then on, I was part of her team—along with Rodianos, Tarsch, and sometimes Brown."

"And what does this team do, exactly?" asked the captain.

Phelana met his gaze. "I can't tell you," she said. "I think you knew that before you asked."

He conceded the point with a smile. "I suspected."

She glanced at his cup. "Your coffee's getting cold."

Kirk looked down and saw the pitiful wisp of steam struggling up from it. "So it is."

He took another sip and discovered it was actually hotter than it looked. In the meantime, his guest took advantage of the respite to begin munching on her corn, in which she took obvious pleasure.

The captain imagined he would have a hard time getting the Andorian to talk about her job any further. It was pretty clear that she had changed the subject for a reason.

So he was surprised when she put her corn down suddenly, looked into his eyes, and said, "I want you to know something."

"What's that?" he asked.

Her antennae curled forward, signaling sincerity. "I don't like the idea of withholding information from you."

"Oh?" said Kirk.

"It's just that Starfleet demands it of me," she told him, her eyes sparkling like liquid obsidian.

He tried to ignore them. "Whatever you say."

Phelana sighed. "I know what you're thinking—that I still go strictly by the book. That I don't like to take chances any more than I used to. But that's not true, Jim. I've learned to take chances when I have to. I've learned to bend the rules."

The captain didn't know how to respond to that. "I'll take your word for it," he said at last.

"But Starfleet's asked me to keep my mouth shut about this mission," the Andorian went on. "And as long as they do that, I've got to go along with it." She tilted her head. "You understand that, don't you?"

"You have your orders," Kirk acknowledged. But it wasn't without a hint of unintended bitterness in his voice.

Phelana gazed at him sympathetically. "I know how you feel. I felt that way myself once, remember? Back on the *Republic?* Cheated, in a way. Left out. It seemed to me that Starfleet was pulling the . . . what's that expression you have? Pulling the wool . . . ?"

"Over your eyes?" he suggested.

"Yes. That's the phrase," she confirmed. "I know how terribly frustrating that can be."

The captain nodded. "I appreciate your candor."

He also appreciated the sensual fullness of her lips, and the long, gentle curve of her neck, and the intoxicating smell of her. He appreciated the way the light glinted off her hair and the deep darkness of her eyes. But he refrained from mentioning any of that.

After all, it had been a long time since the days and nights they had spent together on the *Republic.* If Kirk diverged from the "old friends" tone of their conversation, if he suggested something of a more intimate nature between them, he might only succeed in making his guest uncomfortable . . . and he didn't want that.

"So," the commander said in another obvious effort to change the subject, "have you kept in touch with your friends from the Academy? Other than Mr. Mitchell, I mean?"

The captain shrugged. "A few. Do you remember Karl-Willem Brandhorst—Gary's roommate his first year?"

Phelana thought for a moment. Suddenly, her eyes brightened. "Yes," she replied. "He was the tall fellow with the red hair?"

"That's the one," Kirk told her. "He's the chief science officer on the *Potemkin* now. And he's doing good work, from what I hear."

She nodded. "That's good." Her delicate brow creased ever so slightly. "What about . . . what was his name again? The one who became angry with you after you pointed out his oversight?"

The captain knew just whom she meant. "Ben Finney."

"Yes . . . Finney," said the Andorian, sampling her kaizis sprouts. "Do you know what became of him?"

"As a matter of fact," Kirk told her happily, "he forgave me a few years after I graduated and we became friends again. Good friends, I might add. He even named his daughter after me."

She smiled. "Really?"

"Uh huh. He's the records officer on the *Excalibur* these days," said the captain, "but I'm hoping to get him transferred to the *Enterprise.* It'd be nice to have him around."

"No doubt," Phelana replied, returning her attention to her kaizis sprouts. "It's always good to see old friends again . . . even if you only knew them for a short while."

Kirk couldn't be sure, but it sounded as if she were talking about *him.* After all, their affair had been a painfully short one, though it was wonderful while it lasted.

"And you?" he asked, watching her features, trying to divine her intentions. "Do you see anyone?"

She shook her head, making her antennae bob. "I'm . . . unattached," she told him plainly.

The captain felt a rush of embarrassment. "No," he said gently, wishing he had phrased his question a little more carefully. "I meant . . . do you see anyone with whom we attended the Academy?"

Phelana turned a darker shade of blue. "I see." She paused to gather herself. "Actually, I don't. See anyone from the Academy, that is. At least, I don't think I do. I don't have a good memory for faces."

Kirk grunted. "Some people are like that."

Neither of them said anything for a moment. However, the captain was all too aware of the nearness of her . . . the way she smelled, the way her nostrils flared when she spoke.

The Andorian hadn't changed at all, he reflected. She was just as beautiful, just as desirable as the day he said goodbye to her.

"Funny," she said, echoing his thoughts. "It's been fourteen years and it seems like it all happened yesterday."

"Yes," he agreed. "It does."

Phelana winced as if at some invisible injury. "Do you remember when we were on that rooftop on Heir'tzan?" she asked. "And we saw those kidnappers making off with one of the telepaths?"

Kirk remembered it only too well.

The Heir'och and the Heir'tza, who had originally grown up as one people, had come to a point where they wished to reconcile their differences. Unfortunately, they had spilled so much of each other's blood, they no longer trusted each other.

That's where their telepaths came in. With one representing the Heir'tza and the other the Heir'och, they could agree to peace and simultaneously vouch for each other's honesty in the matter.

As cadets serving on the *Republic,* Kirk, Phelana, and Gary were part of a landing party assigned to Heir'tzan. Their assignment was to lend a Federation presence to the Heir'tza security force overseeing the ceremony—not to do any real security work themselves. But when they saw one of the telepaths being kidnapped by terrorists, they realized they had to intervene.

As it happened, they were standing on a roof forty feet off the ground when they witnessed the abduction. Kirk and Gary had resolved to make the jump. But when Kirk turned to Phelana, he could see the hesitation in her eyes.

Not out of fear that she might be hurt, though that was a very real concern. The Andorian had hesitated because their orders had been to remain where they were.

Kirk and Gary had jumped. Phelana hadn't.

Until that moment, she and Kirk had appeared to have a future together. But afterwards, he hadn't been able to see her in quite the same light, despite her outward beauty.

"I remember," he told her.

The Andorian smiled a sad smile. "You know, I have only two regrets in life," she told him.

"Two?" the captain asked.

"I wish I had jumped," she said.

He wished she had jumped, too, but he declined to say so for the sake of her feelings. "And your other regret?" he wondered.

Phelana looked at him for a moment. A long moment. Finally, she shrugged. "Never mind. It's nothing, really."

Kirk couldn't help feeling that he had been on the brink of a secret as great and mysterious in its own way as Admiral Mangione's. He felt he should press the matter, get his guest to tell him what that other regret was.

But it wouldn't be fair to her. After all, if she did tell him, he wasn't sure what he would do in response.

"I ought to go," the Andorian said, pushing back from the table. "I have preparations to make."

"Of course," he answered.

The captain would have given a great deal to know what kind of preparations they might be. But Phelana had already told him she couldn't divulge anything about their mission, and he didn't believe it was likely the woman would change her mind.

Phelana rose from the table, leaving her tomato juice untouched. Perhaps she didn't like it as much as she used to, Kirk thought. Or had it been a faulty recollection that she had liked it at all?

"I guess I'll see you later," the Andorian said.

Her host rose to be polite. "Later," he agreed.

Then Phelana departed his quarters, leaving the captain of the *Enterprise* with a great deal to think about.

Chapter Nine

FOR MORE THAN a week, Mitchell refined the *Enterprise*'s course by day and contrived to bump into members of Mangione's team by night.

It wasn't easy. The admiral convened meeting after meeting, commandeering the briefing room four and sometimes five times a day. The navigator wasn't sure if Mangione's people really had that much to say to each other or if she simply wanted to keep them apart from Kirk's crew.

Maybe the admiral had learned about Commander Yudrin's lunch with Mitchell's friend Jim. And then again, maybe not, considering no one but the captain, the Andorian, and the navigator knew anything about it . . . and Kirk had made Mitchell swear not to say anything.

In any case, Mitchell remained determined to corner one of the officers with whom Mangione had arrived. Finally, the night before they were to reach their destination, he got his wish.

"Hey," he said, catching sight of Hogan Brown in the corridor outside engineering. The man must have been comparing notes on something with Mr. Scott. "Wait up, Commander."

The engineer glanced back at the navigator and stopped. "Mr. Mitchell. I had a feeling I would be running into you a little sooner."

"And why's that?" the navigator inquired, smiling the most charming smile he could manage as he caught up with the man.

Brown shrugged. "Oh, I don't know. It's just that, as I recall, you seemed pretty eager to find out what was going on back on the *Republic*. I guess I just assumed you'd still be pretty eager."

"And if I were?" Mitchell asked.

The engineer grinned back at him, putting the navigator's smile to shame. "It would be understandable, I suppose. Nobody likes to be left out of anything important, Commander—least of all a naturally inquisitive young man like yourself."

"You sympathize, then," said the navigator.

"Completely," Brown replied. He took Mitchell's arm. "Come, let's walk."

The navigator accompanied the engineer down the hall. "You know what I want to know, don't you?"

The engineer chuckled. "I'd be some kind of fool if I didn't."

Mitchell looked at him. "And what would you say are my chances?"

"Of finding out something about this mission?" Brown asked. He shook his head. "Not good, I'm afraid. Not good at all."

"So what's the purpose of this stroll?" the navigator asked.

"We're going down to the rec lounge," the other man told him. "For a game of three-dimensional chess. You see, I've gotten to be quite an aficionado of the game in my old age, and I've heard you're quite the player."

"Then you heard wrong," said Mitchell.

Brown's eyes narrowed. "I beg your pardon?"

"I'm not the three-dee chess fanatic on the ship," the navigator told him. "That would be Captain Kirk."

The engineer looked at him for a moment. Then he smiled a big, sad smile. "In that case, Commander, I'll see you in the morning."

And he continued along the corridor on his own.

Kirk leaned back in his captain's chair. It was time. "Slow to impulse," he told his helmsman.

"Slowing to impulse," Kelso responded.

His console chirped and the *Enterprise* dropped out of warp. On the bridge's forward viewscreen, converging trails of multicolored starlight shortened and were transformed into tiny pinpricks of illumination.

"Magnify—factor five," the captain ordered.

"Factor five," Gary confirmed from his seat at the navigation console.

Suddenly, a bright red world seemed to appear in front of them. The outermost planet in a three-planet star system, it looked exactly the same as the captain remembered—and he remembered it quite vividly.

"Class-M," said the navigator.

But then, he was only confirming what Kirk already knew. After all, both he and Gary had seen this world before.

For that matter, so had Admiral Mangione, who was standing behind the captain's center seat like a ghost, observing without speaking. The woman had come out onto the bridge several minutes earlier—no doubt, in anticipation of this very moment.

Out of the corner of his eye, the captain saw Spock look up from his science monitors, his lean features caught in their red orange glare. He turned to the Vulcan.

"Sir," Spock announced, "sensors indicate an ion trail in the vicinity of the planet."

An ion trail meant that a ship had been there. Or possibly that it was still there, albeit hidden from view on the planet's other side.

The captain glanced over his shoulder at Mangione, but the admiral remained silent. "Helm," he said, "swing us out to starboard. Let's get a different perspective on the situation."

"Aye, sir," Kelso replied.

His console beeped and the class-M world began to revolve—or appear to. Actually, it was the ship that was moving, revealing more and more of the planet's surface with each passing moment. After a minute or so, Kirk thought he noticed something near the horizon line.

"A ship," he said out loud. "Magnify again—factor seven."

"Factor seven," Gary echoed.

The vessel seemed to jump closer to them. It was recognizable now, easy to identify for what it was.

"My god," breathed Kelso.

The captain reminded himself that his helmsman hadn't been present on the bridge of the starship *Constitution* seven years earlier. Therefore, when Kelso peered at the angular, blue Klingon battle cruiser that was filling their viewscreen at that very moment, its nacelles extended like the wings of some monstrous avian predator, it was understandable that he would be more surprised than Kirk was.

But surprised or not, the captain had a crew to protect. "Go to red alert," he barked, the muscles working in his jaw. "Raise shields and power up the weapons array."

In his mind, he could hear Captain Augenthaler uttering the very same commands, his voice booming throughout the bridge of the *Constitution*. He could see his own fingers flying over the helm controls as the very air seemed to turn the color of blood. He could feel the tension all around him like something palpable.

"Shields up," Spock confirmed back in the here and now. "Weapons batteries approaching full strength."

"You won't need them," Mangione said with calm assurance.

The captain whirled in his chair to regard her. "You knew we'd find this, didn't you?"

"I knew it was a possibility," the admiral replied.

"You might have warned me," Kirk told her.

Mangione's eyes blazed all of a sudden. "I'll warn you if and when I believe it's necessary, Captain. Now power down your weapons and relax."

The Vulcan looked to his commanding officer. Reluctantly, Kirk nodded and turned back to the forward viewscreen.

Seven years ago, the Klingon vessel they encountered had slowly wheeled to face them. This one didn't even bother. It simply maintained its attitude and its orbit as if the *Enterprise* didn't exist.

"Establish a synchronous orbit," said the admiral, "on the side of the planet opposite the Klingon vessel—just in case someone decides to get an itchy trigger finger."

"No one on my ship would do that," the captain pointed out.

"I'm not just talking about your ship," Mangione responded. "Believe me, Captain Kirk, those Klingons don't like the sight of us any more than we like the sight of them."

Kirk turned to his helmsman. "You heard the admiral, Mr. Kelso. Establish an orbit."

"Aye, sir," came the reply.

A moment later, the *Enterprise* began to veer to port—away from the battle cruiser and toward the point on the planet's equator directly opposite. The captain stole a glance at Mangione. She seemed satisfied with the way things were going.

And still Kirk had no idea what his ship and his crew were doing there. It was like tearing through the void without a forward sensor array, he thought. In the old days, before the advent of interstellar flight, they would have called it flying blind.

As they neared the planet, the Klingon battle cruiser began to vanish over the horizon, setting like a small, defiant sun. Finally, it drifted out of sight altogether.

"My team and I will be beaming down to the planet's surface," the admiral announced abruptly. "We'll supply your transporter technician with the coordinates at the appropriate time."

"I see," said the captain. "And can you tell me how long you intend to remain down there?"

Mangione's expression became a wary one.

"It makes sense for me to know," he insisted. "If something's gone wrong, I'll need to pull you out."

The admiral thought about it a moment longer, then nodded. "Half an hour, tops. Anything longer than that and there's been a screwup. But I must tell you, I don't expect anything of that nature."

Who ever does? Kirk mused. But he kept the question to himself.

Deftly, Kelso slipped the *Enterprise* into orbit around the planet. As soon as he disengaged the impulse engines, Mangione left the bridge.

The doors closed behind her with a soft hiss. That's when Gary turned around in his seat to look at the captain, the sourness of his expression a mirror of Kirk's own.

The navigator seemed on the verge of passing a comment about the admiral, but thankfully he refrained. After all, Mangione was still their superior officer and this was still a Starfleet ship.

The captain glared at the viewscreen, where the planet's raw, red surface seemed to mock him. What was waiting down there? he wondered. What was so important to both the Klingons and the Federation that both sides were willing to suspend their customary hostilities for it?

Too many questions, Kirk reflected, and not nearly enough answers. And the way it looked, that wasn't likely to change anytime soon.

"Captain," said Alden, "Mr. Kyle reports that the admiral's team has beamed down safely."

Kirk nodded. "Thank you, Lieutenant."

Any moment now, he told himself, Mangione and the others would be wading into the heart of one of Starfleet's biggest mysteries. They would be basking in the knowledge of it.

He would have given anything to be down there on the planet's surface among them . . . to see with his own eyes, once and for all, what in blue blazes was going on down there.

As he thought that, he saw Gary turn around again. But this time, he didn't look quite so disgruntled. He tilted his head toward his monitors as if he were inviting the captain to see something.

Kirk approached the navigational controls and peered over his friend's shoulder. Most of Gary's monitors reflected the *Enterprise*'s position in space. Only one of them showed him something else—the prevailing conditions at a particular spot on the planet's surface.

The captain scanned the information on the monitor. The sensors were reading five life-forms—three humans, one Vobilite, and one Andorian—not far from the planet's north pole. No other signs of sentient life.

But there was also evidence of an energy barrier—no, two of them. And each one was blocking one end of a twisting, high-walled box canyon. Unfortunately, the ship's sensors couldn't penetrate either of the barriers—no surprise there—or the canyon walls. Obviously, there was some mineral in the latter that resisted long-distance sensor scrutiny.

And just as obviously, there was something in that canyon that the Federation didn't want seen. Something it didn't want released, even if it was just on the planet.

Intriguing, Kirk thought. His friend's expression said that he found it intriguing, too. But neither of them had the information they needed to solve the admiral's mystery.

"Carry on," the captain told his navigator with a sigh. Then he returned to his center seat and awaited word from Mangione.

Phelana Yudrin shielded her eyes from the blue green oven of a sky. Then she gazed at the immense, yellow graviton field that stretched majestically across the entrance to the rust red box canyon.

The graviton barrier seethed with phase-synchronized energies strong enough to withstand even a prolonged, type-X phaser barrage. In fact, she reflected, this was the same technology that Federation starships used to deflect space debris in flight.

There was just one problem with it.

Wiping perspiration from her brow, the Andorian

turned her attention to the small, black, eight-sided energy storage unit she held in her hand. The device's readouts were dead, signifying that it had malfunctioned—which meant that the graviton projector it powered had malfunctioned as well.

Yudrin turned left and then right, taking stock of the site's two dozen other graviton projectors, each one set up on a tripod on the planet's rocky, red terrain. They were all working perfectly.

It was only the projector directly in front of her, from which she had removed the faulty energy storage unit, that had gone dead as a stone. Fortunately, the Andorian told herself, its malfunction shouldn't have had any significant repercussions.

It would only have left a narrow, barely noticeable gap in the graviton field—a gap the other projectors' sensors would have noticed after thirty seconds. Then the projectors on either side of the gap would have widened their emitter apertures to fill it in.

But what if something had happened in those thirty seconds? she asked herself. What if . . .

She stopped herself, deciding to act rather than continue to speculate. Removing her communicator from her belt, she flipped it open. "Commander Yudrin to Admiral Mangione. Come in, Admiral."

Mangione's reply came almost instantly. "What is it, Commander?"

"I've got a bad projector here," the Andorian reported. She wiped her brow again, resenting the intense heat that seemed to come from all around her. "Its energy storage unit stopped working."

The admiral cursed, then said something Yudrin

couldn't hear. It seemed she was speaking to one of the other officers on the team. The other officer appeared to say something back.

"Commander," said Mangione, "we may have a problem."

Despite the temperature, the Andorian felt a trickle of icewater in the small of her back. "What kind of problem?" she asked.

"We haven't scanned the entire canyon yet," she said, "but one of our subjects may be missing."

Yudrin's mouth felt uncomfortably dry all of a sudden. "Missing?" she echoed, trying not to let her trepidation enter her voice.

"It may be nothing," said the admiral. "But considering what you've told us about that projector, we've got to be as cautious as possible. You know how dangerous it could be if there was a security breach."

The Andorian drew her phaser with her free hand. "Yes," she replied with forced calm, searching the nearly barren countryside all around her. "I'm well aware of how dangerous it could be."

"Good," Mangione told her. "I'll alert the others. In the meantime, I want you to work your way east. Commander Rodianos and I will maintain our position until you get here."

Of course, the admiral could simply have had them beamed back to the *Enterprise*. But they had to remain on the planet's surface until they determined if there had been a breach or not.

"Acknowledged," she said. "Yudrin out."

With another quick look around, she started off in Mangione's direction at a trot. Her antennae leaned forward in a position of alertness—not that they would help her in the least. Over millions of years, her people's cranial appendages had become as vestigial as a human appendix.

Leaving the last of the three-legged graviton projectors behind, the Andorian hugged the sheer, red cliffs that rose on her left. On her right, the rock formations were shorter and a good deal less smooth, but just as devoid of vegetation—and therefore, she observed gratefully, devoid of hiding places as well.

Though she was in good shape, the heat began to get to her with surprising quickness. Her heart began to pound harder than normal and she could hear her breath rasping loudly in her throat.

Hang in there, Yudrin told herself, using her whole hand to wipe the perspiration away this time. *Mangione's position was less than two kilometers away when you started out. You'll see it in just a few minutes.*

Then something on her right caught her eye—some kind of movement. Instinctively, she whirled and fired her phaser at it.

The ruby red beam raised a cloud of ocher dust from the hillside and sprayed debris around. But as the dust cleared and the Andorian slowed down to see what she had shot at, it became apparent that there wasn't anything there.

She swallowed, no easy task with her mouth so unbearably dry. She wasn't mistaken, she told herself. She had seen something. But—

A sound drew her out of her reflection. A sound like the pelting of feet against the hard ground.

As Yudrin whirled, a shadow fell across her, blotting out the sun. She tried to fire at it, but something hard and viselike crushed the strength from her wrist, forcing her to release her phaser. Then a terrible weight slammed her to the ground, knocking the wind out of her.

The bronze sun above her backlit her adversary's shaggy countenance, making it difficult for the Andorian to get more than a glimpse of it. But what she saw was cruel, almost demonic.

A massive fist seemed to ascend into the sky, then plummet in her direction. The impact felt as if it broke her jaw and maybe her cheekbone as well. But somehow Yudrin clung to consciousness, the metallic taste of blood strong in her mouth.

"VeQ," snarled her adversary.

Too late now, she realized what must have happened. He had concealed himself in a fold of the cliff face on her left, waiting for her to walk by. When he caught a glimpse of her, he had tossed a rock onto the slope to her right, hoping to draw attention away from him. And like an idiot, Yudrin had fallen for it.

Then he had raced across the distance between them and borne her down. And now, with the Andorian pinned beneath him, he was going to kill her out of his hot-blooded need for revenge.

Mustering what was left of her strength, the commander tried to push her way up toward her enemy's eyes. If she could dig her nails into them, she thought, it would get him to roll off her.

But he was too quick for her, too powerful. He grabbed both her hands in one of his. Then he wrapped the fingers of his other hand around her throat and squeezed.

Yudrin gasped desperately for air, but to no avail. A terrible pressure built up in the base of her throat. She could feel herself ebbing away, see the darkness closing around her.

Then she felt and saw nothing at all.

Chapter Ten

KIRK REALIZED that he was tapping his fingers on the armrest of his chair and forced himself to stop. On the other hand, he couldn't blame himself for being impatient.

It was bad enough to be denied knowledge of whatever Mangione was doing down there on the planet's surface. But to have to wait up here in orbit the whole time . . . that was pushing it.

Then he heard someone say "Sir?" in a taut, clipped tone of voice.

Turning, he saw that it was Spock who had asked for his attention from his post at the bridge's science station. No, the captain thought, not just asked for his attention. *Demanded* it.

In the months that Kirk had known the Vulcan, Spock had barely exhibited so much as a frown. Yet now, he looked positively agitated, his dark eyes wide with apprehension.

"What is it?" the captain asked.

"The admiral's team is no longer alone," the first officer reported with a distinct sense of urgency. "Sensors register other life signs in close proximity to the landing party."

Kirk understood Spock's concern. Getting to his feet, he emerged from the command center and ascended to the level of the communications station. Alden, having heard Spock's announcement too, was already trying to raise Mangione and her officers.

"Anything?" the captain asked, grasping the back of the communications officer's chair and hovering over him.

Alden shook his head unhappily. "Their communicators seem to be working, sir, but there's no response."

Kirk swore beneath his breath and made his way back to his center seat. Punching the stud that would give him a direct line to the transporter room, he snapped, "Mr. Kyle!"

"Aye, sir!" came the technician's startled-sounding response.

"Get a lock on the admiral's landing party and beam them back," the captain told him.

"Will do, sir," Kyle assured him.

Kirk turned to his friend Gary. The navigator looked more than a little concerned, as if one of his famous flashes of insight had shown him something he didn't want to see.

The captain glanced at Spock again. "Any more information on those life signs?" he asked the Vulcan.

Spock's features were bathed in the crimson illumination of his monitors, his brow creased with concentration. "I believe—" he started to say.

"What?" Kirk prodded.

The first officer's frown deepened. Then he returned the captain's gaze. "I was going to say they were Klingon life signs, sir. But I cannot be sure of that conclusion."

Kirk's teeth ground together. What if Mangione had been wrong to trust the Klingons on that battle cruiser? he asked himself. After all, treachery seemed to be a Klingon speciality.

"Kyle's got a lock on them," Alden announced suddenly.

The captain glanced at the viewscreen, as if daring the red orange world to try to stop him from reclaiming his people. Then he tapped the intercom stud on his armrest again.

"Energize," he snapped.

Seconds passed. There should have been a response from the transporter technician, but there wasn't any.

"Mr. Kyle," said Kirk, "is something wrong?"

That's when he heard something . . . but not what he had expected. The intercom brought him a series of snarls and guttural curses—the kind a pack of bloodthirsty Klingons might have made.

And suddenly, the captain understood.

Whirling to face Gary, he said, "Disable the transporter!"

The navigator worked at his console for a moment. But when he looked up, it was with a look of frustration on his face.

"Too late," he reported, "it's in operation again!"

And the system couldn't be disabled in the middle of a transport, Kirk reflected. It had been designed that way out of necessity, but now it was working against them.

Suppressing a curse, the captain tapped another stud on his armrest. "Security," he said, "this is Kirk. We've got an intruder situation in the transporter room. Be advised that there may be hostages, including Admiral Mangione and her team."

By that time, of course, the intruders might have killed them. But the captain didn't care to contemplate that possibility yet.

"I'm on my way," he added. "Kirk out."

He had barely gotten the words out when it occurred to him he might want to take someone else with him, in case the security team wasn't enough—someone who would know what he wanted before he wanted it. There was only one man on the ship who fit that description.

"Mr. Spock," said the captain.

The Vulcan turned to him expectantly. "Aye, sir?"

"You've got the conn," Kirk told him. Then he glanced at Gary. "Mr. Mitchell, you're with me."

Spock seemed surprised for a fraction of a second. Then he got up obediently and moved across the bridge to the captain's chair. At the same time, Kirk led the way to the turbolift, telling himself he would ponder the implications of the moment later on.

The lift doors opened and the captain entered the

compartment. By the time his navigator joined him inside, he had already punched in the code for the transporter room.

Gary looked at him. "We'll need phasers," he said, as the turbolift motors began to whine.

"There's a locker in the corridor," Kirk replied, referring to the passageway between the turbolift and the transporter room.

His friend seemed to picture it, then nodded. "Right."

They shot through the ship at a speed only suggested by the hum of the turbolift's motors or the vibration in the floor beneath their feet. Before the captain knew it, the lift doors hissed open and they were swinging out into the corridor.

As he had pointed out to Gary, there was an emergency phaser locker a few meters down on the left. They paused long enough to open it with a command code and extract two of the phasers within. Then, as the panel slid closed again over the storage compartment, they pelted down the hall with their weapons in hand.

Approaching a left turn in the corridor, Kirk slowed down and peered past the corner. His friend did the same. At the end of the passageway, the captain could see the orange doors of the transporter room. In between, there was nothing and no one.

"The invaders got away," said Gary.

Kirk turned to look at him. "Is that your sixth sense talking?"

"It's my *common* sense," Gary told him. "If the security team had caught up with them, the battle would still be raging."

The captain nodded, then eyed the doors again. "Good point. But let's be careful nonetheless."

Then he approached the transporter room. Naturally, his friend was right behind him.

Just before they would have registered on the bulkhead sensors and activated the entry mechanism, the captain gestured for Gary to veer off to the left. Kirk himself then moved to the right.

For a moment, the captain studied the corridor behind them, to make sure he and his navigator wouldn't be ambushed from behind. Then he slid a half-meter closer to the transporter room entrance and raised his phaser. On the other side of the hallway, Gary did the same.

The doors parted, revealing several figures from Kirk's perspective. Three of them were lying on the deck. Two more were kneeling beside them and two others were standing.

When the latter four caught sight of the captain, their phasers swung in his direction. Then they glimpsed Gary as well and two of them trained their weapons on him. But before they could unleash a barrage, Kirk shouted at them to hold their fire.

"It's the captain!" he added.

"And Lieutenant Mitchell!" said the navigator from his position on the other side of the passage.

The armed figures within, all of them security officers in scarlet uniform shirts, relaxed and lowered their weapons. They looked tense, drawn.

"Sorry, sir," one of them told Kirk.

"That's all right," said the captain.

Tucking his phaser into the back of his waistband, he entered the transporter room and took a closer look at the bodies stretched out unceremoniously on the deck—six of them in all. The admiral and her landing party, he realized, as well as Lieutenant Kyle.

For a moment, Kirk feared they were all dead—all victims of whatever or whoever had beamed up with them. Then he saw one of the victims move her head, as if trying to shake off the effects of a stunning blow.

It was Phelana. She groaned, tried to sit up and was eased back to the floor by one of the security officers. The captain knelt beside the Andorian and took note of the dark blue bruises on her face.

"Call Dr. Piper," he told the officer nearest to him—a man named Rayburn. "Tell him to hurry."

"Aye, sir," said the security officer.

Kirk turned to Matthews, another security officer. "I take it you found them like this?"

"We did, sir," Matthews reported.

"You didn't get a look at the intruders?" the captain asked.

The man nodded. "That's correct, sir."

Kirk gazed at Phelana, brushing a stray strand of platinum hair out of her face. "Commander Yudrin," he said softly, trying to keep his anger and concern in check, "what happened down there?"

As the Andorian gazed back at him with her large, black eyes, her antennae bent needfully in the captain's direction. "They took me by surprise," she responded hoarsely. "I thought I was . . . thought I was dead. Then I woke up and found I was being carried over someone's shoulder."

Kirk bent closer. "Carried by whom?"

Phelana's eyes narrowed and she shook her head slowly from side to side. "That's classified—"

"Don't give me that!" he rasped. "They're loose on my ship, dammit! I need to know what's going on!"

The Andorian seemed ready to hold fast to her position for a moment. Then she must have seen the sense in what he was saying, because she relented. "They're Klingons," she told him.

The captain absorbed the information, but it didn't seem to ring true. Mangione and her people had gone down to the planet armed with phasers and presumably knowing what to expect. And they had been caught unaware by a bunch of unarmed Klingons?

"There's more to it," he concluded. "There's got to be."

Lieutenant Kyle stirred then. One of the security officers went to see to the man.

Phelana licked her lips. "They're not ordinary Klingons," she explained. "They've been enhanced. Made stronger and quicker."

Kirk shook his head. "How?"

"I'm not sure," she told him.

Hearing a tapping sound, the captain looked up and saw Gary drumming his fingers on the surface of the transporter console. No doubt, he was inspecting the system's log.

"One thing's clear," said the navigator, "and that's the way they got up here. They waited until the admiral and her party were caught in the transporter effect and then they hitched a ride."

"How many of them?" asked Kirk.

Gary frowned as he consulted the log again. "Judging from the amount of material that came through the pattern buffers, it looks like there were five or six of them."

"Bloody bastards," growled Kyle, propping himself up on one elbow despite a security officer's attempts to restrain him.

Kirk turned to the transporter technician and saw the bloody gash over the man's eye. "It's not your fault," he told Kyle.

The man sighed. "I noticed something was wrong, sir, but it was too late by then. They were through already."

"And after that, they brought some friends up," the navigator noted, still analyzing the transporter log. "Ten more of them, to be precise." He regarded the captain. "That would make fifteen or sixteen intruders in all."

Fifteen or sixteen intruders didn't appear to pose that serious a problem, Kirk reflected, even if they were armed with the weapons Mangione's party had been carrying. And despite what had happened, he doubted these Klingons were as dangerous as Phelana seemed to believe.

He had barely completed the thought when Dr. Piper rushed into the room with three of his nurses in tow. The security officers backed off to give him room. Bending over the nearest injured party, who happened to be Admiral Mangione, the doctor ran his medical tricorder over her. Then he checked his readings and turned to the captain.

"She's suffered severe head trauma," said Piper.

"I'm going to have to move her to sickbay and keep her under close watch."

Kirk nodded. "Whatever you say, Doctor. But you can't take her there through the corridors. Whoever caused that trauma is still running loose on the *Enterprise.*"

Piper looked ready to protest. Then he appeared to remember that there was an alternative.

Gary must have understood, too, because his fingers were already flying over the transporter controls. "Be with you in a minute," he said.

By the time he was ready, the doctor's nurses had reported on Tarsch, Brown, and Rodianos. Their injuries were serious as well, it seemed, though Mangione's remained the worst of them.

"Energize," said the captain.

In the next second, Piper, his nurses, Mangione, Rodianos, and Tarsch were enveloped in shimmering cylinders of light. Then they vanished as if they had never been there in the first place.

"Captain Kirk," said Phelana.

He turned back to her. "Yes?"

"Let me help," she asked. With a loud grunt, she dragged herself up to a sitting position.

Kirk knew what she was asking and he admired her courage, but he had to deny her request. "You're no good to me like that," he told her. "Besides, we've got a good security force on this ship. We'll find those Klingons before they do any harm."

The Andorian looked more than a little skeptical. But what she said was, "I hope you're right."

The captain would have reassured her, but he

didn't get the chance. Before he could get a single word out, Phelana was claimed by the splendor of the transporter effect.

Kirk watched her disappear, along with Brown and Kyle. Then he turned to his navigator and the team of security officers.

"We've got work to do," he told them.

Chapter Eleven

SCOTTY CURSED beneath his breath. "Klingons, sir?" he asked. "Right here, on the ship?"

It was difficult to believe. Nonetheless, Kirk's intercom voice cut through the throbbing sounds of the engineering room, confirming what he had said a moment earlier.

"Right here on the ship, Mr. Scott—as many as sixteen of them, some armed with phaser pistols. And that's not all," the captain elaborated. "These Klingons have been enhanced somehow. They're stronger and faster than the kind we're used to."

Scotty glanced at the half dozen engineers sitting at control consoles or working up on the catwalk. They looked worried about the news. To be honest, the chief engineer reflected, he was a bit worried himself.

Kirk went on. "It's possible that they'll try to find

the engine room and take the place over, then use it as a bargaining chip. Certainly, that would be one of the options *I'd* consider if I needed a way off the ship."

"Aye, sir," Scotty agreed. "What is it ye'd like us t' do?"

"There's a security team on its way," said the captain. "In the meantime, keep these Klingons away from the engines. It'll be a lot easier to deal with them if they're not holding a gun to our heads."

The engineer nodded. "I understand, sir. An' ye need nae worry—we'll take care o' the place until help comes."

"Thanks, Scotty. Kirk out."

The Scotsman looked around at his staff. Naturally, they were all Academy trained, all capable of handling themselves in an adversarial situation. But they weren't armed.

And if the captain's report was accurate, the Klingons *were.* If that wasn't cause for concern, Scotty didn't know what was.

If he were an intruder on the *Enterprise,* Kirk had decided, one of the first places he would try to reach was the shuttlebay.

After all, there was little chance that the Klingons could secure a well-fortified, largely inaccessible place like engineering before they were stopped. The odds were much better that they could get hold of a shuttle, sneak it out of the larger vessel and find a hiding place for it on the planet's surface.

Then the shuttle's rightful owners would be forced to beam down or descend in another shuttle to locate it, opening themselves up to all kinds of perils and uncertainties. And Kirk dearly wanted to avoid all that.

So once he had contacted all the intruders' most likely targets and lodged warnings with the personnel in charge of them, the shuttlebay became the captain's top priority. And it remained that way until he and his security team reached the corridor that led to it . . . and established that the area was devoid of Klingon life signs.

"Are you sure?" asked Kirk.

Rayburn consulted his tricorder, aiming it at the orange doors that led to the shuttlebay. "Aye, sir," he responded. "There aren't any Klingons here. At least, not—"

Suddenly, a bloodred phaser beam blasted the man in the back, slamming him facefirst into the bulkhead in front of him. As Matthews and the other two security officers rounded the corner to return fire, Kirk and Gary pulled Rayburn back out of harm's way.

Fortunately, the security officer was still alive. The beam that hit him hadn't been discharged at a lethal setting, the captain reflected.

But then, the Klingons probably weren't all that familiar with Federation technology—especially if they had been on the planet for the last fourteen years or more. It might not even have occurred to them that a phaser *had* more than one setting.

Suddenly, a beam caught another of the security officers square in the chest and sent him sprawling. As Gary went to pull him out of the line of fire, Kirk took the man's place.

It was then he saw what they were up against. There were four dark, hulking, wild-haired forms in leathery garb at the far end of the passageway, each one armed with a phaser.

But if they were Klingons, they weren't like any Klingons the captain had ever seen. Their brows jutted out over small, wild eyes, they had bony foreheads that receded well past what should have been their hairlines, and their teeth were long and savage looking.

Before Kirk could squeeze off a shot, he saw one of the intruders point his weapon at him. Flattening himself against a bulkhead, he saw the bright red phaser beam zip within centimeters of his face and splatter against the duranium wall behind him.

Damn, he thought. If the behemoths didn't know anything else about phasers, they sure knew how to aim them.

The captain fired back, but to no avail. His Klingon target ducked in time to avoid his phaser beam. Then, more quickly than Kirk would have imagined possible, the invader unleashed another beam of his own.

As it happened, he missed the security officer at whom he appeared to have aimed. But he didn't miss by much.

Clearly, thought the captain, the Klingons had them at a disadvantage here in the open. He hated the idea of backing off from a threat on his own vessel, but the smarter move was to regroup and make use of the opportunities the *Enterprise* offered them.

"Fall back!" Kirk shouted, his voice ringing in the

corridor over the shrill whistling of competing energy volleys. "Somebody contact the shuttle chief and tell her to open those doors!"

He waited just long enough for the two officers with him to retreat beyond the bend in the hallway. Then he fell back as well, just in time to avoid another fiery red blast from the enemy.

Behind the captain, Gary and one of the security officers were lugging their stunned comrades back down the corridor, while the other security officer used his communicator to contact the shuttle chief.

Kirk didn't know how long it would take for the Klingons to press their advantage. A second? Two, maybe? If the shuttlebay doors didn't open by then, they'd be fish in a barrel.

But the doors *did* open, sliding apart with an audible exhalation of air. They revealed the tall, blond figure of Njalsdottir, the woman in charge of the shuttlebay this shift, and a couple of her technicians.

All three of them were armed with phasers. But then, the shuttlebay had a dedicated weapons locker for just such emergencies as this one.

"Hurry!" bellowed the captain, training his phaser at the bend in the hallway as he backpedaled.

"Move it!" added the navigator, dragging Rayburn toward the shuttlebay as fast as he could.

Then the Klingons made their move. They poured into the corridor like a dark wave, snarling with bloody intent and filling the place with one fiery discharge after another.

Unfortunately for them, Kirk and his crewmen weren't the least bit taken by surprise. The captain's shot struck an invader's shoulder, sending him spinning into one of his comrades. Njalsdottir's beam hammered another one in the midsection, dropping him to his knees.

The shuttle technicians and the unburdened security officer were busy as well. Their phased emissions lanced out and skewered the intruders, hitting them in the knee, in the chest, and even in the face. One by one, the Klingons staggered and fell.

But to Kirk's dismay, the invaders didn't remain there on the deck. They dragged themselves to their feet again and returned the defenders' fire, shrugging off the effects of stun-level phaser beams the way a boxer might shrug off a glancing blow.

Gritting his teeth, the captain delivered another blast, catching one of his adversaries beneath his hairy chin. Then he glanced over his shoulder to see how the others were doing.

Gary and Matthews had dragged the two unconscious security specialists past the threshold of the shuttlebay. Njalsdottir and her people were standing inside the threshold as well.

Only Kirk and a single security officer were still left out in the corridor. If the shuttlebay doors closed, they would be trapped outside them. On the other hand, they didn't dare wait much longer to secure the area.

"Shut the doors!" the captain bellowed over the din of the battle. Then he whirled and squeezed off another shot, driving one of the Klingons into the bulkhead behind him.

For a moment, nothing happened. Then Kirk heard the first, subtle stirrings of the door motors, telling him he had maybe two seconds to retreat or get torn limb from limb.

"Go!" he commanded the security officer.

Without any choice in the matter, the man fell back behind the threshold. At the same time, the captain seared the air with another phaser assault. Then, without waiting to see what effect it had, he turned and took a couple of steps and then launched himself through the air.

He could see the shuttlebay doors sliding purposefully toward one another, directed energy beams kicking off their duranium surfaces with spectacular effect. For a single, panicky moment, Kirk was certain that he wasn't going to make it. Then he hit the deck and slid forward on his stomach, and his momentum carried him through the steadily narrowing gap.

Pulling his legs in after him, he eluded the closing of the doors by a hair. Then he took a deep breath, basked momentarily in the knowledge that he and his people were safe, and got to his feet.

"Are you all right, sir?" asked Njalsdottir, who was kneeling on the floor and had covered his retreat.

"I'm fine," the captain assured her, brushing himself off.

"I thought you might have been exaggerating about those Klingons," the shuttle chief confessed to him, glancing at the doors to her facility. "But you weren't."

"Not even a little," he agreed.

Kirk empathized with Njalsdottir. After all, he hadn't had any firsthand knowledge of the enhanced

Klingons to go by before this. But he could see now that Phelana hadn't overestimated the intruders' abilities. They were every bit the threat she had described.

"Now what?" asked Gary, who was kneeling alongside the unconscious form of Rayburn. "We call security for help? Or just change the settings on our phasers and try again?"

The captain frowned. It was difficult to know how much phaser power it would take to bring these Klingons down. Too much might be lethal, and he didn't want to kill the intruders if he could avoid it.

The former option was more appealing. With the help of reinforcements, they could catch the Klingons in a crossfire.

"We call security," he told the navigator.

And quickly, he added inwardly. Otherwise, the invaders would figure out how to adjust the settings on their own weapons, and then—

Before Kirk could complete the thought, his eye was attracted to the doors. It seemed to him there was a discoloration in one of them. No—not a discoloration, he decided. A hot, red glow . . .

And that could mean only one thing.

"They've figured out how to use the phasers," Gary said hollowly.

Cursing inwardly, the captain nodded. "So they have."

Security officer Scott Darnell was getting dizzy trying to track the Klingon intruders' progress on the security section's massive array of internal sensor monitors.

The largest concentration of the invaders had just appeared outside the shuttlebay and forced the captain to retreat behind the facility's doors. That situation at least appeared stable for the moment.

But the rest of the Klingons had split up, making them a lot more difficult to find—and therefore, a lot more dangerous. In fact, it was Darnell's guess that a couple of the invaders had already crawled into Jefferies tubes and were making their way who knew where.

"I still don't get it," the security officer told Ensign Beltre, who was standing next to him and peering at the monitors over his shoulder. "How did these creeps get on the ship in the first place?"

Beltre shook her head. "They didn't tell me either, sir. But then, does it really matter? The job is still the same—locate the Klingons, flush them out and neutralize them."

Darnell grunted, trying to follow the progress of an armed invader on Deck Three. "It may not be as easy as you make it sound, Ensign. Did you see what that group of four did to the captain's party?"

Beltre's brow creased and she pointed. "What are they doing now?"

Darnell turned to the indicated monitor, where the Klingons were attacking the shuttlebay doors with high-intensity phaser beams. "Damn," he said. "The doors won't last long under that kind of barrage."

Suddenly, the captain's voice rang out in the security station. "This is Kirk," he said. "We need help down here in the shuttlebay."

Darnell was about to contact a team in the field

when some abrupt movement on one of the other monitors caught his eye. It turned out to be a skirmish between a couple of Klingons and a squad of security officers.

"Where did *they* come from?" Beltre asked.

Darnell didn't know either. But then, that no longer mattered very much. What mattered was that the security specialists were getting the stuffing beaten out of them. As Darnell watched, horrified, the intruders took the officers down with one vicious phaser strike after the other, then stepped over their bodies as if they were just part of the scenery.

"My god," said the ensign.

Darnell was about to say something too. Then a flurry of action on another monitor drew his attention. Again, a firefight exploded in front of his eyes. And again, his comrades got the worst of it.

Beltre pointed to a third monitor. "Look!"

It was the same story. The Klingons seemed to come out of nowhere, catching a security team unawares and raking them with phaser fire.

Suddenly, the captain's voice broke through over the intercom. "Repeat," he said, "this is Kirk. We can use a hand down here."

Darnell licked his lips, unable to take his eyes off his monitors. As he looked on helplessly, a fourth battle erupted near engineering.

"This is Darnell," he managed to respond. "I'll send some of our people over as soon as possible, sir. But I should tell you, we've got trouble all over the ship."

"Be more specific," the captain told him, obviously less than thrilled at the news.

Darnell tried to stay calm, tried to remember his training. But it wasn't easy watching his friends get their heads handed to them.

"I don't know how, sir," he told Kirk, "but the Klingons keep getting the jump on us. They've hit three—" His eyes were drawn to yet another violent confrontation. "Make that four security teams. We're not hunting *them* anymore," he concluded bitterly. "They're hunting *us.*"

The captain seemed to ponder the information for a moment—then a curse exploded over the intercom. "It's their sense of smell," he concluded. "It's got to be."

Distracted by the carnage he was witnessing on his monitors, the security officer shook his head. "I don't understand, sir."

"A normal Klingon has a sense of smell superior to yours or mine," Kirk explained succinctly. "But a Klingon whose natural abilities have been boosted, amplified . . ."

Suddenly, Beltre yelled for help. As Darnell whirled to find out why, he saw a dark, shaggy form fling the ensign into a bulkhead. She hit the duranium surface with a thud and slumped to the deck.

By then, Darnell's training had taken over. He reached for the phaser pistol on his hip, intending to knock the intruder senseless with a directed energy beam. But the Klingon was on top of him before he knew it, dragging him to the deck and pinning him with his weight.

The security officer got in a blow beneath his adversary's hairy chin, snapping his head back. The maneuver would have staggered a human being, maybe even maimed him. But the Klingon just shook it off. And before Darnell could strike again, his enemy grabbed him by the throat.

Darnell tried desperately to break the Klingon's grip, to pry his long, thick fingers away, but he couldn't do it. Despite his best efforts, he felt consciousness begin to ebb.

Then the intruder leaned in closer, his breath stinking of something foul, and growled something Darnell could barely make out. When he didn't answer, the Klingon growled again—this time, taking a bit more care to make clear what he wanted.

"Life-support," he rumbled, his eyes glittering with a hideous bloodlust. "Where are the controls, human?"

The security officer knew the stakes. If he didn't answer, his life might be forfeit. But there were more important things than his own survival.

The Klingon's mouth twisted with frustration and his grip tightened on Darnell's throat. "Answer me! Where are the life-support controls? Answer or I'll snap your neck!"

Darnell didn't answer the invader's question. All he said to the Klingon was "Go to hell."

Then came the darkness.

Chapter Twelve

Kirk stuck his head into the shuttlecraft *Galileo,* where Njalsdottir and a couple of her red-suited technicians were hunched over a section of exposed propulsion circuitry.

As the captain looked on, the shuttlebay chief applied a needle-thin phaser beam to one of the circuit junctions. Njalsdottir's features were caught in a bright red glow for just a second. Then the blond woman rocked back on her heels and turned to Kirk.

"That should do it," she said.

The captain nodded. Then he drew back from the shuttle and took another critical look at the doors to the place. What had been an almost imperceptible glow a couple of minutes earlier was now a dark, defined hot spot the size of his fist.

In another minute, maybe less, the Klingons' phaser beams would blacken the duranium surface of the door and punch through it. Then the wound would widen, little by little, until the enemy could get inside and eventually take over the facility.

But that wasn't the worst of Kirk's problems. After all, he had heard what sounded like a skirmish and then lost contact with Darnell, which forced him to believe that security had fallen to the Klingons. And judging from what Darnell had said before he was cut off, the invaders were prevailing in other parts of the ship as well.

The captain's jaw clenched. Obviously, he had underestimated the enemy. But he still believed that, in the end, he and his people would prevail. And in the meantime, the Klingons would find their prize—their escape route, which had to lead through this shuttlebay—had effectively been eliminated.

Suddenly, Gary was beside him. "We haven't got much time," the navigator reminded his friend.

"I guess not," Kirk agreed. "How are Rayburn and Keyes?"

"Could be worse," said Gary.

The captain grunted. "We'll need to be ready for the Klingons when they penetrate the doors. You and Matthews will take up positions on the right side of the shuttlebay. Njalsdottir and I . . ."

He stopped himself, realizing that something had changed. He sniffed the air once, then again.

"What is it?" the navigator asked him.

Kirk held his hand up and drew in another breath. It confirmed his suspicion. There was a strange smell in the air, as if something had gone wrong with the ship's ventilation system.

What's more, he knew what had caused it. "Life-support."

Gary regarded him. "What are you saying?"

The captain frowned. "There are life-support controls in security. The Klingons have found them."

Understanding dawned on the navigator's face. "They've changed the mixture of breathable gasses." He took in the expanse of the shuttlebay with a glance. "We're breathing something meant for another species."

Kirk nodded. "That's my guess."

A few moments ago, he had been thinking about how to fight the Klingons outside in the corridor. Now, he had an adversary on his hands that he couldn't fight—an enemy that couldn't be seen or heard or touched.

On the other side of the shuttlebay, Njalsdottir began to cough. "The air," she said wonderingly. "It's getting hard to breathe . . ."

"It's the Klingons," one of her technicians concluded, a worried expression on his face.

"The Klingons," the captain confirmed.

"They got hold of the life-support system?" asked another technician.

"Right again," said Gary. He turned to Kirk. "Which means we're in a lot more trouble than we were before."

The captain got an idea. "Not necessarily," he replied.

He turned to the orange doors and saw the sullen glow of the hot spot their adversaries had created. That meant the Klingons outside hadn't yet received word from their allies in the security section. Ignorant of the life-support situation in the shuttlebay, they were still trying to create an entrance for themselves so they could take the place over.

"Not necessarily, sir?" the navigator said.

Kirk thought it through as he spoke. "Those Klingons out in the hallway obviously don't know we're having trouble breathing. If we supplement their energy barrage with one of our own, we can poke a hole in that door before they know what's happening. Then we'll have access to what they're breathing—which will probably be fine for us."

"But we'll still have to worry about the Klingons themselves," Njalsdottir pointed out, her breathing noticeably labored.

The captain was feeling light-headed, too. "One thing at a time," he told the shuttlebay chief. Making an adjustment on his weapon, he raised his voice so everyone in the shuttlebay could hear him. "Set your phasers on maximum intensity and aim for the glow. If those Klingons want to get through the doors so badly, we'll give them a hand."

Then he pointed his weapon at the hot spot and fired.

Lieutenant Commander Spock had been aware that there was a problem on the bridge for some time. After all, Kelso, Alden, Brent, and Yeoman Smith had all begun to complain of difficulty in breathing.

Then Captain Kirk contacted the bridge and confirmed it.

"The Klingons control the *Enterprise*'s life-support?" Spock echoed, confirming the captain's report.

"And maybe . . . other systems as well," Kirk told him over the intercom, clearly starved for oxygen himself. "But we don't need . . . to worry . . . about anything else right now. Just life-support."

"Understood," said the Vulcan, who was only beginning to experience some discomfort himself. "Did you have a plan in mind, sir?"

"Affirmative," came the captain's response. "But I don't . . . want to discuss it . . . over the intercom . . . in case our friends the . . . the Klingons are listening in. Just do what you can . . . to defend the bridge, Commander."

Spock frowned, troubled by the lack of information but forcibly resigned to it. "Aye, sir."

"Kirk out," said the captain.

The Vulcan looked around at his companions. All four of them were waiting for him to say something, waiting to see how Spock would respond to Captain Kirk's orders.

The first officer acknowledged the weight of the phaser hanging at his hip. Fortunately, he had thought to ask Yeoman Smith to bring a handful of the weapons up to the bridge, just in case. Now, it seemed, the decision might prove to be a critical one.

That is, if Kelso, Alden, Brent, and Smith could maintain consciousness—a circumstance which was far from assured. All of them were red faced already, making subtle wheezing noises. If the Klingons continued to poison their air at the same rate, it would be impossible to mount the level of defense the captain required of them.

"Sir?" said Kelso, a little impatiently.

Spock returned the man's scrutiny with characteristic calm. Until something changed, he told himself, there was only one tack he could take—only one thing he could say.

And that was "Carry on."

Kirk's throat hurt as he tried desperately to suck in oxygen that was no longer available to him.

Holding on to a bulkhead for support, knees weak almost to the point of buckling, the captain continued to train his phaser beam on the hot spot in the shuttlebay door. However, only Gary and Matthews were still alert enough to join him, their faces as red as their energy emissions and their eyes popping with their efforts to breathe.

Most everyone else had already succumbed to the decline in breathable air, joining the two injured security officers on the floor. Njalsdottir was the only exception, and she wasn't far behind. The shuttlebay chief had dropped to her knees and was struggling just to stay conscious, her phaser lying unused on the deck beside her.

Kirk's head swam. If they didn't punch through to the corridor soon, he told himself, they might never do so.

At this point, the captain could no longer tell if the Klingons were still working on the door from the outside. All he could see was the fiery splash of red emissions.

Kirk had barely completed the thought when he

saw Njalsdottir slump to the floor. Then Matthews's phaser stopped emitting its beam—a bad sign, the captain knew. A moment later, the security officer clutched at a bulkhead, spun around and fell.

It left just Kirk and his friend still standing—still firing at the hot spot. Somehow, the captain continued to drag air into his tortured lungs and fight the darkness at the edges of his vision.

A heartbeat later, Gary fell to one knee. But he didn't stop firing. His phaser beam continued to eat at the hot spot, reinforcing his friend's beam, testing the durability of the duranium surface.

Kirk's jaw clenched. *I won't fall,* he promised himself. *I won't.*

But he did. He felt his knees give way and he fell in a heap at the foot of a bulkhead. And in the process, his finger slipped off the trigger of his weapon, allowing its beam to die.

No, thought the captain. Not now. Not when we're so close.

Forcing himself to stay awake, to concentrate, he found the trigger again, took aim and pressed down on it. Once again, the ruby red phaser beam shot out and attacked its target.

But only for a few seconds. Then Kirk found that no matter how hard he tried to pull in oxygen, he couldn't find any. His hand went numb and his weapon clattered to the floor.

He looked to his friend. Gary had stopped firing as well. He was on all fours now, his face the color of blood. The tendons in his neck standing out like cables, he fought to hold on to his senses.

As the captain watched, the navigator lost his

battle. He fell over on his side, having spent his last iota of energy. Kirk stared at him for a moment, hating the sight of Gary lying there.

Then he felt the cold of the deck against his face. And a moment later, he didn't even feel that.

Phaser in hand, senses alert, the Klingon called Qadar coiled behind the lift doors. When they opened in front of him with a rush of air, he took in the enemy's bridge with a single, economical glance.

He saw five figures—four males and a female, all of them dressed in Starfleet garb and all of them sprawled on the floor. Keeping his weapon trained on the nearest of them, Qadar came out on the bridge and gestured for his fellow M'tachtar to follow him.

The place still stank from the exotic gasses the M'tachtar had introduced to this place. However, Qadar and his comrades—who didn't need much oxygen in the first place—had brought enough of it up in the turbolift to keep them going for a minute or two. Later, they could figure out how to contact security and have an oxygen mixture pumped in again.

Chi'ra grunted. "It was too easy. I had hoped for more opposition."

"You hoped for too much," said Rokh'ma.

Qadar ignored his warriors' remarks. The engines throbbing beneath the deckplates, a counterpoint to the eager beating of his hearts, the Klingon approached the nearest of the Starfleet officers—a dark-skinned man lying face up beside a peripheral console. Reacting to the return of oxygen to the enclosure, the human was starting to wake, to open his eyes—to cough and draw in air in great gulps.

Bringing his booted foot back, Qadar kicked the officer in the face, eliciting a groan of pain and surprise. Then the man's head lolled to the side and he lay still again, though his chest continued to rise and fall as his lungs drank their fill.

The other humans were showing signs of waking as well. Qadar was about to instruct his followers to handle them as he had handled the dark-skinned one. But before he could open his mouth, one of their adversaries sprang to his feet and drove his fist into Chi'ra's jaw.

Chi'ra didn't fall. But he didn't strike back, either. Obviously, the blow had stunned him.

Qadar was confused for a moment. He hadn't thought humans capable of such resilience—or such power. Then Chi'ra absorbed a second blow and staggered backward, giving Qadar a better look at the Starfleet officer . . . and in that instant, the Klingon's confusion was dispelled.

It wasn't a human at all, he realized. It was a Vulcan—a member of a much stronger and more durable species. And at the moment, he was bolting for the still-open turbolift, no doubt hoping to escape this place and report what had happened here to his superiors.

Qadar's mouth twisted. There would be no escapes. He had waited much too long for this opportunity to leave the tiniest detail to chance.

As the Vulcan tried to slip by him, the Klingon reached out and grabbed him by the arm. Then he planted his feet and whipped his adversary over the orange red rail, sending him flying into a freestanding console.

The Vulcan hit it with enough force to knock out most sentient species. Nonetheless, he found the strength to grab hold of the console and pull himself up to one knee.

Qadar respected strength. He admired dedication. But his respect and admiration didn't outweigh his need to accomplish his objective—and accomplish it quickly.

Extending his phaser pistol in the Vulcan's direction, he unleashed a sudden, bloodred beam. The officer recoiled from the impact, hit the console again and lay still.

Qadar grunted. "See to the others," he told his followers.

Glaring at the Vulcan, Chi'ra used his knuckle to wipe crimson spittle from the corner of his mouth. "I'll see to *him,"* he said.

Qadar grinned as the other Klingon advanced on the unconscious officer. "Just leave him alive, Chi'ra. Who knows? I may need him."

After all, he mused, examining the bridge a little more closely, this was a big vessel—and an unfamiliar one. He didn't know yet who among its crew he might keep and who he might decide to throw away.

Kirk regained consciousness in the grasp of two burly but unarmed Klingons, each of them a full head taller than he was, in what he immediately recognized as one of the ship's turbolift compartments.

His head hurt and his lungs hurt even worse. He

could only guess how he had wound up here or where he was headed. But he knew one thing for certain—he wasn't about to let the element of surprise slip away from him.

Driving the heel of his boot into the side of one captor's knee, the captain used the leverage it gave him to smash the other one in the jaw with his elbow. The Klingons groaned and cursed at him, and for just a fraction of a second he was free to maneuver.

But his adversaries recovered more quickly than he would have liked. As he launched another blow at the one he had kicked, the other one caught him from behind with a savage strike to his shoulder.

It drove Kirk to his knees and numbed his right arm. And before he could get up again, he felt a second punch knock him flat. Nor did the Klingons let him lay on the deck for long. They dragged him to his feet and held him as they had before, except more securely.

The captain resolved to wait until the compartment came to a halt before making another attempt at escape. But a moment later, as the lift doors slid aside, he realized the futility of such a plan.

Even before Kirk saw the Klingons on his bridge, he heard them. The sounds they made were deep throated, savage, more like rocks grinding together than actual language.

Glancing about, he saw that the invaders were everywhere—at the communications console, at engineering, at the science station, at the helm, and at navigation. And, of course, in the captain's chair.

The Klingons behind him shoved Kirk out of the

lift compartment. He stumbled, then caught himself and looked around some more.

For a second, the intruders stopped to study him or, in some cases, to chuckle at the human's helplessness. But only for a second. Then they returned to their respective duties.

Only then did the Klingon in the center seat rise and turn around to regard him. Coming around the sleek, dark chair, he ascended to the level of the lift doors as if to get a better look at his captive.

The captain looked up into the Klingon's face. It was craggier than any of the others, his forehead bonier, his eyes more deeply set and more malevolent over a cruel gash of a mouth. And unlike his brethren, he exhibited no facial hair—only a thick, dark mane gathered in a long, plaited pigtail.

He glanced at Kirk's sleeves, which bore the gold stripes of a Starfleet captain. "You are the commander of this vessel," the invader snarled, his voice deep and guttural. "True?"

Kirk shrugged. "Who wants to know?"

He had dealt with Klingons before, after all. He knew that he had to maintain an air of bravado if he was to maximize his chances of survival.

But this was not the kind of Klingon he had dealt with in the past. Instead of sneering at his remark, the warrior brought his hand back almost too quickly for the captain to follow and lashed him across the face.

Kirk's head snapped back under the impact, his mouth filling with the taste of blood. Turning and spitting it out, he glared at his tormentor.

"He looks angry," one of the other Klingons taunted.

"Perhaps we should be frightened," another gibed.

They laughed at the remark. But not all of them—not their leader. He just gazed at the captain appraisingly.

"If you are seeking to impress me," the Klingon growled, "I should tell you I am not easily impressed. Now I ask you again, for what I assure you is the last time . . . are you the commander of this vessel?"

Kirk raised his chin. "I am."

The Klingon's eyes narrowed. "You are trainable. That is surprising. I had heard your species was slow to learn."

Again, there was rough laughter among the Klingons. And again, it didn't come from their leader.

Instead, he stroked his chin. "You disabled your shuttlecraft," he told the captain. "What was your purpose in this?"

"To keep you from escaping," the captain responded defiantly.

His captor's mouth crinkled at the corners—as close as it seemed he would come to a smile. "To keep *us* from escaping?" he said.

The invaders laughed again, perhaps harder than before. Kirk felt his face heat up. "What's so funny?" he asked.

The Klingon eyed him. "We never had any intention of escaping your vessel," he replied.

Not until then had the captain been able to appreciate the full scope of the invaders' arrogance.

Now, however, he saw it in all its savage splendor. "Then you wanted to get into the shuttlebay—"

His captor made a derisive sound deep in his throat. "To keep *you* from escaping," he said, finishing the human's sentence.

Kirk swallowed back his humiliation. What a fool he had been. What a smug, overconfident fool.

What's more, the Klingon knew it.

"When they come for you," he grated, "as they surely will, tell them it was Qadar who took your ship and made you an object of ridicule." He leaned closer, so that his aquiline nose was mere centimeters from the captain's. "Don't forget, human—it was *Qadar.*"

Kirk didn't know what the Klingon meant by that. "When they come for me . . . ?" he repeated.

Qadar didn't answer, he just made a quick, sharp gesture of dismissal. As the Klingons on either side of him reached for his arms, the captain wondered if he was going to be executed or just taken away—and decided he didn't want to wait to find out.

Driving his elbow into the midsection of the Klingon on his right, he doubled the warrior over. That freed up his right hand, which he then drove into the jaw of the Klingon on his left.

As the invader staggered, the captain reached for the phaser pistol the Klingon had tucked into his belt. If he got it, he told himself, he would have a fighting chance—especially in such close quarters.

But he wasn't quick enough. Before his fingers could close on the weapon, Kirk felt his wrist encased in the hardest grip he had ever felt. Then his hand was wrenched away from its objective.

And he found himself looking up into Qadar's face again.

Still holding the captain's wrist, the Klingon glared at him for a moment, his eyes dark and supremely contemptuous beneath his brow ridge. "Remember" was the only word he said.

Before Kirk could even think of responding, Qadar belted him hard across the face again. Stunned and bloodied, the human fell backward—and found himself grabbed by two strong pairs of Klingon hands. Then he was dragged forcibly away from the center seat. What's more, his captors continued to drag him until he was back inside the turbolift.

Then the doors closed, obscuring the Klingons from view—and the captain was forced to wonder if he had seen his bridge for the last time.

Chapter Thirteen

KIRK DIDN'T GO DOWN to the planet's surface without a struggle.

In the turbolift, he tried again to free himself from his Klingon captors. And again, he was beaten down for his trouble.

Then, as they pulled him out of the lift compartment on the transporter deck, the captain attacked them again. He got in two good blows before they slammed his head against a bulkhead.

After that, he drifted in and out of consciousness. The next thing he knew, he was lying on hard ground under a blazing hot sun, Nurse Hinch's face swimming over his.

"Try to lie still," he heard her say, her voice deep with concern. "You've been beaten pretty badly, sir."

Ignoring her, Kirk rolled over on his side and

propped himself up. He could see where he was now, but it wasn't a pretty sight—not for him or for the hundreds of other crewmen who stood in the lee of a line of gigantic, ocher-colored cliffs, looking lost and defeated.

The whole crew, he thought at first. Then he realized it was only part of it. A little more than half, maybe.

And they were on the planet's barren, craggy surface—the same unforgiving landscape that had served as a prison all those years for Qadar and his enhanced Klingons. In fact, the captain could see an immense yellow forcefield in the distance.

They had no food, he thought, no water—other than what they could scratch out of the land. Poetic justice? he wondered. At least from Qadar's point of view?

Kirk found he didn't care about the motive. All that mattered to him was that the Klingon had spared them.

"Captain," said a familiar voice.

Kirk shielded his eyes and turned to it. There was a dark, slender figure standing over him, backlit by the sun but nonetheless recognizable.

"Spock," he said.

The Vulcan held out his hand and the captain took it. As he pulled himself up with Spock's help, he felt all the places where he had been pounded and pummeled in his attempts at resistance.

Then Kirk got a better look at his first officer and realized he wasn't the only one who had suffered at the Klingons' hands. An entire side of Spock's face was a mess of dark green bruises and there was dried blood in one corner of his mouth.

"You look awful," the captain said.

The Vulcan grunted softly. "I am not the only one, sir."

Kirk looked around at the vast stretches of fiery terrain, at the cloudless, blue-green sky. Then he looked at his people. "We're not all here. Any idea what happened to the others?" he asked soberly.

Spock nodded. "Before I was beamed down, I heard a discussion among our captors. Their leader opted to keep half the crew as hostages—to make sure the *Enterprise* is not fired on by other starships."

The captain was relieved. It meant the other part of his crew was still alive. But as he thought about it, he realized they might not stay that way for long.

"Unfortunately," he said, "hostages are no assurance. Starfleet will do whatever it takes to stop the Klingons from making off with the *Enterprise*—even destroy her, if it comes down to it."

"Of course," the Vulcan replied, "the Klingons don't know that."

Kirk frowned. He wished Gary was with him and Spock on the planet's surface. But he knew in his heart that his friend was among those who had been kept on the ship.

"I wonder where they'll take her," the captain said out loud.

Spock shook his head ruefully. "Under the circumstances, sir, there is no way of knowing."

"Yes, there is," said a feminine voice.

Kirk turned and saw Phelana approaching them. The Andorian was still bruised and battered from her encounter with the Klingons, but she didn't look any worse than the captain felt.

"You know more than you told me," he concluded.

"A little," she said, her black eyes glinting in the strong sunlight. "According to the admiral, those Klingons are renegades of some kind. They have reason to hate the High Council."

"So they're headed for the Klingon homeworld?" Kirk gathered. "To seek their revenge?"

Phelana nodded. "That's my guess."

The captain swore to himself. His ship and half his crew were under Qadar's control. If a starship on the Federation side of the neutral zone hailed them and got an inkling of what was going on . . .

"Our comrades are in great danger," Spock concluded.

"Yes," said Kirk, "they are."

Not that any of them could do anything about it. Not down here, alone and cut off from—

Suddenly, the captain stopped himself. After all, they weren't alone . . . were they? "The Klingon ship!" he breathed.

The Vulcan's eyes narrowed. "What about it, sir?"

"If we can get their attention," the captain explained, "let them know what's happened on the *Enterprise* . . ."

Phelana sighed. "But we haven't got any communications equipment. Our captors made certain of that."

Kirk wiped his brow with the back of his hand. *There's got to be a way to contact those Klingons,* he thought. *There's got to be.*

The commander of the Klingon vessel *Doj* turned to his right and eyed his communications officer with a certain amount of skepticism. "A signal from the surface?" he said. "Are you certain, J'likh?"

"Quite certain," came the response from the communications officer, his features bathed in the faint, green glare of his monitors.

The commander grunted and turned to his hexagonal viewscreen again. As before, it showed him a sweep of red-orange terrain, somewhere in which the M'tachtar's prison was located.

But how could the M'tachtar have sent out a signal? And why hadn't the Federation vessel on the opposite side of the globe already done something about it?

The commander scowled in his beard and listened to the drone of the *Doj*'s engines. Unfortunately, his orders prevented him from initiating any communications with the Federation ship. But clearly, the matter needed to be investigated.

He got up from his seat and gestured for his second in command to take charge. As Tupogh moved to the commander's chair, the commander himself left the dimly lit bridge and headed down the even more dimly lit main corridor of his ship, his destination the *Doj*'s transporter facility. En route, he told himself, he would gather some warriors to accompany him.

Then the commander would see for himself how the M'tachtar had managed to send a signal out—and he would make sure it didn't happen again.

For what must have been the twentieth time, Kirk pressed the stud on the jury-rigged graviton projector and watched it send a narrow, yellow beam into the aquamarine sky.

But, just like the first nineteen times, there was no response. The captain rocked back on his heels and wiped the perspiration from his brow. The heat was starting to get to him, he reflected.

"Perhaps their sensors are not calibrated to receive such a signal," Spock suggested. "Or they may have moved out of range."

"Or a great many other possibilities," Kirk conceded, a little annoyed with the scope of the first officer's conjecture. "But that doesn't mean we're going to stop trying, Mr. Spock."

The Vulcan arched an eyebrow. "I did not mean to suggest we should," he replied. "Only that we may wish to examine other options."

"Such as?" asked the captain.

Spock frowned. "I am working on it," he responded without rancor.

Kirk sighed. The Vulcan was only trying to be helpful, he told himself. He was wrong to have snapped at him. Just as he had been wrong to think the enhanced Klingons were just another group of intruders.

"I apologize, Mr. Spock." He glanced at the expanse of bright, empty sky, then at the large group of crewmen who had gathered on the rust red bluff behind him, and back again at the first officer. "It's just that I was so certain this would work."

"So was I," said Phelana.

The Andorian was standing just a few meters away, in the shade of a rocky upthrust, alongside Alden, Kyle, and Kelso—the team that had helped the captain and Spock alter the projector into a narrow beam device. Their uniforms were all soaked through with perspiration.

"Maybe we didn't calculate the wavelength right," Kyle suggested.

"Or the conversion ratio," Kelso allowed.

Alden shook his head. "No . . . we did everything right. The Klingons should have received our signal and beamed down a long time ago."

"You should be grateful," said a deep, guttural voice, "that we responded at all."

Whirling, the captain saw a squad of five armed Klingons advance to the forward edge of a rocky, red shelf. But to his relief, they were the kind of Klingons he had encountered before—tall, dark, and lean, with high cheekbones and upswept eyebrows. Nothing like the muscular, bumpy-headed supermen who had taken over the *Enterprise*.

Kirk got up and took a step toward the bluff. Spock came along.

"That's far enough," said the foremost Klingon, pointing his weapon at the captain. "Identify yourselves."

"I'm Captain James T. Kirk of the starship *Enterprise,"* the captain said, his voice echoing from rock to rock. He tilted his head to indicate the Vulcan.

"And this is Spock, my first officer. We're the ones who sent you that graviton pulse."

The Klingon regarded Kirk with dark, suspicious eyes. "You claim that you sent the signal?"

"I did," the captain confirmed.

The Klingon shook his head. "Why?" He gestured with his weapon at the sea of *Enterprise* crewmen. "And what are so many of you doing down here?"

Kirk explained as briefly as he could. When he got to the part about Qadar and his warriors escaping, the Klingon's eyes opened wide. And when he added that Qadar and his men had seized the *Enterprise,* the Klingon's mouth twisted with disgust.

"You let him take your *ship?"* he said incredulously.

The captain met the affront without flinching. "If he had wanted yours, he would have had that as well."

The Klingon shook his head defiantly. "You say that because you don't know me, human."

Kirk felt a bead of sweat trace its way down his face. He held his hands out. "Listen . . . we can stand here talking all day, if you like. Or you can beam us up to your vessel and break orbit as soon as possible. Because if you don't, you're going to lose your quarry."

The Klingon made no effort to hide his disdain. "Beam you up? And why should I take *you?"*

"Because I know my ship," the captain replied coolly, "every inch of it. With my assistance, you'll catch those other Klingons and stop them. Without my assistance . . ." He shrugged.

The Klingon's lips pulled back, revealing a set of

sharp, predatory teeth. "Very well," he said. "You'll come with me." He gestured with his weapon in the direction of Spock, Phelana, Alden, Kyle, and Kelso. "These five as well. But no more."

Then he turned to Kirk again, as if he expected a challenge. The captain wasn't going to give him one. After all, he had gotten further with the Klingon than he had expected.

The Klingon gestured again—this time to a point just below the bluff on which he was standing. "Gather here," he instructed Kirk and the others. "Apart from the rest of your comrades."

The captain and his designated officers did as they were told. Then the Klingon leader removed a mechanism from his belt that looked vaguely like a Starfleet communicator.

"Eleven to beam up," he said, speaking into the device. "Two parties—ours and theirs. Keep them separate."

A rough acknowledgment came from the communications device. Then the Klingon put it away and gave Kirk a sidelong glance.

"Do not try any tricks," he declared. "If you do, you'll regret them a thousand times over."

"We'll be peaceful as lambs," the captain replied, though he allowed a note of irony to creep into his voice.

A moment later, the Klingons vanished. Kirk looked at his officers. "Be ready for anything," he told them.

After all, no Starfleet officer had ever seen the inside of a working Klingon vessel. Whenever a Klingon commander lost a battle, he would destroy his ship rather than allow a conqueror to set foot in it.

Of course, Kirk and his people were hardly conquerors in this instance. To the Klingon leader and his crew, they were closer to being laughingstocks—bumblers who had lost their ship to a clever intruder.

The captain had barely completed this thought when he realized his surroundings had changed. Instead of the open, barren terrain on which he had been abandoned, he found himself in the cramped, dark atmosphere of what appeared to be a Klingon transporter room.

Getting his bearings, Kirk saw that his officers were present as well—all five that had been designated for transport. He also saw the half dozen Klingon warriors gathered in front of the hexagonal transport grid with their disruptor pistols aimed at their guests.

"Put your weapons down," said their leader, making his way through the assembled Klingons. "Captain Kirk and his people are harmless."

The warriors grinned and exchanged amused glances. Some even chuckled at their superior's remark.

It was a slap in the face, Kirk knew, even if the conclusion was a reasonable one considering the circumstances. The captain didn't know a great deal about Klingons, but he knew one thing—it was required of him to take umbrage with the Klingon's comment.

Without hesitation, Kirk walked up to him and looked him in the eye. "Send your guards away and

I'll show you how harmless I am. Or do you only know how to make insults when you've got an army behind you?"

The Klingon's eyes flashed black fire and his lips pulled back in anger. For a moment, it appeared he would reach for the weapon at his hip. Then his fury seemed to cool.

"I'll be glad to oblige you when my duty has been discharged," the Klingon growled at him. "Until then, you are too valuable to kill—as you yourself were quick to point out."

Inwardly, the captain breathed a sigh of relief. But then, he didn't want to fight any more than the Klingon did. He still had a ship to get back.

The Klingon took in his warriors with a glance. "Spread the word," he said. "Our guests are not to be harmed." He glanced at Kirk again. "That is the command of Kang, son of K'naiah."

Kang, thought the captain. At least now he knew who in pity's name he was dealing with.

Chapter Fourteen

KIRK STOOD at the broad, hexagon-shaped portal and watched the stars wheel by. "They're coming about," he noted.

Spock, who was standing beside him in the Klingons' dark, brazen version of a briefing room, nodded slowly. "No doubt, their sensors have confirmed our suspicions about the *Enterprise*'s heading—perhaps from her ion trail—and they have decided to offer pursuit."

The captain turned to Kelso. "Your observations, Lieutenant?"

The helmsman shrugged, his features caught in the yellow glare of one of the room's few lighting sources. "Looks to me like they're setting a course for the Klingon Neutral Zone, sir."

"Just as I thought they would," said Phelana.

Kirk glanced at her. "Yes. Just as you thought."

"Sir," said Alden, "what about the others? The ones we left behind on the planet's surface?"

"They'll have a difficult time of it without supplies," Kyle pointed out.

"Don't worry," the captain told them. "I'll see to it that our people are taken care of."

Suddenly, the doors to the room parted and Kang walked in accompanied by a trio of his warriors. All four of them still wore their disruptor pistols, as if they were expecting trouble.

Then again, this was a vessel full of Klingons. If the stories were true, Kirk told himself, they fought among themselves more often than they fought their enemies.

"We have identified your *Enterprise*'s heading," Kang told the captain without preamble. "In time, we will overtake her."

That depends on how fast she's going, Kirk remarked inwardly. But he didn't express the concern out loud.

"Meanwhile," said Kang, pulling out a chair from the bloodred, hexagon-shaped table that dominated the room, "I want to know how this shameful situation came about." He leaned forward, skewering Kirk on his gaze. "I want to know how the M'tachtar escaped."

The captain looked at him. "The M'tachtar?"

The Klingon frowned. "Qadar and his fourteen followers."

Kirk nodded, filing the name away. He looked to Phelana. "We'll be glad to tell you all about it, of course. But first, we've got to send a message to the nearest Federation starbase, alerting the fleet to the plight of my people on the prison planet. Otherwise, they may not live long enough to see the outcome of our pursuit."

Kang looked at him for a moment, no doubt weighing the wisdom of complying with the captain's wishes. Finally, he came to a decision. "Very well. One of your officers may send such a message, Captain. I will have my communications officer assist you in this."

Kirk eyed him back. "I'm grateful."

The Klingon shrugged. "As you should be."

The captain turned to Alden. "Lieutenant?"

Alden rose and waited for Kang's reponse. A moment later, the Klingon leader signed to one of his men, who got up and led the way out of the briefing room. The lieutenant was right behind him.

Kang eyed Kirk again. "And now . . . ?"

"And now we'll tell you what we know," the captain told the Klingon. "But after that, I want to know something also—and that's how the M'tachtar came to be so powerful."

Kang regarded him fiercely. For all the human knew, he had pushed the Klingon leader too far and would pay the price for it—in blood, perhaps.

Then the corners of Kang's mouth pulled up and he grinned a wolfish grin. A grin of respect, Kirk hoped.

"You want to know how the M'tachtar became so powerful, Captain?" The Klingon nodded, still amused. "I believe that can be arranged."

Kirk grinned, too. But then, he couldn't afford not to.

* * *

Gary Mitchell sat in one of the *Enterprise*'s gray, dimly lit cargo bays, surrounded by fifty or sixty of his fellow crewmen, and stared resentfully at the glittering energy barrier blocking their access to the corridor outside.

Beyond the barrier, there was a strapping Klingon guard in dark, leathery garb, a phaser pistol clutched in his big, scarred fist. And though he and one of his comrades had spoken at length just a few minutes earlier, he didn't look like he was eager to speak that way with any of his captives.

"We've got to get out of here," Mitchell said.

"Any ideas?" asked Scotty, who was sitting beside him.

The navigator turned to him. "You're the idea man, Mr. Scott."

The engineer frowned. "I've got t' admit, I'm at somethin' of a loss. At least, for the time bein'."

Sulu, who was sitting on Mitchell's other side, said, "Maybe it would help to take stock of our situation. Tally up what we know and see if we can use any of it."

"All right," the navigator agreed. "So what do we know?"

Scotty shrugged. "That a bloody bastard named Qadar has taken control of our ship."

"That some of us are captives here and some others were left on the planet," Sulu offered.

"And that the captain was one o' those left behind," said the engineer, a note of bitterness in his voice.

On the other side of the cargo bay, Admiral

Mangione groaned and rolled over onto her side. Dr. Piper propped up the uniform shirt under her head to make her more comfortable, but without his hypospray he was limited in what he could accomplish.

"And that some of us need medical attention," Scotty added, "the admiral foremost among 'em."

Mitchell's teeth ground together. He understood why the Klingons would want to keep someone like him imprisoned in a cargo bay. But Mangione . . . a woman suffering from a concussion, who was clearly in no condition to undermine Qadar's efforts? What did their captors have to gain by holding the admiral here instead of in sickbay? Was it some kind of payback for what the Klingons had endured on the planet they had left behind?

The navigator cursed beneath his breath. He felt so helpless here, and he hated feeling helpless. Unexpectedly, he felt a hand on his arm.

It was Scotty's hand. "I know how ye feel, lad," said the engineer. "And believe me, I feel the same way."

It helped Mitchell to know he wasn't alone in his anger and frustration. But to tell the truth, he thought, it doesn't help *enough.*

The navigator wished he were at his friend Jim's side, plotting to rescue both halves of the crew. He wished he were hiding somewhere on the ship where the Klingons couldn't find him. In fact, he wished he were anywhere but behind an energy barrier.

"Hey," he said.

Both Sulu and Scotty turned to him.

Mitchell tilted his head toward the forcefield. "Remind me never to get penned behind one of these things again."

Sulu chuckled dryly. "Whatever you say."

The navigator thought again about his friend the captain. Of course, he had every confidence in the man. He knew Jim Kirk could beat anything the Klingons threw at him, with or without his old pal Gary.

But as he had said not so long ago, he was the captain's rabbit's foot, his good luck charm—and as such, he had the gall to believe Kirk was better off with him than without him.

Still marveling that he was in a Klingon briefing room, Kirk sat back in his hard, metal chair between Kelso and Phelana and listened as the Andorian provided an answer to Kang's question.

"From what I could see," Phelana said, "the energy storage unit in one of the graviton projectors that kept the M'tachtar incarcerated met with some malfunction—even though the devices were checked every six months, along with the M'tachtar themselves."

The Klingon leader scowled. "Was there no back-up measure?"

"There was," the Andorian responded. "But it wouldn't have kicked in until the projector was down for thirty seconds. Normally, that would have been little enough. Unfortunately, one of Qadar's people must have been in the right place at the right time. Seeing the gap, he would have taken advantage of it to escape."

"And once he was free," the captain speculated, "he must have worked on some of the other projectors, enabling his friends to get out as well."

Kang didn't say anything. However, his scowl had deepened.

"Of course," Phelana went on, "getting past the energy barrier was only the first step. They also had to get hold of a ship. So they waited until our regularly scheduled visit and concealed themselves in the vicinity of the cliffs, which our sensors couldn't penetrate."

"They jumped our landing party," Kirk noted. "And when we realized something was wrong and attempted to beam them up, the M'tachtar came along for the ride."

The Klingon leader grunted. "Obviously, your Federation technology is untrustworthy and your technicians are sloppy. It's a good thing my vessel was waiting in orbit as a precaution, or the M'tachtar would have gotten away without a trace."

This time, the captain ignored the detraction. "We've told you what you wanted to know," he declared. "Now tell us about the M'tachtar."

Kang snorted. "The M'tachtar," he said, as if it were a curse. He looked at the warriors who flanked him at the bloodred table. "As little as sixteen years ago, they did not exist. Then a scientist whose name you will recognize decided to dabble in previously forbidden arts."

"Qadar?" Kirk suggested.

"Qadar," the Klingon confirmed.

"It would never have been permitted," one of the

other warriors said with a sneer, "except he was the emperor Grannoch's ruustai-cousin."

"True, Tupogh," said Kang, taking no apparent exception to the interjection. "But whatever the reason, it *was* allowed. Qadar introduced certain substances into the blood of his experimental subjects, causing changes in muscle mass, perception thresholds, and reaction times. These altered Klingons, whom he selected from his house's retainers, he named the M'tachtar . . . an ancient term for the ultimate Klingon warrior. And Qadar, by his own design, became the ultimate of ultimates."

The phrase sent a chill down the captain's back. *The ultimate of ultimates.* A faster, stronger, more predatory Klingon than those the Federation had faced anytime before.

And Qadar could have repeated the process over and over again, until every warrior in the empire was on a level with the M'tachtar. Kirk couldn't imagine anything more frightening.

"Unfortunately for Qadar," Kang continued, "he was not a patient individual. Perhaps it was the change in his biochemistry. Perhaps it was a lust for glory he had harbored all his life."

"Perhaps it does not matter," Tupogh laughed, his voice echoing throughout the briefing room.

Kang laughed with him, his dark eyes flashing. "Perhaps not. In any case, Qadar thirsted for blood. And he hoped to quench that thirst by spearheading an attack on the Federation."

"Charming," said Kelso.

The Klingon leader glanced at him with hooded

eyes, then turned to Kirk again. "Qadar found it so," he replied. "So did the emperor, for that matter. However, he had been working on a plan of his own, which hinged on his nurturing certain alliances."

"With whom?" asked the captain.

"If I told you," said Kang, "I would be forced to destroy you. Suffice it to say they would have been *powerful* alliances, had they taken place. As you can see, they did not—because your Federation still exists."

Lucky us, Kirk thought.

The Klingon went on. "The idea of making alliances did not appeal to Qadar. So, without the emperor's support, or even his knowledge, Qadar secured a battle cruiser—on which he hoped to take his M'tachtar into bloody battle against your Starfleet."

Phelana looked at him. "The entire fleet?"

Kang shrugged. "If you wish to kill a serpent, you cut off its head. That is what Qadar planned to do—deprive your fleet of its head."

The captain was stunned by the audacity of what the Klingon was suggesting. "Qadar planned to attack Starfleet Command?"

"On your human homeworld," his host confirmed, letting the remark hang in the air.

A century earlier, thought Kirk, the Romulans had come within a hair's breadth of invading Earth. They had fallen short of their goal, thanks to the courage and tenacity of her human defenders.

But what Kang was describing was a different threat entirely—a surgical strike at the most critical and well-guarded link in the Starfleet chain of command. And judging by what Kirk had seen of the M'tachtar, he wasn't all that confident the attack wouldn't have worked.

"Then," said the Klingon leader, "the emperor got wind of Qadar's plan. He had to have been intrigued by it, as it would have removed Starfleet and the Federation from the path of Klingon conquest. However, he couldn't allow it to be carried out."

The captain understood. "Because Qadar's effort might have placed the emperor in a bad light."

"A bad light indeed," Kang agreed. "If the M'tachtar emerged victorious, what would that have said about the emperor and his supporters on the council? The people of the empire might have turned away from them and embraced Qadar's group instead. And if the M'tachtar had died in their quest, they might have been revered as heroes—and again, the emperor and the council would have suffered in comparison."

"What did the emperor do?" asked Spock, who had been as silent as the void until that moment.

Kang grunted. "Something he never thought he would even consider. To begin with, he gave Qadar the impression that he was giving in to his arguments—and dispatched the M'tachtar to an unpopulated planet in Federation space, where they would remain until they received further orders. Then he contacted Starfleet Command and sent a warning concerning the M'tachtar's arrival—effectively setting a trap for Qadar and his warriors."

A trap, Kirk reflected. For his own people. It left a bad taste in his mouth and he wasn't even a Klingon.

"The emperor fully expected your Starfleet to destroy the M'tachtar," Kang noted, rapping the briefing room table with his knuckles. "After all, that was what any Klingon would have done. He was taken aback when the return message asked him in what manner he wanted the M'tachtar returned to him."

The captain had never met the emperor, but he could imagine the Klingon's reaction. Not a happy one, he thought, considering Grannoch believed his problem had been solved already.

"The emperor sent a second transmission," Kang said, "advising your Starfleet of the danger presented by Qadar and his people. He recommended that the M'tachtar be executed at the earliest opportunity. The return message wasn't long in coming, apparently. Citing some Federation code of honor, it said your people wouldn't kill the M'tachtar under any circumstances."

Tupogh laughed again, even louder than before. "Honor? Among humans?" he growled derisively.

Kirk looked at him. "You find that difficult to imagine?"

"No," said the Klingon. "I find it impossible."

"A discussion for another time," Kang told them, displaying little patience for the digression this time.

"How was the matter of the M'tachtar finally resolved?" asked Spock, in an obvious attempt to bring the conference back on track.

Kang seemed to approve of the question. "As I said, your people refused to kill the M'tachtar. They also refused to send the M'tachtar back, claiming to be concerned that we Klingons would kill them."

"Which a spineless p'takh like Grannoch would no doubt have done," Tupogh observed slyly.

"Without hesitation," Kang agreed. "But to his mind, what your Starfleet eventually proposed was the next best thing—to catch the M'tachtar unaware and destroy their vessel, giving them barely enough time to beam down to the planet's surface. Then energy barriers would be set up to contain them—along with a handful of surveillance devices, so you might be warned when Qadar and his people made attempts to escape."

"That wasn't the only reason for the surveillance equipment," Phelana pointed out, her antennae extended forward. "We also wanted to make sure the M'tachtar were all right. That they were in good health."

Kang frowned across the table at her. "So the Federation has always maintained."

The captain regarded the Andorian. "Let me get this straight," he said. "Qadar's people were thought to be too dangerous to set free, so you exiled them to an unoccupied planet?"

The Klingon nodded. "A harsh planet, I might add. Where they would be forced to fight for their survival."

"It was that," Phelana explained, "or try to move them to an easier environment. And considering what we knew of them—"

"Moving them didn't seem wise," the captain finished for her. "I understand what you're saying."

What's more, he found he approved of it. As tough as the M'tachtar were, it was hard to imagine a life-supporting environment that could have been too harsh for them. And Qadar *had* proposed to destroy Starfleet Command.

Nor was it difficult for him to see why Starfleet would keep the M'tachtar situation a secret. First off, anyone who beamed down to the planet would be in danger. Secondly, any contact with the outside could have resulted in the M'tachtar's escape—as Kirk had seen firsthand.

But there was a third reason, as well. Starfleet couldn't have been very proud of maintaining a prison—no matter how necessary or humane that prison might be.

The captain turned to Phelana again. "The *Republic* had a part in closing the trap on the M'tachtar . . . didn't it?"

The Andorian returned his gaze with her shiny, black eyes. "By the time Bannock arrived, the M'tachtar had already been attacked and forced to the planet's surface. The *Republic*'s role was to set up the forcefields and the surveillance equipment that surrounded them, while other personnel stood guard over the operation."

Kirk nodded, absorbing the information. "And the time when I was serving on the *Constitution* under Captain Augenthaler? When Mangione and the others commandeered the ship?"

"One of Starfleet's occasional visits to the planet," Phelana explained.

"Attended by a Klingon vessel, as always," Kang noted from across the table.

The Andorian nodded. "For the sake of protocol," she said, "a Klingon ship was allowed to slip through Federation defenses and attend each visit—scheduled or otherwise. In the instance you're speaking of, a vessel full of renegade Klingons had gone through the neutral zone in an attempt to free the M'tachtar. The *Constitution* came close to engaging the renegades."

"But in the end," Kang pointed out, "it was the Klingon ship *jevSuS* that engaged them. I know, because I was a junior officer on that vessel. Then, as now, you were fortunate there were warriors in the vicinity to clean up your Federation mess."

"As I understand it," said Phelana, "the *Constitution* was ordered to withdraw at the request of the Klingons—so the renegades could be handled as an internal matter. There was a mention of . . . honor at stake."

Kang's mouth pulled up ever so slightly at the corners. "Of course," he said, declining to address the Andorian's comment, "the problem we have now is much more serious than that of the renegades. For the last fourteen years, the M'tachtar have been gnashing their teeth and longing for the day they can avenge themselves on the ones who betrayed them—starting with the Klingon emperor and his council."

"And," Tupogh added, "thanks to the ineptitude of the Federation, that day has come."

Kelso reddened. "If the Klingons had taken care of the M'tachtar on their own fourteen years ago, none of this would have happened."

Tupogh's eyes narrowed. "If you of the Federation had killed them in battle, as you should have—"

"Enough!" snarled Kang, his voice filling the

briefing room like thunder. "Bickering will get us nowhere."

Kirk put a hand on Kelso's arm. "He's right, Lieutenant. Let's stick to the facts here, shall we?"

Kelso nodded, though it was clear he was still simmering. "Of course, sir. The facts."

"I wonder," said Spock, "how difficult will it be for Qadar and his people to get to the emperor?"

"I can't imagine it'd be too easy," Alden opined. "Especially now that Grannoch has been warned."

Tupogh made a sound of derision. "Once he gets into Klingon space, there will be nothing easier. Grannoch cannot hide from the M'tachtar. It would be unseemly. If there is a challenge to be faced, he must face it head on—regardless of who brings it or why."

Kang nodded. "Which is why we must stop Qadar's vessel before it reaches Klingon space—or the empire is liable to have a mad dog on the throne before very long."

"Indeed," Tupogh remarked soberly. "And wouldn't that bode well for our survival as an empire."

It wouldn't bode well for the Federation either, the captain reflected. If Qadar was successful in destroying his ruustai-cousin and seizing control of the High Council, his next step would likely be to finish the job he started—the conquest of Starfleet.

"If we're to help you stop Qadar's vessel," said Kirk, "we need to know more about Qadar and his people—what they can and can't do."

Kang shrugged. "The M'tachtar are just like regular Klingons," he explained, "but their abilities are amplified. Their strength is greater, their speed is greater, and their eagerness for battle is greater."

"Then," said Spock, "their weaknesses must also be greater."

Kang's dark eyes narrowed. "Weaknesses are for other races," he replied confidently. "Klingons have none."

Unperturbed, the first officer met the Klingon's glare. "Every species has a weakness," he insisted. "It is simply a matter of finding it."

Kang leaned forward over the briefing room table. When he spoke, his voice was low and dangerous. "I repeat, Vulcan—Klingons do not have weaknesses."

"Mr. Spock—" Phelana began, no doubt concerned that her colleague was going too far.

But Kirk put his hand on her arm, stopping her. He sensed that the Vulcan was up to something, though he didn't see what it was yet.

In the meantime, Spock went on. "As I understand it," he said, "the Klingons have engaged in war with several other spacegoing species. And in most every instance, they have been beaten."

The captain could see Kang react. The Klingon's lips drew back like those of a Terran wolf.

"For instance," said the Vulcan, "approximately fifty years ago, your people encountered the Abbutan. An armed conflict ensued in which you were beaten back from three separate Abbutan colonies."

The muscles writhed in Kang's temples. Clearly, he was less than pleased with Spock's recital.

But the first officer didn't show any signs of stopping. "Three years later," he noted, "the Empire clashed with the Renns'ala. Once again, there were hostilities, which culminated in the decisive Renns'alan victory at Romenthis Three."

Kang's nostrils flared and his complexion darkened. "I have listened to enough," he rumbled.

Spock seemed not to have heard him. "Then there was the Battle of Donatu Five, in which—"

The Klingon shot to his feet, wide-eyed with fury at the Vulcan's insolence, and bellowed, "I said it was *enough!*"

And with that, he brought his fist down like a hammer on the end of the hexagonal conference table. The table splintered under the impact, sending tiny fragments of wood flying through the air.

For the next few moments, there was silence. Kang looked down at his hand, which he had bloodied in hitting the table. Then he looked at Spock.

What's more, thought Kirk, he seemed to understand what the Vulcan had been up to—and perhaps even respect him for it. By then, of course, the captain understood as well.

"I think," he observed in front of all parties present, "we've identified the Klingons' weakness."

Kang regarded him for a long time, then sneered—but only halfheartedly. "At least in theory," he replied.

But Spock had made his point, Kirk reflected. If anger was a weakness in a normal Klingon, it might be an even greater weakness in the M'tachtar. No one said it out loud—but then, no one had to.

"I have set aside quarters for you and your officers," Kang informed the captain in a tone used to being obeyed. "Tupogh will take you there now. I will send for you when I again require your counsel."

Kirk frowned. "I trust we won't be kept waiting long," he said.

Kang frowned more deeply. "That remains to be seen."

Then he got up and led the way out of the room, and Tupogh followed directly behind him. But the other Klingon, who hadn't spoken a word, remained there until Kirk and his people had filed out. Then he came after them, his hand on his weapon and a look of vigilance on his face.

After all, thought the captain, they were still the enemy in many respects, and Kang didn't want them straying from the path he set out for them. It was a reasonable precaution.

In fact, if his position and Kang's were reversed, Kirk would undoubtedly have done the same thing.

Chapter Fifteen

KANG SAT in the dark, elevated center seat of his vessel, stared at the stars streaming by on his hexagon-shaped viewscreen, and pondered what the one called Spock had taught him.

Klingons didn't normally consider their anger a point of vulnerability. If anything, they saw it as a tool to be honed and used in combat.

But the Vulcan had shown him that his wrath could be used against him. And though the notion made Kang uncomfortable, it also made him stronger—for the victor was often the one who knew himself the best.

Abruptly, Kang's sensor officer swiveled in his chair and turned to him. "Commander," he said, "I have established the coordinates of the Federation vessel on long-range scan."

Kang felt a surge of anticipation—an awakening

of his peculiarly Klingon lust for battle. Keeping it tamped down lest he be disappointed, he stood up and crossed the bridge to join the sensor officer at his control console. Peering over the other man's shoulder, he gazed at the green, orange, and blue graphic on the screen.

There was a long blue oval evident in the center of the graphic—the symbol for a Federation ship. As the sensor officer had noted, they had established a fix on the *Enterprise.* And from all appearances, they were closing the gap with each passing second.

"Their heading?" asked Kang.

"Without question, the homeworld," said the sensor officer. "Just as you speculated, Commander."

Kang grunted and eyed the graphic again. Then he glanced at his helmsman. "Accelerate to warp seven," he said.

The helmsman regarded him with obvious concern. "At warp seven, we may damage the engines."

"Then damage them," Kang snarled, not at all pleased that the wisdom of his command had been questioned. "But first, bring me in range of the *Enterprise.* Is that understood?"

The helmsman nodded. "It is understood, Commander."

Kang nodded. "Good. I would not want to have to eject you through a torpedo tube due to a simple misunderstanding."

The other man's lip curled at the rebuke, but he turned back to his control panel and carried out

Kang's orders. Clearly, he wasn't ready to challenge his superior's authority.

But he would be someday, Kang mused, having been hardened by experience. And when the helmsman posed his challenge, the son of K'naiah would be ready for him.

Kirk surveyed the quarters Kang had "set aside" for him—a space barely big enough to be a closet on the *Enterprise,* with lurid red lighting and two hard, blockish looking bunks.

Not unreasonably, Kang had assumed the captain would want to room with his first officer. As a result, Kirk found himself watching Spock examine the room for surveillance devices.

"They're there," the captain assured him, having already resigned himself to the fact. "Even if you can't find them, they're there."

The Vulcan turned to him. "In fact, I *have* found them. All three of them," he said.

"How do you know there aren't more?" Kirk asked him.

Spock shrugged. "Because if there were, I would have found those as well."

The captain smiled. "You're that confident?"

His first officer nodded, his countenance utterly devoid of hubris. "I am," he replied.

Kirk decided it was pointless to pursue that avenue of inquiry any further. Instead, he opened another one.

"Tell me," said the captain. "What made you decide to provoke Kang back in that briefing room?"

Spock looked at him, as dispassionate as ever. "A great many chemical reactions require the application of heat, sir. It was only logical to apply heat to Kang as well."

Kirk shook his head in wonder. It was logical, all right—but he didn't know anyone else who would have looked at the problem quite that way.

"You know," he responded, "I don't believe I've been giving you enough credit, Commander."

The Vulcan didn't speak for a moment. Then he said, "I believe that only you would know if that was so, sir."

The captain felt the sting of the remark. It was as close as Spock was likely to come to saying "I told you so."

He made a mental note to rely more on Mr. Spock's advice—assuming, of course, that he ever got his ship and the other half of his crew back.

As soon as the turbolift doors whispered open, Mitchell was catapulted onto the bridge by one of his captors. Then he looked back to see Corbet and Swift, a couple of science officers, shoved out after him.

Noticing their arrival, Qadar got up from his seat and loomed in front of them, his massive hands on his hips. The navigator had seen friendlier expressions on a Vicarian razorback.

With a glance at the viewscreen, Mitchell understood why. A rear-view perspective showed him a Klingon battle cruiser in pursuit. The same battle cruiser, no doubt, that they had seen orbiting the prison world.

A mixed blessing, the navigator thought. As much as he wanted to stop the M'tachtar, he didn't want to get blown out of space in the process.

"We are having some difficulty wringing maximum speed out of your engines," Qadar told them, his voice seething with frustration.

Mitchell turned to the helm-navigation console, where one of the M'tachtar was handling the piloting controls a lot more roughly than he needed to. And judging from the speed at which they were leaving stars behind on the viewscreen, the warrior still hadn't coaxed the propulsion system to do better than warp six.

"I need this ship to go faster," Qadar rumbled menacingly. "And I need it to do so now."

The navigator frowned. "It's not possible," he said. "Not with all the damage you did to her."

It was a lie, of course. He could have accelerated their progress if he wanted to. All it took was a little know-how.

But Mitchell wasn't going to tell Qadar that. Not if it would help him to accomplish whatever the Federation had been trying to prevent for the last fourteen years.

Qadar eyed him for a moment, as if trying to decide if the human was telling the truth. Then he reached into his belt with terrible quickness, took out his phaser, and shot at Corbet.

The red beam hit the science officer in the throat, breaking his neck even before it sent him slamming into the console behind him. Limply, Corbet slumped to the deck and came to rest in an awkward heap.

Mitchell swallowed, sickened by the sight. And angered as well, though there wasn't anything he could do about it—not with two other M'tachtar training their weapons on him and Swift.

Qadar turned to the navigator a second time, his eyes full of hatred, and pointed his phaser at him. "I don't believe you," he said savagely.

Mitchell winced at the nearness of the energy weapon's aperture. But he wasn't going to give in to this monster, he told himself. Not even if it cost him his life.

"It's the truth," he insisted, lying a second time. "The ship needs repairs. Until she gets them, she won't go any faster."

He could see Qadar's finger starting to press down on the trigger. Suddenly, the Klingon swiveled his weapon away from the navigator and unleashed a burst of energy at Swift instead.

The crewman flew backward under the force of the crimson beam and hit the bulkhead with a disheartening thud. By the time Swift hit the deck, he was as dead as Corbet before him.

The navigator wanted to howl with pain and rage. He wanted to take Qadar by the throat and make him feel what Corbet and Swift had felt before they died. But he did neither of those things.

He just stood there, controlling himself as best he could, because there was something hanging in the balance that was more important than his life or the lives of Corbet and Swift.

Mitchell didn't want to help the M'tachtar make the *Enterprise* go any faster. But he also didn't want any more of his comrades to be killed. So he had to sell Qadar on the idea that he had to make repairs before Qadar could get what he wanted—or perish with the sad, awful knowledge that the M'tachtar would keep on spilling blood until they found someone weak enough to bend to their demands.

Qadar turned his phaser on the navigator again, holding it just a few inches from the man's chest. "I ask for the last time, human. Show me how to make this ship accelerate."

Mitchell eyed the aperture on the M'tachtar's weapon as if it were an enemy unto itself. "Shoot if you want," he declared. "But it's not going to get you what you need. And if you keep slaughtering us, there'll be no one left who can give it to you."

Qadar became so angry that his eyes looked as if they would pop out of his skull. His mouth twisted and the hand that held the phaser trembled with raw, naked fury.

This is it, the navigator thought. *This is where he kills me.* He braced himself for the bone-jarring impact and the cold touch of death.

But it never came.

Slowly, gradually, the Klingon got his rage under control. His teeth still clenched, he took a deep, rasping breath and lowered the phaser. Then his eyes narrowed beneath his brow ridge and he nodded.

"Very well, human. Make your repairs," he snarled. "But you will do so under the eyes of an armed guard. And if he believes you have lied to me, I will kill you and twenty of your comrades before you have any idea what might have happened." He leaned closer to Mitchell—so close that the navigator could smell the stench of his breath. "Is that clear?"

Mitchell nodded. "It's clear," he replied, still shaky from his ordeal and not at all ready to believe his good luck.

Qadar turned to one of his warriors and gestured to the turbolift with a thrust of his chin. The M'tachtar nodded and shoved the navigator back in the direction of the double doors.

As they slid open, the Klingon leader said, "One more thing, human."

Mitchell turned back to him, wondering if his luck had run out after all. "Yes?" he answered.

Qadar scrutinized him with a dark malevolence. "Few of your kind understand that individual lives are meaningless compared to the triumph of the group. But the way you accepted your comrades' deaths a moment ago . . . you seem to be an exception." He grunted. "If I did not know better, I would suspect you were a Klingon in disguise."

Thanks for nothing, the navigator thought. But what he said was "If that's a compliment, I accept."

The M'tachtar leader seemed to find amusement in the remark—but only for a moment. Then he returned to the center seat.

"Take the human where he needs to go—but watch over him," said Qadar.

"As you wish," said Mitchell's escort.

Then the navigator was shoved back into the waiting turbolift.

* * *

As the lift doors slid apart, Kirk got his first look at a living, working Klingon bridge. Having studied the operations of Klingon ships based on fragments recovered from military encounters, he wasn't surprised by what he saw—a place that was cramped, dimly lit except for the ghostly red or green glow of monitors, with a high, dark chair looming over four freestanding consoles and a number of peripheral stations.

The chair was Kang's, of course. He was sitting in it at that very moment, his back to the captain. On the hexagon-shaped viewscreen ahead of him, Kirk could see a distant but eminently familiar shape.

"The *Enterprise,*" he breathed.

Kang turned in his chair and acknowledged the human's presence. "So it is," he confirmed. "And now is the moment of which I warned you, Kirk—when I again require your counsel."

Leaving his escort behind, the captain advanced to the Klingon's side—continuing to peer at the viewscreen all the while. He had never seen his ship from so far away. But then, under the circumstances, it felt pretty damned good to see her at all.

"Before long," said Kang, "we will come within tactical range. No one knows the *Enterprise*'s vulnerabilities better than you do. In the interest of our common goal—our common interest in stopping the M'tachtar—I urge you to divulge those vulnerabilities to me."

Kirk looked at him askance. "And place the Federation's Constitution-class fleet at the mercy of the Klingons?"

Kang's eyes narrowed. "What is the alternative?"

It occurred to the human that there *was* an alternative. "I can disable my ship," he said, "without divulging a thing about her."

The Klingon commander looked skeptical, even suspicious. "And how can this be accomplished?" he wondered.

The captain frowned. After all, he didn't like the idea of giving away even this much. "My ship is programmed so that certain command codes will shut down her engines and key operating systems. All I have to do is transmit those codes at a frequency the *Enterprise*'s comm system will recognize and the computer will take care of the rest."

Kang looked at him. "And you can do this from here?"

Kirk nodded. "I believe so. But I'll need some privacy if I'm even to make the attempt."

The Klingon grunted. "So your worthy enemy doesn't witness the procedure, I take it."

"Exactly," the captain responded.

Kang pondered the problem for a moment. "Very well," he said finally. "I will allow you to use an auxiliary tactical facility. But first, we will block its ability to interface with the ship's other systems—so you don't learn any of *our* procedures."

"Agreed," Kirk replied. "And while you're at it, you can disable the facility's connection to your main computer. I wouldn't want to leave a record of the proceedings for you to study later."

The Klingon regarded him with a hint of a smile on his lips. "Of course not," he said.

The captain glanced at the viewscreen, where the *Enterprise* looked marginally closer than when he had looked at her last. He felt he had taken at least a half-step toward recovering her.

"So what are we waiting for?" he asked Kang. "Let's get cracking."

Chapter Sixteen

KIRK WATCHED the dark, heavy door slide closed behind him, leaving him alone in the dimly lit tactical facility—alone, that is, except for the throbbing of the Klingon vessel's warp engines and the bleating of the room's only control console. He planted himself on the seat in front of it and studied its large, hexagonal screen.

It was divided into orange, blue, and green fields. The captain had a pretty good idea what the various colors represented. In effect . . . nothing.

Or at least, nothing yet.

Plying the console's unfamiliar controls as best he could, Kirk established a link with the battle cruiser's external sensor grid. Then he brought up a schematic of the *Enterprise,* which appeared in a brilliant white across the three colored fields.

Finally, the captain assigned each of the three

colors to an aspect of the data collected by the sensors. As he did this, the outline of the *Enterprise* turned green and the area where its engines were located became orange. Blue vanished from the screen altogether, though Kirk trusted it wouldn't be gone too long.

Step one was complete. Now it was time for step two.

Working the control panel, the captain accessed the Klingon vessel's communications grid. Then, making certain there were no recording devices creating feedback on the line, he punched in the command code known only to him and his Vulcan first officer.

The code had been designed for just such an emergency as this one. It provided a starship's captain with a way to immobilize his vessel without doing any real harm to her. Thank god for the foresight of Starfleet engineers, Kirk reflected, sitting back in his chair and keeping an eye on the sensor screen.

For a while, nothing happened. The captain began to wonder if something had gone wrong—if, for instance, the Klingon vessel had failed to send out the code exactly as he had tapped it in.

Then the orange part of the schematic began to fade, indicating that the *Enterprise*'s engines were shutting themselves down. At the same time, a smaller blue area began to assert itself—an area that represented the ship's auxiliary power generators.

Of course, Kirk reflected, they wouldn't provide enough power to keep propulsion or any of the *Enterprise*'s tactical systems alive. However, they would provide plenty of juice for essentials like life-support and communications.

The captain smiled grimly. He had done it. He had incapacitated his ship. Now the rest was up to Kang, he thought, as he got up from his seat and headed for the door.

Qadar was livid.

One moment, he had been sitting in the captain's chair on the bridge of the *Enterprise,* watching stars stream by on the forward viewscreen and picturing Grannoch's throat in his grasp. The next moment, both the bridge and the viewscreen had gone dark.

Almost immediately, Qadar had been able to see again by the faint, blue glow coming from a series of recessed light panels. But the viewscreen was still dead—and judging by the looks of dismay on his followers' faces, it wasn't the only thing in that state.

"My lord," one of them growled in shock, "the engines have stopped! We have no power!"

"The ship's weapons are useless!" reported another, his voice thick with disgust.

A third warrior pounded his fist on his console. "Shields and tractor beams have been sabotaged as well!"

Part of Qadar wondered how his enemies had crippled his ship. But another part of him didn't care. It only wanted to splinter the bones of whoever was responsible for it.

"Life-support?" he demanded.

One of his men checked his monitors, their crimson glow bathing his craggy features. "Still operational," he responded.

Of course, Qadar mused. Without life-support, his Federation captives would begin to perish. It only lent more credence to his observation that this was no accident.

"Lord Commander," said another of his followers, who had been sitting at the communications console, "the ship received a data transmission just before everything went dark."

Eyes narrowing, Qadar turned to him. "What kind of transmission?"

The Klingon pored over her monitors for a moment. Then she looked up, her mouth twisted with hatred. "It came from the battle cruiser behind us."

Qadar felt his jaw clench. *I should have killed the Federation captain when I had the chance,* he told himself. *I should have split his skull open and drunk his blood.*

But he hadn't. And this was the result.

"What are your orders?" asked one of his followers.

What indeed? thought Qadar, his belly roiling like the fabled fire mountain at Kri'stak.

For more years than he cared to count, he had been imprisoned on an alien world, cut off from his rightful place in the universe. Finally, by dint of painstaking vigilance, he had freed himself from that prison—only to find himself incarcerated in another one.

A prison whose walls were duranium bulkheads, Qadar reflected. A place from which there was no escape except the airless cold of space. Unless . . .

Stabbing the intercom stud on his armrest with a

gnarled forefinger, he said, "Chi'ra, this is Qadar . . ."

As Kirk returned to the bridge of Kang's ship, he noticed three things. First, that the Klingon was busy giving orders. Second, that on the hexagonal viewscreen, the *Enterprise* hung in the void with no illumination except her emergency lights.

And third, that Spock and Kelso were on hand, flanked by a pair of Kang's guards. The captain looked at them, wondering why they had been brought there. But before he could ask, another concern reared its head.

"He's going to blow up the *Enterprise!*" Kelso blurted.

The guard nearest to him responded by shoving him hard into the bulkhead. But the Vulcan was still free to speak.

"It is true," said Spock. "Commander Kang intends to take advantage of the ship's lack of defenses by destroying her."

The second guard tried to silence him the way the first had silenced Kelso, but the Vulcan was too quick for him. He grabbed the Klingon's wrist and bent him back over a console.

Kirk was about to go to Spock's aid when he heard a voice ring out. It belonged to Kang.

"Enough!" the Klingon bellowed.

Turning to him, the captain saw that Kang had trained his disruptor on the Vulcan. The captain locked eyes with his opposite number.

"I thought we were allies," he said.

Kang kept his weapon aimed at Spock. "We were," he replied without inflection. "For a time."

Kirk shook his head. "What does that mean?"

"It means we have your ship in our sights," the Klingon explained. "And, as your officers have told you, we are going to reduce her to debris."

The captain glanced at the Vulcan. "Stand down," he commanded.

Spock hesitated for just a moment. Then he said "Aye, sir," and released the Klingon in his grasp.

Kirk glared at Kang. "I thought Klingons prided themselves on how well they kept their word. I see I was wrong."

Kang looked as if he had been slapped in the face. Lowering his weapon, he spat, "This is not a matter of holding to one's word. It is a matter of necessity. I must destroy the M'tachtar while I have the chance."

"You had this in mind all along," the captain realized.

"Ever since you mentioned that you could disable the *Enterprise,*" the Klingon conceded. "The only reason I allowed you to return to the bridge was so you could witness your contribution to the success of our mission."

"My contribution . . . ?" Kirk sputtered angrily. "Of all the—"

Kang didn't wait for his guest to finish. Instead, he turned to his weapons officer. "Arraq?"

The Klingon looked up from his console. "Commander?"

"Target the *Enterprise,*" said Kang.

"No," said Kirk. He started for the Klingon leader

but found his arms pulled back by the guards who had brought him up here. "You can't do this," he told Kang.

The Klingon returned his look. "I have no choice."

"Targeted," said Arraq, a distinct note of eagerness in his voice.

But Kirk wasn't about to let him go ahead with his assignment. "You're not firing on my ship," he insisted.

Kang eyed him wearily. "And why is that?"

"Because," the human told him, "she's *my* ship—and half my crew is still aboard. I'll be damned if I'm going to let you blast them all to atoms for no good reason."

"No good reason?" the Klingon echoed. "Open your eyes, Kirk. You have seen the M'tachtar and what they can do. If I give them even the smallest opportunity to survive, they will make us regret it."

But the captain stood his ground. "All I need is a small team and an hour—no more. If I don't take my ship back by then, you can go ahead and blow her out of space."

The Klingon's brow creased as he considered the proposition. "You could not beat the M'tachtar before, even with your entire crew behind you. What makes you think you can beat them now?"

Suddenly, Spock spoke up. "It is said that four thousand throats can be cut in one night by a running man."

Kirk looked at him. Then he looked at Kang. The Klingon's eyes had narrowed with suspicion. No—not suspicion, the captain realized. Puzzlement.

"You are familiar with our proverbs?" Kang asked the Vulcan.

"Only some of them," said Spock. "Specifically, the ones mentioned in a tape to which your crew allowed me access. I believe it is called 'The Battle Cry of Kahless.'"

The Klingon grunted. "I am familiar with it."

"Then you understand my point. No matter the magnitude of the odds against Captain Kirk, one cannot say with certainty that he will fail in his effort. To deprive him of a chance to regain his ship would be . . ." The Vulcan hesitated. "I believe the term is *dishonorable.*"

Kang's lips spread into a thin, grudging smile. Clearly, Spock's words had struck a chord in him. "You are clever," he told the first officer. "But do you honestly think your captain can be the running man of the proverb? You think he has the courage?"

Spock answered without hesitation. "I have never encountered a sentient being as courageous or dedicated as Captain Kirk. If bravery is the only quality he requires in order to succeed in the task at hand, you may already consider it done."

The Klingon eyed him a moment longer. Then he turned to Kirk. "Your first officer is most accomplished at bending the truth."

The captain shook his head. "That's where you're wrong, Kang. Commander Spock may be accomplished at a great many things, but bending the truth isn't one of them."

The Klingon mulled what he had heard. "Very well," he said at last. "I'll give you your hour, Kirk. See that you make the most of it."

"Believe me," the captain told him, "you won't be disappointed."

At least that was his fervent hope. And if he was even half as courageous as Spock had made him out to be, maybe his gambit would find a way to succeed after all.

Chapter Seventeen

THE ENGINE ROOM had been dark for several seconds, its only illumination that of its emergency lighting strips, when Mitchell heard Qadar's intercom voice cut into the string of curses coming from his guard.

Hearing his master speak his name, the Klingon stopped swearing and looked up. "This is Chi'ra," he answered. "What has happened, my lord?"

"The Federation captain has found a way to cripple us from a distance," Qadar told him, his tone full of undisguised bitterness. "But we will not sit here and let them beat us without a fight. We will make them sorry they ever tried to stop us."

The guard eyed his human captive. "Shall I start by destroying the one you sent me here to watch?"

The M'tachtar raised his weapon to the level of Mitchell's face. The navigator refused to flinch.

"No," Qadar responded. "Do not destroy him,

Chi'ra. Take him to the cargo bay he occupied earlier and let me know when you arrive. Then I will give you further instructions."

The guard nodded, still glaring at the human. "As you wish, my lord." But he didn't lower his weapon. "Move," he spat, indicating the exit with a toss of his shaggy head.

Mitchell did as he was told. But somehow, he didn't feel all that grateful for having been spared—not when what awaited him would probably be worse than a quick phaser shot.

Kirk stepped up onto the Klingon transporter pad and watched the rest of his team gather around him.

"All right," he said, rechecking the charge on his disruptor pistol. "Listen closely, everyone, because I doubt I'll have an opportunity to repeat this."

It was no more than the truth. The captain had been granted little enough time as it was, and assembling a boarding party had taken several precious minutes of it.

"Our mission," he went on, "is to transport over to the *Enterprise,* locate the M'tachtar, isolate them and put them out of action as quickly as possible. If that means killing them, I can live with it—but it's a last resort. Everyone got that?"

"Check," Alden told him.

Spock nodded. "Acknowledged."

"Aye, sir," replied Kyle.

"I'm with you, sir," said Kelso.

That left only one member of the team. Phelana finished examining her handheld sensor device, then looked up and regarded Kirk. "Ready to make the jump," the Andorian responded with a grim smile.

The others might not have perceived the layers of meaning in her answer, but the captain did. And perceiving them, he couldn't help smiling back at her.

Then he turned to the Klingon standing at the freestanding console at the opposite end of the room. "Energize," he said.

The transporter pad spawned spirals of green energy that gradually enveloped them in emerald brilliance. And before Kirk could draw another breath, he found himself in a dark but familiar place.

Right where he and the others were supposed to wind up, the captain told himself. The eerie, emergency-lit sickbay of the *Enterprise.*

After all, it was the last place one of the M'tachtar was likely to be found. Beings that hardy weren't apt to injure themselves very often. And even if they did, their Klingon machismo wouldn't have allowed them to make use of the facility.

All that notwithstanding, Kirk didn't even whisper until he and his people had checked the place out. Finally, satisfied that their arrival had gone undetected, he led the way out through the sliding doors.

His handheld sensor told him that there wasn't anyone in the corridor ahead of them. That meant they could proceed unimpeded to the nearest Jefferies tube, which was only a few dozen meters away.

When they reached the duranium ladder, the captain climbed it until he could reach the tube's hatch door and swing it open. Then he crawled inside and the others followed, with Kyle closing the hatch after them.

The tube was long and cramped, thanks to the conduits and flashing circuitry that covered its inner walls like an alien fungus. Normally, it would also have been loud with the sound of the engines, but now it was almost disturbingly quiet. Kirk made his way through it on elbows and knees, holding his disruptor in one hand and his Klingon sensor in the other.

A turbolift would have been a lot more comfortable, he mused. But with the ship operating on emergency power, there would be relatively few lifts in service, and they didn't want to take a chance on running into a M'tachtar before they were ready for him.

It took several minutes for them to reach the appropriate deck. When they got there, the captain opened their exit hatch and peered out into the corridor. It was illuminated only by the soft, blue glow of emergency lighting, but it appeared to be clear in both directions.

Slipping out of the tube, he grasped the ladder next to it and descended, then watched the rest of his team do the same. When they had all joined him, he led the way again.

Kirk had selected the auxiliary control room as their first destination because it seemed likely that one of the M'tachtar would be there—especially during a shipwide malfunction. As it turned out, he had guessed right. At least, that was what his hand-held sensor told him as he approached the room's double set of red orange doors.

The captain gestured for the others to gather around him and told Phelana what he wanted her to do. Once he was sure she understood, he and the rest of the team withdrew to the cover of the nearest junction.

As they watched, the Andorian concealed the disruptor and the handheld sensor device she had received from Kang's Klingons. Then she came close enough to auxiliary control to encourage its doors to open.

From where he stood, concealed by a bulkhead, Kirk didn't have a very good angle on what was going on inside the control room. All he could see was Phelana standing at the threshold, looking around.

Then he heard a deep-throated challenge from within and saw the Andorian whirl as if she had been taken by surprise. Pausing just long enough to make sure her adversary was in pursuit, she bolted down the corridor.

Phelana had been exceptionally fleet of foot in her Academy days, which was why the captain had picked her for this chore, and it looked to him as if she hadn't lost a step. But the M'tachtar was still faster.

Fortunately, it wasn't destined to be a long race. As the Andorian got closer, Kirk and the others raised their weapons. Then Phelana came tearing around the corner, glancing off the bulkhead in front of her in her haste. And half a heartbeat later, her pursuer shot into their sights.

As the captain had planned, they caught the M'tachtar in a crossfire. Five blazing blue disruptor beams hit him at once, jerking him in one direction and then in another. Battered by the onslaught and given no respite, the Klingon collapsed in a heap.

At a signal from Kirk, Alden took out a device

Kang had given them—a Klingon incapacitor designed to temporarily inhibit certain brain functions. According to Kang's supply officer, the thing was best applied behind the right ear.

But just as Alden bent to affix the incapacitor to the fallen M'tachtar, the warrior stirred and took a swipe at the man. Alden straightened in time to keep his head from being torn off, but was still sent flying willy-nilly into the bulkhead.

The captain tried to take aim at the M'tachtar, but couldn't. The warrior was moving too quickly in these painfully close quarters, consciously or unconsciously using Kirk's comrades for cover.

One would never have known that the M'tachtar had absorbed a half dozen disruptor blasts. He was still as strong as a rampaging bull and twice as fast. Kelso charged him to try to subdue him, but was hurled away with savage force. Then Kyle attempted the same thing, but with no more success.

Kirk took his shot too, trying to tackle the M'tachtar around the middle and at least slow him down a little. But as soon as he latched on, his opponent drove him to the deck with a two-handed blow.

Dazed by the impact, the captain tried to roll out of harm's way—even as the M'tachtar drew back his heavily booted foot for a kick at Kirk's ribs. But before the Klingon could land his blow, another gold and black figure came hurtling at him, slamming him into the bulkhead behind him.

The captain looked up and saw that it was Spock.

The first officer was grappling with the M'tachtar, fighting for leverage. Unfortunately, even his Vulcan strength proved to be no match for the Klingon's muscle.

With an almost bestial cry of triumph, the M'tachtar flung Spock away. However, the first officer had given the others the opening they needed.

As soon as Spock was clear, Kirk nailed the Klingon with a dark blue disruptor beam, pinning him to the wall at least for a moment. Then Kyle, Kelso and Phelana added their own barrage, and Alden joined in as well.

The M'tachtar tried with all his strength to break free of the punishment they were inflicting on him, but it was no use. Even his prodigious strength was no match for a prolonged and concentrated dose of directed energy.

His head lolled to the side and he went limp, apparently unconscious. But even then, the captain continued to fire his disruptor until he was certain of the outcome. Only then did he discontinue his beam and signal his officers to do the same.

As soon as their disruptor blasts died, the M'tachtar fell to the deck. And though Kirk and the others waited patiently, he didn't move again. The captain signaled to Alden, and this time the communications officer affixed the incapacitor without any trouble.

Kirk kneaded his shoulder where the Klingon had clocked him and breathed a heartfelt sigh of relief. One down and fourteen to go, he told himself. But they had taken too long to bring down a single target. If they expended this much time with all the M'tachtar, Kang would destroy the *Enterprise* before they were halfway done.

The captain looked at the others. "Come on," he said. "Let's go."

Mitchell felt himself shoved into the cargo bay, joining Scotty and Sulu and the others. They looked relieved to see him again.

"Are ye all right, lad?" asked Scotty.

"What about Corbet and Swift?" asked Sulu.

The navigator frowned and shook his head. "Don't ask," he said.

The M'tachtar who had brought Mitchell back to the cargo bay didn't bother to reactivate the force-field. He just tapped an intercom grid set into the wall. "This is Chi'ra," he said. "I have arrived at the cargo bay, my lord."

"Good," said Qadar, his voice malevolent even when watered down by the intercom. "Is our friend Mitchell listening?"

The guard glanced at him. "He is, lord."

"Excellent. Now tell him we need to reverse what has happened to the *Enterprise*—and that if he refuses to tell us how, you will kill one of his comrades every thirty seconds."

"No!" cried the navigator, taking an involuntary step toward Chi'ra.

He heard savage laughter over the intercom. "Perhaps I was wrong, human," said Qadar. "It seems you are not quite a Klingon after all."

Mitchell's heart was pumping with fear—but for the others, not for himself. "Listen to me, Qadar. I don't know what's happened to this ship or how to deal with it. You've got to believe that."

It was another lie, of course. He had his suspicions

about what was going on, but he wasn't about to share them with the M'tachtar.

Unfortunately, Qadar wasn't buying what the navigator was selling. He didn't even bother to answer Mitchell's protest. All he said was "Follow my orders, Chi'ra."

The guard's mouth twisted into a cruel grin. "Gladly, lord."

"Let me know when you have achieved some results," said the leader of the M'tachtar. "Qadar out."

The one called Chi'ra eyed Mitchell. Then he planted his hand against the human's chest and sent him flying backward past his comrades. Before Mitchell could do anything to help himself, he felt something hard and unyielding slam into the back of his skull.

The bulkhead, he thought dully, finding himself slumped at the base of it. Spitting blood, the back of his head throbbing with pain, he tried to get to his feet.

"Leave him alone," said Sulu, moving toward his friend as if to defend him from the M'tachtar.

"No," the navigator groaned. "I'm all right."

Come on, he told himself, using the bulkhead for support. *Don't let this sorry excuse for a sentient see you squirm. Show him you can take whatever he dishes out.*

But despite his warning, Mitchell found Sulu kneeling at his side, trying to help him up. "Come on," said the helmsman. "I've got you."

Suddenly, the navigator saw the point of the Klingon's phaser appear in front of Sulu's face. Mitchell looked up into the guard's eyes, which had widened with fury in the shadow of his brow ridge.

"You heard the master," he snarled, glaring at the

helmsman but addressing the navigator. "You have ten seconds to tell me what to do . . . or you will watch this one die in agony."

Mitchell swallowed. He didn't doubt the Klingon meant it—or that he would stop with Sulu. But at the same time, he didn't want to undo whatever his friend Jim was trying to accomplish.

Just as he thought that, he saw something out of the corner of his eye—a movement in the vicinity of the entrance to the cargo bay. However, he didn't turn his head to get a better look at it. If it was what he suspected it was, what he hoped it was, he didn't dare to do anything but continue staring at the M'tachtar looming over him.

"Ten," said their bony-headed tormentor, his voice growing thick with anger. "Nine. Eight . . ."

The navigator's teeth ground together. *Whatever you're doing,* he told the captain silently, *do it quickly. Otherwise, I'm a goner—because I'm not going to let this bastard blow Sulu away.*

"Seven," the M'tachtar hissed, his lips pulling back to reveal long, sharp canines, his eyes bulging with bloodthirsty anticipation. "Five," he spat. "Four. Three . . ."

Mitchell tensed, the fingers of his right hand coiling into a fist. *Hurry, Jim,* he urged in the privacy of his mind. *For godsakes . . .*

"Three," said the guard. "Two . . ."

The navigator pulled his hand back, ready to drive it forward into his enemy's chin. But before he could do that, he saw a dark blue beam skewer the Klingon between the shoulder blades.

Crying out in pain, the M'tachtar clutched at his

back and staggered away from Mitchell and his comrades, but he didn't fall. Instead, he looked around frantically for the source of the attack.

That's when a second beam smashed into his ribs, doubling him over sideways and forcing him to drop his weapon. Still, he remained on his feet somehow. It took a third assault and a fourth to finally topple the guard and send him crashing to the deck.

But even then, the disruptor barrage didn't stop. The beams smashed into the M'tachtar's inert body, buffeting him for another several seconds before they finally relented.

As the navigator scrambled to secure the Klingon's weapon, he saw someone come out into view. It was his pal Jim, looking more deadly serious than he had looked in years.

The captain regarded the body of the unconscious Klingon warily, then signaled to someone out in the corridor. A moment later, Spock appeared too. Then he was joined by Phelana, Kyle, Alden and Kelso.

"Cutting it a little close?" the navigator asked, posing a question that his friend had posed often enough to him back at the Academy.

Kirk brushed the sweat from his face with his sleeve and smiled wearily. "I prefer to think of it as split-second timing," he replied, using Mitchell's stock answer to the question.

"Corbet and Swift are dead," the navigator reported.

The captain winced. But he said, "They're probably not the only ones."

"Have any of the rest of you been injured?" Spock inquired of Mitchell and his fellow captives.

Sulu grunted. "We've *all* been injured, Commander. But we're not in need of any immediate attention."

"Good," said Kirk. "Because we're going to need your help." Without any further preamble, he brought Mitchell and the others up to speed.

"Then you're on a deadline," the navigator concluded. "If you don't work quickly, Kang will blow up the *Enterprise.*"

The captain nodded. "You've got it." He handed Mitchell, Sulu and Scotty a phaser. "That's why we need everyone's help—yours included, Commander."

"What can I do?" asked the navigator, expecting to have to lead a team against the M'tachtar despite his injuries.

Kirk looked at him, then gestured to the crewmen with whom Mitchell had shared the cargo bay. "You can transport these people to the Klingon ship," he answered, "with the help of the command codes I'm about to give you. Then you can transport yourself there as well."

The navigator didn't believe what he was hearing. He felt an impulse to protest the order, but he managed to stifle it.

"Aye, sir," he said at last. "That is, if you're certain, sir."

The captain nodded. "I'm certain, all right."

But he continued to look at his friend a while longer. It was as if Kirk was saying he had done fine to this point, even without his lucky rabbit's foot—and that he could finish the job on his own just as well.

Under the circumstances, it was a hard conclusion

to argue with. Mitchell held up his phaser. "Are you sure you won't need this?" he asked.

The captain shook his head. "Hang on to it. For all we know, there are a couple of M'tachtar posted in the transporter room. And as for the command codes . . ."

He whispered them in the navigator's ear. Mitchell repeated them to himself, then nodded. "Got 'em."

Kirk smiled. "Good luck, Commander."

His friend smiled back at him. "We make our own luck, sir."

"I suppose we do," the captain conceded.

Then he gestured to Spock and the others who had come in with him, and they left in a group—no doubt headed for the next cargo hold and its dangerous M'tachtar watchman.

Mitchell turned to his companions. "Well?" he asked. "What are we waiting for? We've got a transporter room to get to."

And he led the way.

Chapter Eighteen

QADAR DRUMMED his fingers on his armrest, growing angrier than ever. Entire minutes had passed, and there had been no word from Chi'ra—even though, by then, the Klingon had to have destroyed four or five of the prisoners.

Was it possible the Starfleet targs were refusing to talk anyway? Had the M'tachtar somehow underestimated their stubbornness?

He brought his fist down on the intercom stud embedded in his armrest. "Chi'ra?" he demanded gruffly.

There was no answer.

Cursing Federation technology, Qadar brought his fist down on the stud a second time. "Chi'ra?" he rumbled.

Still no answer.

The Klingon felt his lips pulling back from his

teeth. Something was wrong, he told himself. He could feel it.

This time, he didn't attempt to contact Chi'ra. He tried Molta instead. However, Molta didn't respond either. Nor did Drabbak or Yarruq when Qadar called their names in mounting rage and frustration.

But there were sounds that came to him over the intercom system—grunts and curses and muffled thuds, and something shrill as well. The sounds of a fight, he realized.

The M'tachtar brought his fist down on his armrest again—but this time, he put a significant dent in its control panel. Either the prisoners had revolted, he told himself, or the *Enterprise* had been boarded.

Either way, Qadar decided as he tried not to choke on his fury, the matter demanded his personal attention.

Spock stood in the *Enterprise*'s computer room, a fallen Klingon giant at his feet, and frowned at the captain's suggestion. "Sir—"

"I know," Kirk told him, his face caught in the crimson glare of the room's overhead lighting. "We're taking a chance here, Mr. Spock. Unfortunately, we've no longer got a choice."

He pointed to the chronometer readout in his handheld sensor device. It indicated that thirty-two minutes had expired since they left the Klingon battle cruiser.

"In another twenty-eight minutes," the captain noted over the hum of the computers, "Kang is going to assume we've failed and hit the *Enterprise* with everything he's got—and so far, we've only run down seven of the M'tachtar."

"Eight," said Kelso, straight faced. "That is, including the one in the transporter room that Mr. Mitchell no doubt took care of."

Kirk smiled grimly. "Including that one, Lieutenant—assuming he was posted in the transporter room in the first place, and assuming Mr. Mitchell did, in fact, take care of him."

"Which leaves at least seven of them still standing," Kyle observed.

The captain turned to the Vulcan again. "Seven, Commander. So—"

"I agree," said Spock.

Kirk's brow knit as he tried to absorb his first officer's response. "You do? But judging by your expression—"

"I am not enamored of the strategy," Spock admitted. "It was difficult enough to incapacitate the M'tachtar when all six of us acted in concert. But as you point out, our choices are limited by our circumstances."

The captain grunted. "In that case, we'll split up into three teams. Spock and Kyle will head for engineering. Yudrin and Alden will make their way to security. And Kelso and I will try to take back the shuttle bay."

Phelana nodded. "Done."

"Afterward," Kirk went on, "we'll meet back here."

"And then?" asked Alden.

The captain looked at him. "Then we'll head for the bridge and confront our friend Qadar."

An ambitious plan, the first officer thought, as he and his comrades left the computer room. But then, Captain Kirk was an ambitious man.

As Kirk and his helmsman approached the doors to the shuttle bay in the ghostly light of the emergency strips, he couldn't help noticing the blackened spot where the M'tachtar had tried to punch their way in.

Now their positions were reversed, he thought. It was he and his companions who were trying to take over the *Enterprise,* and the Klingons who were trying to defend themselves against the intruders.

The captain signaled to Kelso to stop a good ten meters shy of the entrance. Then he used his handheld sensor to scan the area beyond the doors. As he had suspected, there was a M'tachtar warrior within—but only one.

Kirk was grateful there weren't any more of them. Otherwise, he and Kelso might have had an impossible task ahead of them.

Unfortunately, the captain mused, his boarding party had probably lost the element of surprise. With seven and possibly eight M'tachtar down, Qadar must have taken notice—and warned his remaining followers.

So he wouldn't bother trying to lure his adversary out into the corridor, the way Phelana had drawn out the Klingon in auxiliary control. Instead, he would be forced to go charging in.

Kirk shared his thinking with Kelso, who just held on to his disruptor a little tighter and nodded. Then the two of them moved closer to the phaser-scarred shuttle bay doors.

As the doors reacted by starting to slide open, the captain began to advance a little more quickly. Then, when the opening was just wide enough to admit him, he accelerated to a sprint and used his momentum to hurl himself into the shuttle bay.

Kirk didn't take the time to see if Kelso was diving in behind him. He just rolled with his weapon extended and tried to find his target in the twilight glow of the backup lights.

But as it happened, his target found him first. The captain saw a ruby red phaser beam scald the air near his face, missing him by inches. Drawing a bead on its source, which looked to be in the vicinity of the bay's control console, he fired back with his disruptor.

However, the dark blue beam failed to hit the M'tachtar, spattering spectacularly on the bulkhead behind the console instead. And a moment later, a second dark blue spurt of energy hit the console itself—but like the first one, it missed their adversary.

As Kirk saw what looked like the business end of a phaser, he dove for the shelter of a shuttle. What's more, he moved just in time, because the ensuing phaser blast barely missed him.

Glancing back at Kelso's shadowy form, the captain saw him scramble for cover as well. Somehow, the helmsman eluded a fiery shaft of directed energy and disappeared behind one of the other shuttlecraft.

But Kirk and his comrade had a problem. After

all, the M'tachtar held all the cards. He had established a position from which it would be difficult to dig him out, and their time was quickly expiring.

Then the captain remembered the point Spock had made about Klingon vulnerabilities in Kang's briefing room. If a short fuse was a weakness in a normal, unenhanced Klingon . . .

"Coward!" Kirk roared suddenly, his voice echoing from bulkhead to bulkhead. "You don't have the guts to show your face to us!"

He heard an inchoate snarl come from somewhere behind the console. "You dare to call Mezarch a coward, human? I'll tear your eyes from their sockets and stuff them down your throat!"

"Not if you cower behind that console," the captain returned mockingly. "We're taking our ship back deck by deck, Mezarch. You can't hide there like a frightened child!"

"I am not a frightened child!" the Klingon thundered, his voice ringing off every surface in the shuttlebay. "I am a M'tachtar!"

"You are nothing!" Kirk rumbled back at him. "You are less than nothing! And your craven, misshapen head will adorn my bridge before I sit down to eat my dinner tonight!"

He was laying it on a bit thick, he had to admit. But that was the way he had heard Klingons speak to one another.

"I will show you who is a craven!" Mezarch growled.

The next thing the captain knew, the M'tachtar was rushing him like a maddened bull, paving the way for himself with a blaze of phaser fire. Kirk took a couple of steps back behind the shuttle and raised his disruptor, bracing himself for the Klingon's attack.

A moment later, Mezarch came swinging around the side of the vehicle, his eyes red and protuberant beneath his craggy brow, his teeth bared like those of an animal. Knowing all too well what the M'tachtar would do if he got his hands on him, the captain squeezed off a dark blue burst.

It struck the Klingon full in the chest—and barely even slowed him down. As Mezarch fired back, Kirk was forced to duck the blast and retreat. As soon as he could, he unleashed another energy attack, but this one was no more effective than the last.

Just as he was about to turn up the disruptor's intensity to a kill setting, the captain saw the M'tachtar grimace and twist his body around. Then Kirk saw what had drawn Mezarch's attention. Kelso had begun firing at him from behind.

Hissing with rage, the Klingon whirled and aimed his weapon at the helmsman—but before he could get off a shot, the captain skewered him in the back with another disruptor blast. And Kelso was still pounding him from the other side, refusing to stop for even a nanosecond.

Mezarch writhed in torment, too beleaguered to hit either of his targets. Instead, his phaser volleys slammed into ceiling and bulkhead and shuttle hull—just about everywhere except where he wanted them to go.

After what semed like an eternity, the M'tachtar succumbed to the disruptor barrage. First, he sank to his knees. Then he dropped his phaser. And finally, eyes rolling back in his shaggy head, he landed on his bony, bearded face.

As he had done with the other Klingons he encountered, Kirk continued to fire even after his adversary appeared to have lost consciousness. Kelso did the same. But after a minute or so, when they were sure Mezarch wouldn't rise up and bite them, they discontinued their fire.

The helmsman studied the Klingon for a second in the light of the emergency strips, still wary despite all appearances. Then he took out an incapacitor, applied it behind Mezarch's ear and stood back.

"Well," he said to the captain, "I guess we can head back to the computer room. This one's not going any—"

Kelso never finished his sentence. Before that could happen, something big and dark loomed up behind him and slammed him into the shuttle with bone-crushing force. Swearing to himself, Kirk realized what it was.

Another of the M'tachtar—and not just any of them. It was the most vicious and powerful of them all.

It was Qadar.

"Kirk," he spat, making it sound like a curse.

His face was distorted with rage, his hands opening and closing as if they couldn't wait to take hold of the captain's throat. Backing off from the M'tachtar, Kirk raised his disruptor and unleashed a brilliant burst of energy, hoping only to buy himself a little time.

He didn't even accomplish that.

Qadar absorbed the blast and kept on coming.

And before the captain could change the setting on his weapon, the Klingon reached out and knocked the disruptor from his grasp.

As the weapon clattered on the deck, Kirk looked disbelievingly at his empty hand. He had never seen anyone move with such blinding speed. Clearly, Qadar had amplified his own abilities even more than he had amplified those of his followers.

"You will die for what you've done," the M'tachtar rumbled.

It was the only warning the captain got, but he took it to heart. Hurling himself backward as fast as he could, he avoided Qadar's closed-fisted blow—but only barely.

Nor could he continue to avoid such attacks. In a closed space, the Klingon had the decided advantage, and he wouldn't hesitate to use it. In fact, Kirk had only one thing going for him—the insight given to him by his Vulcan first officer.

"It's no use," he told Qadar, lying through his teeth. "My people are all over the ship." And as he said it, he moved away from the shuttle.

His dark eyes smoldering, the M'tachtar took another violent swipe at the captain. Unable to dart away completely this time, Kirk absorbed a glancing but painful blow on the shoulder.

"You've lost," he said. "There's nothing left to fight for." And he moved again, a critical destination taking shape in his mind.

Qadar shook his head. "No, human. It's you who have lost. And your broken body will be proof of it."

He lashed out again, and the captain leaped backward. But the Klingon's long sharp nails raked the captain's chest, drawing blood and tearing his gold uniform shirt open.

On the bright side, Qadar hadn't gotten in a crippling blow yet. That meant that Kirk could still maneuver, still try to carry out his plan.

"Why bother to go on with this?" he asked. "Why not admit that your experiment was a failure?"

The M'tachtar's face darkened with anger. His hands began to clench and unclench faster than before.

"In the final analysis," the captain persisted, "despite all the pain and dishonor you suffered, you're no better than any other Klingon. In fact, you're something less."

Qadar's breathing began to accelerate. His eyes looked as if they were struggling to free themselves from their sockets.

Kirk pressed his point relentlessly. "A real warrior would have caught me and finished me by now," he chuckled. "But you . . . in all those years you spent in a Federation cage, you forgot what it was like to be a warrior."

The Klingon couldn't seem to speak anymore. He was too incensed, too consumed with blind, unreasoning rage.

"Go ahead," said the captain in his most scornful voice. "Kill me, Qadar. Or do you no longer have the guts?"

That did it. A strangled cry erupted from the M'tachtar's throat and he came flying at Kirk with all the speed and fury of a striking rattlesnake.

Though the captain was ready for him, it took every iota of his agility and training to throw himself out of Qadar's path.

Unfortunately for the Klingon, he had put too much power into his lunge to stop himself. And even more unfortunately, there was an unyielding duranium bulkhead just ahead of him.

Which was exactly the way Kirk had planned it.

Qadar struck the bulkhead with enough force to shatter the skeleton of an ordinary Klingon. But the impact didn't kill him. In fact, it didn't even knock him out.

But it gave the captain a chance to dart across the shuttle bay and reach the control console. Grabbing hold and swinging around behind it, he dragged down the lever that controlled the bay doors.

Gradually, they began to slide apart, revealing the starry blackness of space—and without a forcefield to separate the bay from the void, the air in the place began to rush out.

Kirk felt a terrible stormwind rip past him, tugging him in the direction of the sliding doors. But it was nothing compared to the force that tore at Qadar, who was just a couple of meters from the opening.

His long, coarse hair whipping about his head, the M'tachtar screamed his defiance at the stars and fought the pull of the vacuum, but it was no use. Finally, he had met an adversary he couldn't withstand.

With a bellow of rage, Qadar lost his footing and went sliding toward the infinite. Just as it looked as if he would be sucked out of the *Enterprise* altogether, he managed to grab hold of one of the doors. But then, even that precarious handhold was lost to him, as the door buried itself in the slot designed for it.

Hanging on by nothing more than his fingertips, the Klingon looked back at the captain. His face was a mask of unbridled fury.

"Kirrrrrrk!" he yelled over the roar of escaping air.

Then, arms and legs still fighting against the tide, he went spiraling out into the void and was lost to the captain's sight.

Immediately, Kirk pushed the lever back to its previous position, reversing the movement of the doors. As he watched, they began to approach each other again, slowly shutting out the starlit splendor of space.

Automatically, the life-support system began to compensate for the loss of oxygen. As the captain felt the sweet influx of air from the vents above him, he remembered Kelso. A glance across the bay told him that the helmsman was still lying there by the *Galileo,* as still and unmoving as death.

Making his way across the room to Kelso, fighting the still-powerful pull of outrushing air, Kirk dropped at the man's side and felt his wrist for a pulse. To his relief, he found one.

A moment later, the helmsman's eyes fluttered open. It took a bit longer for them to focus and find the captain.

"Sir?" he said haltingly, wondering at the wind, which was diminishing with each passing moment.

Kirk rocked back on his heels, relieved. "You gave me quite a scare there, Lieutenant. I thought you were dead."

With an effort, Kelso raised himself off the deck. "Don't worry," he breathed, his attention drawn to the closing doors. "It takes more than a superman to kill *me,* sir."

The captain smiled. "It certainly seems that way."

Then, as the doors finally met and the stormwind stopped, Kirk helped the lieutenant up, explained what had happened and guided him in the direction of the nearest turbolift.

Chapter Nineteen

As Kirk helped Kelso inside the lift, he had every intention of taking it down to the computer room. Then he checked the chronometer on his handheld sensor and changed his mind.

"Damn," he said.

"What, sir?" asked Kelso.

The captain frowned. "We're not going to the computer room, Lieutenant. There's no time."

Kelso nodded. "If you say so, sir."

As the doors closed behind them with a hiss of air, Kirk punched in their destination. "You know what this means?" he asked, as the lift motors began to skirl with increasing intensity.

"I think I do," said the helmsman. "It'll just be the two of us."

"That's right," the captain told him. "And we don't know how many of the M'tachtar we'll be facing up there. But if we can't take back the bridge, we can't contact Kang."

Kelso took in the information, though it was nothing he hadn't heard before. Then he did something unexpected. He smiled.

"Piece of cake," he said.

Kirk had to smile, too. "Piece of cake," he replied.

But just in case, he set his disruptor pistol on a kill setting, and made sure his lieutenant did the same. The captain hated the idea of spilling blood—but there were Federation lives at stake here, not to mention the survival of his ship. As one of his professors back at the Academy would have said, it was "crunch time."

In a matter of seconds, the lift slowed and the motor cycled down. Kirk raised his disruptor and glanced at Kelso. The helmsman lifted his own weapon and glanced back.

"Here goes nothing," he said.

The captain grunted. "That's as good a battle cry as any, Lieutenant."

Then the doors slid apart and a Klingon came flying at him.

Staggering backward under the weight of the M'tachtar, Kirk pulled his weapon free and started to bring it down on his adversary's head. But before he could do so, the Klingon slumped to the floor of the lift.

The captain looked at him, more than a little surprised. Then he gazed out at his bridge. Spock, Phelana, Alden, and Kyle gazed back at him, their disruptors pointed in his direction.

"I am pleased to see you are unharmed," said the

Vulcan, as if nothing out of the ordinary had taken place.

"Likewise," Kirk responded.

He paused to make sure Kelso was placing an incapacitor behind the M'tachtar's ear. Then he moved out of the turbolift and surveyed the area. He didn't have to go far to see another strapping Klingon sprawled at the base of his center seat.

Spock, meanwhile, had slid over to his science station and was working diligently. The captain glanced at the chronometer on his sensor device and joined him.

"We haven't got much time," said Kirk. In fact, they had less than thirty seconds before they missed Kang's deadline.

"I am aware of that," the Vulcan replied, concentrating on his monitors.

The captain expected to see Spock tapping in the ship's command codes. But he was doing something else instead.

"Commander," said Kirk, "you'll need to—"

"There is no time to input the command codes," the first officer explained, refusing to become distracted. "As an alternative, I am routing emergency power to the communications system." He tapped in a final set of instructions, then looked up. "There."

The captain didn't ask how Spock had routed emergency power to the communications system—he had a feeling the explanation would have taken more time than they possessed. Instead, he hurried over to the communications station, where Alden was already opening a channel to Kang's vessel.

Kirk accepted the headset from the communications officer and held it to his mouth. "This is Captain Kirk," he said quickly, "on the bridge of the *Enterprise.* We've done it, Kang. We've taken the ship back."

There was no response. The captain looked at Alden.

"The channel's open," the lieutenant assured him, running a frantic diagnostic to confirm it. Then, again, he said, "Yes, sir, it's open."

Kirk glanced at the chronometer on his sensor. It gave them ten seconds, no more than that.

"This is Captain Kirk," he said again.

Eight seconds.

"We've taken the ship back," he barked.

Six seconds.

"Dammit, Kang, answer me!"

Four seconds. Three.

"Kang!" he bellowed.

Two. One . . .

The captain braced himself for the Klingon vessel's barrage . . . but to his surprise, nothing happened. Then a deep, by then familiar voice rang out imperiously across the bridge.

"You don't have to shout," said Kang. "I heard you."

Kirk cursed under his breath. "Then why didn't you answer?"

"I don't suppose I felt the same urgency you did," the Klingon replied casually. "Besides, having given the matter some thought, I'd decided I wasn't so eager to destroy your vessel after all."

The captain shared a skeptical look with Alden. "Oh no?" he responded. "And why would that be?"

"It is a matter of honor," said Kang. "No matter what the M'tachtar have done, they are Klingons—and formidable Klingons at that. A warrior hates to destroy a worthy opponent without first looking into his eyes."

Kirk frowned. "I see."

"As for you," the Klingon went on, "I've already looked into your eyes. As a result, your death would not have pained me in the least."

"It warms my heart to know that," said the captain. "In fact, life would be complete if you told me you'd received those of my crewmen the M'tachtar were holding in my cargo bays."

"I have," Kang confirmed. "Every last one of them, I'm told. And now, they are being held in *my* cargo bays."

At least they were safe, Kirk told himself. "It seems we have a few logistical details to work out."

"So it does," the Klingon agreed.

He spent a minute coordinating those details with Kang—the rounding up of the M'tachtar they had incapacitated, the recovery of Gary and the crewmen who had escaped with him and, finally, the rescue of those they had left behind on the prison planet.

"I think that about covers it," Kirk said.

"So it does," said the Klingon. And he signed off.

The captain took a breath, then turned to Spock. "You know, we missed you in the computer room, Commander."

The Vulcan's brow creased in response. "It did not seem prudent to remain in that location with time running out on our deadline, sir. However," he said, "if you feel I disobeyed your orders without cause, I will not resist an inquiry as to the—"

Kirk held up his hand. "Easy, man. That was a joke, Spock. A joke."

The first officer regarded him for a moment. Then he said in a flat, noncommittal voice, "I will take your word for it, sir."

Captain's log, supplemental.

Once again, the Enterprise *is operational. What's more, I have recovered all the crewmen Commander Mitchell beamed over to the Klingon vessel—including the commander himself—and dispatched the worst injured among them to sickbay. Dr. Piper tells me they will all recover—making crewmen Corbet and Swift the only fatalities of the M'tachtar occupation. My next concern is the half of my crew that was stranded on the prison planet. But before I can retrieve them as well, there's another matter that needs to be taken care of—and that's the fate of the surviving M'tachtar.*

Kirk, his chief engineer, and his security personnel didn't have to wait long before Kang joined them in the *Enterprise*'s briefing room—accompanied by four security officers of his own.

Looking around, the Klingon made a derisive sound. "So much wasted space," he said. "If I had this much room at my disposal, I would have filled it with additional armaments."

The captain smiled politely. "Have a seat, Commander. We can discuss the layout of the place some other time."

Kang's eyes narrowed, but he sat. His men didn't, however. They stood at the corners of the room, their hands on their blades—since they had been forced to beam over without their disruptors.

Kirk glanced at Scotty, who was the only senior officer Piper hadn't demanded to see in sickbay. "I think we're ready to begin," he said.

"Indeed," the engineer responded.

The captain gestured to one of his security officers, who left the room for a moment. When he came back, his phaser drawn, he was accompanied by a M'tachtar female with high, bony cheekbones and a long, thick braid running down her back.

Her name, Kirk knew, was Molta. And according to what she had told him earlier, she spoke for all the enhanced Klingons.

As she took up a position at one end of the room, Molta didn't look at anyone. She stared straight ahead, her eyes dark and dangerous looking under her distinctive brow ridge.

"You wanted to speak with us?" Kirk asked.

"I did," she confirmed, her voice echoing in the confined space of the briefing room. "I wish to present you with a request."

Kang made a sound of disgust. "You are the vanquished. You dare to make requests of your conquerors?"

The M'tachtar's eyes slid in Kang's direction and fixed on him. "I am a Klingon," she snapped. "I dare anything."

The remark seemed to catch Kang off-guard. He leaned back in his chair, new respect showing in his expression. "Go ahead," he told Molta in a more reasonable voice. "We are listening."

The M'tachtar frowned. "As you say, Commander, we are the vanquished. But among warriors, even the vanquished have rights. For instance, the right to choose the manner in which they may die."

Kirk shook his head. "No one said you were going to die."

Molta turned to him, her lip curled with restrained anger. "We have already died—and not just once, but many times. Every morning when we woke between your forcefields, caged like animals . . . every night, when we went to sleep hoping to dream of a quick end in battle . . . those were deaths, human. You may not understand the Klingon heart, but those were deaths."

The captain looked at her. "I understand that you don't want to return to the prison world. But the alternative—"

"Is to return to Qo'noS," the M'tachtar said, finishing his thought for him. "We are aware of that. What's more, we welcome it."

Kang stroked his bearded chin. "Do you understand what will happen to you on Qo'noS? Do you appreciate what the emperor's position must be?"

Molta nodded. "He will have us executed as an example to all who might consider defying him. We will die for who we are and what we have done. And in the end, we will join Kahless the Unforgettable and the heroes who attend him in Sto-Vo-Kor."

Kirk sighed. He didn't like the idea of letting the M'tachtar return to the Empire. But then, it wasn't his place as a Starfleet officer to steer the destinies of other beings—only to make sure that they saw clearly where they were going.

"This is what you want?" he asked Molta. "To perish at the hands of your fellow Klingons?"

The M'tachtar nodded, steadfast. "This is what we want."

Kang grunted approvingly and leaned forward. "Then that is what you shall have, Molta of the M'tachtar."

For a moment, the captain thought the woman was going to smile—but she didn't. Instead, she headed for the door. When it slid open for her, Molta left the briefing room without another word, a security guard falling in quickly behind her.

Then the door whispered closed again. Kirk looked at Kang. "Do you think there's any hope for them?"

The Klingon frowned. "You mean in Sto-Vo-Kor?"

"I mean in this world," the captain told him.

Kang considered the question for a moment. "No," he replied at last. "They will die. It is a certainty. And yet . . ."

Kirk looked at him. "And yet what?"

The Klingon shrugged. "There is much in them that can be admired. Perhaps someday the technology that made them can be modulated. And then . . ." His eyes seemed to glaze over.

"And then?" the captain prodded.

Roused from his reverie, Kang shook his head. "Never mind."

But Kirk had an idea where the commander's thoughts were wending. In his next report, he would tell Starfleet Command not to be too surprised if it encountered a stronger, more aggressive breed of Klingon somewhere in the not so distant future.

"Then that's it," said the captain, leaning back in his chair. "We'll gather the surviving M'tachtar and transport them to your vessel as soon as you're ready for them."

Kang turned to him. "And, no doubt, you'll breathe easier when you've gotten rid of them."

"Maybe a little," Kirk replied.

"Honesty, from a human?" asked his guest.

"Always," he said. "Whether you choose to believe it or not."

The Klingon regarded him. "If any other Starfleet captain told me that, I would laugh in his face."

"And in my case?" asked Kirk.

Kang bared his teeth. "I will laugh later, when I speak of it with my comrades over a goblet of bloodwine."

The captain took that as a sign of respect, if not friendship. "You know," he said, "the possibility exists that we'll meet again someday. And if we do, we'll no longer be allies."

"I did not expect that we would be," the Klingon replied. "My people and yours will never be allies."

Kirk shrugged. "Not for more than a day, at any rate."

Kang made a sound of assent. Then he signaled to

his guards, got up, and departed from the briefing room. Like Molta, he received an escort of armed security officers.

The captain watched the Klingon go, then glanced at Scotty. "Nicest coldhearted conqueror I ever met."

The engineer scowled. "Aye, sir. Ye can say that again."

Chapter Twenty

CAPTAIN KIRK looked down at Admiral Mangione, who was resting comfortably on her biobed, not far from the beds of her friends Tarsch, Brown, and Rodianos. "Then you've got everything you need, ma'am?"

"For the moment," Mangione told him, her voice a good deal stronger than Kirk might have expected. "You picked up the rest of your crew, I see."

"Yes," he said. "And none too soon, Admiral. They were beginning to get a bit too comfortable with all that downtime."

Mangione chuckled softly. Then her expression turned thoughtful. "So, Captain. Now you know."

Kirk nodded, understanding exactly what she meant. "At long last, Admiral."

"You know," she said, "you're still under orders

not to speak of this to anyone until Starfleet tells you otherwise."

"I understand," the captain told her.

Funny thing, he reflected. *Now that I know the truth, I almost wish I didn't—considering it cost me the lives of two of my crewmen. And the thought of sending the M'tachtar off to their deaths . . . that'll haunt me for a long time to come.*

"I guess I'll leave you to your rest now," said Kirk.

Mangione grunted. "In other words, you've got some other patients you want to visit." She smiled. "Go ahead, Captain. I'll keep."

Kirk smiled as well. "See you later," he told the admiral.

Then he went to check up on Spock, whose bed was on the other side of sickbay. As he approached, he glanced at his first officer's vital signs, which were displayed on the monitor hanging over Spock's head.

I'm impressed, the captain thought. He had never been to medical school, but he was certain no human could have endured what the Vulcan had endured and remained in that kind of shape.

Spock, who had been studying a monograph on a tensor arm, discontinued library access and pushed away the screen when he saw Kirk coming. "Captain," said the first officer, acknowledging his superior.

Kirk looked at him. "How do you feel, Mr. Spock?"

The Vulcan didn't hesitate. "I am fine, sir. As far as I can tell, there is no reason for me not to report for duty."

The captain admired Spock's eagerness, but Piper had insisted on examining everyone—even Kirk, eventually. "Unfortunately, Commander, that's not our decision to make. It's the chief medical officer's."

The Vulcan showed just a hint of disappointment—which for someone like him was an emotional outburst. "Of course," he responded.

Kirk forged ahead with the reason for his visit. "Mr. Spock, I have an apology to make."

The first officer cocked an eyebrow. "An apology, sir?"

The captain nodded. "For the last several months, I haven't made you feel at home here. I haven't treated you with the respect due an executive officer. But you can be certain that's not going to continue."

Spock regarded him with equanimity. "I see," he said.

"Clearly," Kirk continued, "you're a valuable resource and a hell of an officer, and I'd be crazy not to take advantage of those qualities at every opportunity." He paused. "You understand what I'm saying, don't you?"

The Vulcan looked at him for a moment. Then he shook his head. "No, sir. I do not believe I have the slightest idea."

The captain frowned. "You asked for a transfer, Commander. I'm hoping you'll rescind that request and stay here on the *Enterprise.*" He shrugged. "Where you belong."

Spock considered Kirk's words for what seemed like a long time. Then he said, "In that case, I will stay."

Unexpectedly, the captain felt himself break into a grin. "Good. I mean, I'm happy to hear you say that, Commander. I mean . . . well, never mind what I mean. I'll see you later."

The Vulcan nodded. "Aye, sir. Later, as you say."

Leaving Spock behind, Kirk crossed sickbay again and made his last scheduled stop—his friend Gary's bed. Of course, the navigator wasn't in half the shape the Vulcan was in, but he was still doing fine.

"Captain Kirk," said Gary. "As I live and barely breathe."

The captain scowled. "Seems to me we did this already. You in the biobed, me coming to make sure you were still alive."

The navigator pretended to think about it. "Now that you mention it, it does seem familiar. Except last time, as I recall, I saved your life. And this time . . ."

Kirk held a hand up. "Let's just say we're even."

Gary's eyes widened. "Even? Not by a long shot. According to my records, I've saved your life seventeen more times than you've saved mine. So if I were you, I wouldn't be resting on my laurels anytime soon."

"I wouldn't dream of it," the captain told him.

"Although," the navigator went on, "I will admit you did a pretty good job on those M'tachtar—even without your lucky rabbit's foot."

Kirk nodded, poker faced. "I guess I can make a few decisions on my own when I absolutely have to."

Gary smiled. "I guess Resourceful is your middle name."

"No," said the captain, recalling their old, private joke. "That's Racquetball. Or is it Rhino?"

The navigator shrugged. "I forget."

"So do I," said Kirk.

They were silent for a moment. And neither of them had ever been uncomfortable with that kind of silence.

"Well," said the captain, "I ought to get back to the bridge—before Dr. Piper grabs me and puts me on a biobed of my own. I'll see you when you're cleared for duty."

"If I'm cleared for duty," his friend returned. "I'm starting to like it here. I mean, I get to see more of Nurse Hinch." And he winked.

Kirk shook his head. "You never learn, do you?"

"Never," Gary told him.

Sighing, the captain took his leave of the navigator and headed for the exit doors. But as soon as they parted for him, he saw Phelana out in the corridor. Apparently, she had been called down for a physical as well.

"Commander Yudrin," he said.

"Captain." She inclined her head slightly, her antennae curled forward. Then she gazed at him with her big, black eyes.

"On your way to sickbay?" he asked innocently.

The Andorian nodded. "Unfortunately, yes."

"You know," Kirk said, "it'll be a few days before we reach the nearest starbase. When you're finally emancipated by Dr. Piper maybe we can catch up on old times."

Phelana thought for a moment. Then she shook

her head. "I don't think so, Captain. I'm trying to put one particular old time behind me."

He looked at her, caught off-balance. "Oh?"

"Yes," she said. "A time on a rooftop when I was just a cadet." Her eyes brightened. "On the other hand, I'd love to discuss something else with you—say, over dinner."

Kirk smiled. "And what is it, exactly, that you'd like to discuss?"

The Andorian smiled back at him. "New times." Then she entered sickbay and left him standing there in the corridor.

He sighed. Sometimes, it seemed, people *could* put their past behind them . . .

Chapter Twenty-one

As the memory faded, the captain heard the rain pattering with renewed intensity on the Mitchells' window. Gary's parents were waiting for him to say something, looking more concerned than ever.

The captain swallowed painfully, his throat dry as dust. He hated himself for shying away from his duty to these people. He was here to tell the Mitchells what they had a right to know, not to torture them even more than they had been tortured already.

Finally, he said it. "I killed your son."

Gary's parents stared at him, their expressions unchanged except for a little confusion around their eyes. "I beg your pardon?" Mr. Mitchell replied at last.

Kirk took a breath, then let it out slowly. "I killed your son," he repeated at last, finding it didn't come out any easier the second time than the first. "I killed Gary."

Mr. Mitchell chuckled uncomfortably and said, "What the devil are you talking about? Gary knew what he was getting into when he entered the Academy . . . when he joined the Fleet."

His throat constricting, the captain shook his head. "That's not what I mean," he told the Mitchells. "I mean I killed him. I . . ." He searched desperately for words. "Gary died by my hands."

This time, the Mitchells waited a little longer before they responded. "I don't understand," Gary's mother said softly.

Mr. Mitchell shook his head. "Me, either."

Kirk licked his lips. "We came across an energy barrier in space. It affected Gary . . . changed him into some kind of . . ." He pulled up short of calling his friend a monster. "It made him powerful beyond belief. He could absorb information at a fantastic rate, read people's minds . . . even manipulate objects over long distances."

The Mitchells didn't say anything in response. They just gaped, trying to get a handle on what he was telling them.

"And then, little by little," the captain told them, "he changed in other ways as well. He became aloof, arrogant, cruel . . . the very antithesis of the Gary we all knew. As much as I denied it at first, he became a danger to the *Enterprise* and her crew. So I sedated him and took him to a distant planetoid, where I planned to . . ." Even thinking it made him feel ashamed. "Where I planned to abandon him."

"My god," breathed Mrs. Mitchell. Her husband's forehead creased, but he kept his silence.

Kirk looked down at his hands. "It didn't work. He murdered one of my men and got out of the cell we put him in. I went after him with a phaser rifle, hoping I could put an end to him before he killed anyone else."

He could have told them about Dehner and the way she and Gary had exchanged energy blasts. He could have told them about the grave Gary had dug for his friend and the boulder he had loosened from the cliff face. But at that point, the details didn't seem to matter very much.

"He was much stronger than I was," the captain noted, "but I saw an opportunity and I took advantage of it." He looked up. "In the end, I was lucky—and he wasn't."

Outside the room, rain drummed on the window some more and thunder mumbled something unintelligible. The Mitchells looked dazed and pale, Gary's mother more than his father.

Then, with shocking quickness, her expression changed into something hard and hateful. "You killed my boy!" she moaned, reddening with anger and resentment. "You killed my Gary!"

Mr. Mitchell put his hand on his wife's hands. "Easy, Dana."

Gary's mother shook her head from side to side, her red-rimmed eyes fixed on Kirk. "Gary trusted you," she sobbed, her voice rising in pitch with each accusatory word. "He thought you were his friend. And you found it in your heart to kill him?"

The captain wanted very much to get out of that place. He would have given anything to escape Mrs. Mitchell's withering glare. But he stayed where he was and endured whatever he had to endure—because, in the final analysis, everything Gary's mother was telling him was true.

His friend had trusted him, and he had betrayed that trust. Of course, he hadn't had a choice in the matter, but that didn't change anything. He had murdered Gary and now he was paying the penalty for it.

"I don't know what to say," he rasped.

"Yes, you do," Mr. Mitchell told him.

Kirk regarded him. "Sir, I—"

"You know what to say," the man insisted grimly. He turned to his wife. "You say that you *were* Gary's friend, despite everything. And you say that if you killed him, it wasn't because you wanted to. It was because there was nothing else you could do."

Gary's mother brought her hands up to her face and buried it in them, and shook as she let out a sorrow she hadn't even known was inside her. Her husband ran his hand over her back and watched her sadly.

"And you say something else," he told the captain, his voice little more than a whisper now. "You say you loved Gary so much, you couldn't disgrace his memory by telling a lie about him. You loved him so much you had to come here and tell us the truth about our boy."

Kirk saw Mr. Mitchell's lip begin to tremble, and he found himself going over to the man to put his arm around him. But before he could get there, Gary's mother got up and intercepted him and cried in his arms.

"I'm sorry," she said, wetting his uniform with her tears. "I'm so sorry, Jim. Can you ever forgive me?"

The captain stroked her hair. Could *he* forgive *her?* he wondered in amazement.

"It's all right," he said, swallowing back tears of his own as he gazed gratefully at Gary's father.

Mr. Mitchell was still sitting on the couch, his eyes as red rimmed as his wife's now. But he was smiling.

And the rain washed the windows with its fury, for the rest of the night and all the way to morning.

On the planet Heir'tzan, his bare feet cold on the pink marble below them, Perris Nodarh sighed deeply. The sound seemed to whisper through the Eastern Temple's cavernous primary chamber, disturbing the rintzalaya birds that had gathered on the ledges beneath the chamber's vaulted ceilings.

Perris's attendant, who had been dressing him in a new white robe with blue trim, looked up at the telepath. "Is something wrong, Honored One?"

Perris gazed at the bright yellow eyes and scaly bronze skin of the attendant, who was too young to have waited on him the first time the telepath donned such a robe. Then he nodded.

"Something is wrong," Perris confirmed.

"With your garment?" the attendant asked, concern etched in his face. Then the concern deepened. "Or with you, perhaps?"

It was a valid question. After all, the telepath was

getting on in years. He had not been young the first time he walked from the temple to the government center, and that had been fourteen years ago.

"I am fine," Perris told his attendant. "In body, at least. But I must admit, my spirit is in some discomfort."

The youth shook his head. "I don't understand."

The telepath smiled. "I received news this morning from a starship. Gary Mitchell perished on a distant world."

His attendant's brow creased as if with pain. "The Mitchell . . . dead?" He shook his head, bewildered. "But how could he . . . ?"

"Die?" said Perris, finishing the youth's question. He remembered his human friend and savior, and shrugged. "We all die, Ataan. And the Mitchell led a dangerous life, always pitting himself against great terrors—just as he did here on Heir'tzan."

He glanced at the western wall of the chamber, where some of the greatest events in Heiren history were depicted in a great mural. His eye naturally went to the vignette in which the Mitchell and the Kirk were shown battling festively-robed terrorists.

Had the Starfleet cadets not put their lives on the line, the telepath would never have reached the Eastern Temple and there would have been no Great Reconciliation. And this day, when all Heiren celebrated the reunion of their species, would never have come to pass.

His attendant swallowed. "I did not know, Honored One."

Perris smiled down at him. "Only a very few of us have been made aware of the Mitchell's passing,

Ataan—myself, the other Honored One, Primary Minister Lenna . . . and now you." He gazed at the arched entrance to the chamber, from which he would issue in a few minutes, re-enacting his historic journey to the Government House. "Though soon," he went on, "everyone will know. After all, the Mitchell belongs to all of us."

And so he did. But the telepath, who owed the human his life, would mourn him more than any other, he thought.

Seeing that his attendant was still distraught, Perris put a hand on the young man's shoulder. "Come, Ataan. Finish your work. The Mitchell once went to great lengths to see this ceremony happen on time. I do not think he would want to see it delayed now."

The attendant smiled at him. "As you say, Honored One."

And under the telepath's kindly but watchful eye, the youth went on with his ministrations.

The day of Gary's funeral, the sun shone and the air smelled freshly washed. The rain of the night before was just a dream. Or at least, that was the way it felt to Kirk as he arrived at the simple, sandstone chapel where the service would be held.

The captain had walked the dozen or so blocks from his lodgings, figuring it was silly to call for a taxi to go such a short distance in such beautiful, crisp autumn weather. But that wasn't his only reason for proceeding on foot. He had also needed the walk to settle himself inside.

Halfway up the chapel steps, he heard the call of a

familiar voice. Turning, he saw McCoy hastening to catch up with him.

"Dammit, Jim," said his friend. "It's not a race. Slow down, for pete sakes."

Kirk smiled. "Good to see you, Bones."

The doctor looked at him. "So? Did you . . . ?"

"Tell the Mitchells?" the captain finished for him. He nodded. "I did."

McCoy frowned. "And?"

"And we're all right," Kirk told him. "All of us."

The doctor grinned a sincere grin. "Well, that's great, Jim. Really great. I'll bet you feel worlds better now."

"Worlds," said the captain.

Suddenly, McCoy seemed to realize that something was missing. "Say, where's your cast?" he inquired.

Kirk shrugged. "I didn't feel like I had to wear it anymore. And don't tell me it's too soon to take it off."

"Who, me?" the doctor exclaimed. "I'm the last one to advise anyone to carry any extra baggage." He tilted his head in the direction of the arched chapel entrance. "Shall we?"

The captain eyed the entranceway. "I guess so," he replied.

Then Kirk and McCoy walked up the last few steps together and went inside. And if the captain was a little nervous at what awaited him there, it was nothing compared to how nervous he would have felt if he hadn't made his confession to Gary's parents.

Then he got a look at the large, well-lit interior of

the place, and a sight met his eyes for which he hadn't been the least bit prepared. He clutched the doctor's arm and said "My god."

McCoy took in the same sight and smiled. "How about that."

The chapel was packed with people from wall to wall—not just with friends and relatives of the deceased, though there seemed to be plenty of them as well, but also with a small army of Starfleet officers and crewmen wearing the green or red or blue of their dress uniforms.

"Hey, look," said the doctor. "It's Miyko Tarsch . . . from Starfleet Medical. I didn't know he and Gary had even met."

Kirk followed McCoy's gaze and saw the Vobilite. "Yes," he replied. "We served with him on the *Republic.*"

Then he realized that Tarsch wasn't the only *Republic* officer in attendance. Captain Bannock, the ship's retired commander, was present as well—his eyes as steely as ever, his leathery visage marked by an undiminished air of authority.

So was Jord Gorfinkel, Bannock's science officer, his curly brown hair gone mostly gray. And jovial chief engineer Hogan Brown. And Commander Rodianos, barrel chested and olive skinned.

And Admiral Mangione, who had served on the *Republic* as first officer. She was there to see Gary off, too.

Nor did the list end there. Kirk saw Mark Piper seated along with Lieutenant Alden, Nurse Chapel and Yeoman Smith, not far from Scotty, Sulu and Stiles. And a group from the *Constitution* was a few rows behind them—a group that included Captain Augenthaler, Commander Hirota, Dr. Velasquez, Lieutenant Borrik, and even security chief Gaynor.

McCoy leaned closer to him. "Do you know all these people? The Starfleet types, I mean?"

Swallowing back an unwelcome flood of emotion, the captain nodded. "I know them, all right." He knew something else, too—that some of them were there for him as much as they were for Gary. They had come to pay their respects because the deceased was his best friend.

But that didn't make their coming any less touching, and it didn't make their numbers any less impressive. What's more, Gary wouldn't have cared why they had come—he simply would have marveled that they were there.

"Sir?" said a voice from behind him.

Kirk turned and saw the biggest surprise of all.

"Mr. Spock?" he said wonderingly.

The Vulcan showed no more emotion than usual. "I trust I am in time for the ceremony," he responded.

"Very much in time," the captain assured him.

Spock cocked an eyebrow. "You looked surprised," he observed.

"I . . ." Kirk shrugged. "I didn't think you went in much for funeral services. I mean, back on the ship—"

"On the ship," said the Vulcan, "it was necessary for someone to man the bridge. With the *Enterprise* in Earth orbit, it is no longer incumbent on me to perform that duty."

"I see," the captain replied. "Thank you for

clarifying that." He turned to his companion. "Dr. McCoy, this is Mr. Spock, my first officer."

The doctor extended his hand. "Good to meet you, Mr. Spock."

The Vulcan considered McCoy's hand for a moment, then looked up. "My people try to avoid physical contact."

The doctor frowned and withdrew his hand. "Sorry about that," he told Spock. "I'm a doctor, not a diplomat."

The Vulcan nodded. "I can see that."

McCoy looked at him askance. "And what's that supposed to mean?"

"Your uniform," Spock expanded, "is one that clearly represents the sciences. No one in Starfleet would mistake it for that of an individual in the diplomatic corps."

"Ah," said the doctor. "Of course."

But he didn't seem to quite accept the explanation. What's more, thought Kirk, the first officer had had an edge in his voice that he didn't think he had ever heard there before.

Clearly, there was an interesting interpersonal dynamic going on here. He couldn't wait to see how it developed now that McCoy had agreed to take over as chief medical officer.

In fact, the captain was tempted to inform Spock of that fact then and there. And he might have done it if another old friend hadn't chosen that moment to join them.

"Hello, James," said a blue-skinned Andorian beauty in commander's garb, her antennae bent all the way forward.

Kirk smiled at her, beset suddenly by memories both pleasant and not so pleasant. "Phelana."

The woman leaned forward and kissed him on the cheek. "I'm sorry about Gary," she told him. "I'm going to miss him a lot. I don't think I've ever met anyone quite like him."

"I know what you mean," the captain said.

Phelana looked at him, her eyes black and ever so willing to share his grief. "At least he died a hero. We can all be proud of that."

Unfortunately, Kirk couldn't tell her the truth about Gary's death—not when the official record failed to mention the kind of being he had become, or how he had murdered Lee Kelso in cold blood, or how close he had come to taking over the *Enterprise*.

Gary hadn't liked the idea of keeping secrets from anyone—and the captain didn't either. But in this case, he didn't really have a choice.

Then he saw the Mitchells beckoning to him from the front of the chapel, and he had to excuse himself. Making his way to the first row, he sat down beside Gary's mother, who squeezed his hand.

"It's a pretty big turnout," said Mr. Mitchell.

"Bigger than I expected," said Gary's mother, who looked a little overwhelmed by it.

"Gary had a lot of friends," Kirk noted.

"They must have come from pretty far away," Mr. Mitchell observed.

"That they did," said the captain.

Then the service got underway. Gary's parents ascended to the podium and stood behind a handsome wooden lectern and thanked everyone for coming. They said they would miss their son, but it was good to see that he lived on in the lives of so many other people.

After all, they pointed out, some people live longer than others. But a person's life should be measured not in years, but in the ways it affects others—and by that standard, they told the assembled mourners, Gary's life was as full as anyone's.

Then they asked everyone to listen to what their son's friend had to say about him because Jim Kirk knew Gary better than anyone. And as they left the podium, the captain climbed its steps in the opposite direction.

For a moment, as they passed one another, his eyes met the Mitchells' and found reassurance in them. Go ahead, they seemed to say. Speak from your heart, son, and everything will be all right.

It was good advice, he thought.

Taking his place behind the wooden lectern, Kirk looked out over the sea of people. They waited patiently for him to begin, no doubt sympathizing with how hard it had to be for him.

But for the captain, the hardest part was over, and had been since late the night before. All he had to do now was send his friend off in style.

"Let me tell you about Gary Mitchell," he began.

Spock seemed to sit up a little straighter in his seat. Lieutenant Borrik and Commander Rodianos appeared to do the same.

"Gary Mitchell," he told them, "was a magician. Whether you loved the guy or hated him, you couldn't argue with that. He could take a quiet rec lounge and stir it up with laughter in no time. There was no feeling down when you were with Gary. It just wasn't allowed. Every day, every minute, you had to be as full of life as he was."

In the audience, Scotty nodded in agreement. So did Phelana and Captain Bannock and Dr. Velasquez.

"Let me tell you about Gary Mitchell," the captain continued. "Gary Mitchell was a man of remarkable courage. He saved my life a dozen times . . . though if you asked him about it, he probably would have told you it was twenty or thirty."

That got a ripple of laughter. And from Hogan Brown, a great, broad smile of approval.

"But if you really want to know how brave he was," said Kirk, "you should ask his adversaries. If they were here today, they would tell you he was the most dangerous foe they ever butted heads with. And why would that be? Because Gary didn't know when to give up. He didn't know . . . or maybe just couldn't accept . . . that there was anything in the universe that could beat him if he tried hard enough."

Judging by her expression, Admiral Mangione seemed to agree with that. The same went for Dr. Piper and Yeoman Smith and Chief Gaynor.

"Let me tell you about Gary Mitchell," the captain went on. "Gary Mitchell was a teacher . . . not in terms of cold, classroom facts, but in terms of what he was able to teach us about ourselves. I can tell you that he taught me a few things. He taught me to act on my instincts instead of going by the book all the time. He taught me how important it was to make the tough decisions, the decisions no one else wants to make."

He looked at Gary's parents, who must have known what that last part meant. They were looking back at him with pride as well as sadness.

"At times," Kirk continued, "I felt like I was a project of Gary's as much as his colleague, a lump of clay in the hands of a talented sculptor. And because of what he gave me, he'll always be a part of me."

Sulu smiled at that. Augenthaler and Hirota, too.

"Let me tell you about Gary Mitchell," the captain sighed, playing the refrain one last time. He raised his chin, swallowed back his grief, and made the point he had really come there to make—what, in the end, Gary would have wanted most to hear.

"Gary Mitchell," he said, "was my friend."

Look for STAR TREK Fiction from Pocket Books

Star Trek®: The Original Series

Star Trek: The Motion Picture • Gene Roddenberry
Star Trek II: The Wrath of Khan • Vonda N. McIntyre
Star Trek III: The Search for Spock • Vonda N. McIntyre
Star Trek IV: The Voyage Home • Vonda N. McIntyre
Star Trek V: The Final Frontier • J. M. Dillard
Star Trek VI: The Undiscovered Country • J. M. Dillard
Star Trek VII: Generations • J. M. Dillard
Star Trek VIII: First Contact • J. M. Dillard
Star Trek IX: Insurrection • J. M. Dillard
Enterprise: The First Adventure • Vonda N. McIntyre
Final Frontier • Diane Carey
Strangers from the Sky • Margaret Wander Bonanno
Spock's World • Diane Duane
The Lost Years • J. M. Dillard
Probe • Margaret Wander Bonanno
Prime Directive • Judith and Garfield Reeves-Stevens
Best Destiny • Diane Carey
Shadows on the Sun • Michael Jan Friedman
Sarek • A. C. Crispin
Federation • Judith and Garfield Reeves-Stevens
The Ashes of Eden • William Shatner & Judith and Garfield Reeves-Stevens
The Return • William Shatner & Judith and Garfield Reeves-Stevens
Star Trek: Starfleet Academy • Diane Carey
Vulcan's Forge • Josepha Sherman and Susan Shwartz
Avenger • William Shatner & Judith and Garfield Reeves-Stevens
Star Trek: Odyssey • William Shatner & Judith and Garfield Reeves-Stevens

#1 *Star Trek: The Motion Picture* • Gene Roddenberry
#2 *The Entropy Effect* • Vonda N. McIntyre
#3 *The Klingon Gambit* • Robert E. Vardeman
#4 *The Covenant of the Crown* • Howard Weinstein
#5 *The Prometheus Design* • Sondra Marshak & Myrna Culbreath
#6 *The Abode of Life* • Lee Correy
#7 *Star Trek II: The Wrath of Khan* • Vonda N. McIntyre

#8 *Black Fire* • Sonni Cooper
#9 *Triangle* • Sondra Marshak & Myrna Culbreath
#10 *Web of the Romulans* • M. S. Murdock
#11 *Yesterday's Son* • A. C. Crispin
#12 *Mutiny on the Enterprise* • Robert E. Vardeman
#13 *The Wounded Sky* • Diane Duane
#14 *The Trellisane Confrontation* • David Dvorkin
#15 *Corona* • Greg Bear
#16 *The Final Reflection* • John M. Ford
#17 *Star Trek III: The Search for Spock* • Vonda N. McIntyre
#18 *My Enemy, My Ally* • Diane Duane
#19 *The Tears of the Singers* • Melinda Snodgrass
#20 *The Vulcan Academy Murders* • Jean Lorrah
#21 *Uhura's Song* • Janet Kagan
#22 *Shadow Lord* • Laurence Yep
#23 *Ishmael* • Barbara Hambly
#24 *Killing Time* • Della Van Hise
#25 *Dwellers in the Crucible* • Margaret Wander Bonanno
#26 *Pawns and Symbols* • Majiliss Larson
#27 *Mindshadow* • J. M. Dillard
#28 *Crisis on Centaurus* • Brad Ferguson
#29 *Dreadnought!* • Diane Carey
#30 *Demons* • J. M. Dillard
#31 *Battlestations!* • Diane Carey
#32 *Chain of Attack* • Gene DeWeese
#33 *Deep Domain* • Howard Weinstein
#34 *Dreams of the Raven* • Carmen Carter
#35 *The Romulan Way* • Diane Duane & Peter Morwood
#36 *How Much for Just the Planet?* • John M. Ford
#37 *Bloodthirst* • J. M. Dillard
#38 *The IDIC Epidemic* • Jean Lorrah
#39 *Time for Yesterday* • A. C. Crispin
#40 *Timetrap* • David Dvorkin
#41 *The Three-Minute Universe* • Barbara Paul
#42 *Memory Prime* • Judith and Garfield Reeves-Stevens
#43 *The Final Nexus* • Gene DeWeese
#44 *Vulcan's Glory* • D. C. Fontana
#45 *Double, Double* • Michael Jan Friedman
#46 *The Cry of the Onlies* • Judy Klass
#47 *The Kobayashi Maru* • Julia Ecklar
#48 *Rules of Engagement* • Peter Morwood
#49 *The Pandora Principle* • Carolyn Clowes

#50 *Doctor's Orders* • Diane Duane
#51 *Enemy Unseen* • V. E. Mitchell
#52 *Home Is the Hunter* • Dana Kramer Rolls
#53 *Ghost-Walker* • Barbara Hambly
#54 *A Flag Full of Stars* • Brad Ferguson
#55 *Renegade* • Gene DeWeese
#56 *Legacy* • Michael Jan Friedman
#57 *The Rift* • Peter David
#58 *Faces of Fire* • Michael Jan Friedman
#59 *The Disinherited* • Peter David
#60 *Ice Trap* • L. A. Graf
#61 *Sanctuary* • John Vornholt
#62 *Death Count* • L. A. Graf
#63 *Shell Game* • Melissa Crandall
#64 *The Starship Trap* • Mel Gilden
#65 *Windows on a Lost World* • V. E. Mitchell
#66 *From the Depths* • Victor Milan
#67 *The Great Starship Race* • Diane Carey
#68 *Firestorm* • L. A. Graf
#69 *The Patrian Transgression* • Simon Hawke
#70 *Traitor Winds* • L. A. Graf
#71 *Crossroad* • Barbara Hambly
#72 *The Better Man* • Howard Weinstein
#73 *Recovery* • J. M. Dillard
#74 *The Fearful Summons* • Denny Martin Flynn
#75 *First Frontier* • Diane Carey & Dr. James I. Kirkland
#76 *The Captain's Daughter* • Peter David
#77 *Twilight's End* • Jerry Oltion
#78 *The Rings of Tautee* • Dean W. Smith & Kristine K. Rusch
#79 *Invasion #1: First Strike* • Diane Carey
#80 *The Joy Machine* • James Gunn
#81 *Mudd in Your Eye* • Jerry Oltion
#82 *Mind Meld* • John Vornholt
#83 *Heart of the Sun* • Pamela Sargent & George Zebrowski
#84 *Assignment: Eternity* • Greg Cox

Star Trek: The Next Generation®

Encounter at Farpoint • David Gerrold
Unification • Jeri Taylor
Relics • Michael Jan Friedman
Descent • Diane Carey
All Good Things • Michael Jan Friedman
Star Trek: Klingon • Dean W. Smith & Kristine K. Rusch
Star Trek VII: Generations • J. M. Dillard
Metamorphosis • Jean Lorrah
Vendetta • Peter David
Reunion • Michael Jan Friedman
Imzadi • Peter David
The Devil's Heart • Carmen Carter
Dark Mirror • Diane Duane
Q-Squared • Peter David
Crossover • Michael Jan Friedman
Kahless • Michael Jan Friedman
Star Trek: First Contact • J. M. Dillard
The Best and the Brightest • Susan Wright
Planet X • Michael Jan Friedman

#1 *Ghost Ship* • Diane Carey
#2 *The Peacekeepers* • Gene DeWeese
#3 *The Children of Hamlin* • Carmen Carter
#4 *Survivors* • Jean Lorrah
#5 *Strike Zone* • Peter David
#6 *Power Hungry* • Howard Weinstein
#7 *Masks* • John Vornholt
#8 *The Captains' Honor* • David and Daniel Dvorkin
#9 *A Call to Darkness* • Michael Jan Friedman
#10 *A Rock and a Hard Place* • Peter David
#11 *Gulliver's Fugitives* • Keith Sharee
#12 *Doomsday World* • David, Carter, Friedman & Greenberg
#13 *The Eyes of the Beholders* • A. C. Crispin
#14 *Exiles* • Howard Weinstein
#15 *Fortune's Light* • Michael Jan Friedman
#16 *Contamination* • John Vornholt
#17 *Boogeymen* • Mel Gilden
#18 *Q-in-Law* • Peter David
#19 *Perchance to Dream* • Howard Weinstein

#20 *Spartacus* • T. L. Mancour
#21 *Chains of Command* • W. A. McCay & E. L. Flood
#22 *Imbalance* • V. E. Mitchell
#23 *War Drums* • John Vornholt
#24 *Nightshade* • Laurell K. Hamilton
#25 *Grounded* • David Bischoff
#26 *The Romulan Prize* • Simon Hawke
#27 *Guises of the Mind* • Rebecca Neason
#28 *Here There Be Dragons* • John Peel
#29 *Sins of Commission* • Susan Wright
#30 *Debtors' Planet* • W. R. Thompson
#31 *Foreign Foes* • David Galanter & Greg Brodeur
#32 *Requiem* • Michael Jan Friedman & Kevin Ryan
#33 *Balance of Power* • Dafydd ab Hugh
#34 *Blaze of Glory* • Simon Hawke
#35 *The Romulan Stratagem* • Robert Greenberger
#36 *Into the Nebula* • Gene DeWeese
#37 *The Last Stand* • Brad Ferguson
#38 *Dragon's Honor* • Kij Johnson & Greg Cox
#39 *Rogue Saucer* • John Vornholt
#40 *Possession* • J. M. Dillard & Kathleen O'Malley
#41 *Invasion #2: The Soldiers of Fear* • Dean W. Smith & Kristine K. Rusch
#42 *Infiltrator* • W. R. Thompson
#43 *A Fury Scorned* • Pam Sargent & George Zebrowski
#44 *The Death of Princes* • John Peel
#45 *Intellivore* • Diane Duane
#46 *To Storm Heaven* • Esther Friesner

Q Continuum #1: *Q-Space* • Greg Cox
Q Continuum #2: *Q-Zone* • Greg Cox
Q Continuum #3: *Q-Strike* • Greg Cox

Star Trek: Deep Space Nine®

The Search • Diane Carey
Warped • K. W. Jeter
The Way of the Warrior • Diane Carey
Star Trek: Klingon • Dean W. Smith & Kristine K. Rusch
Trials and Tribble-ations • Diane Carey
Far Beyond the Stars • Steve Barnes
The 34th Rule • Armin Shimerman & David George

#1 *Emissary* • J. M. Dillard
#2 *The Siege* • Peter David
#3 *Bloodletter* • K. W. Jeter
#4 *The Big Game* • Sandy Schofield
#5 *Fallen Heroes* • Dafydd ab Hugh
#6 *Betrayal* • Lois Tilton
#7 *Warchild* • Esther Friesner
#8 *Antimatter* • John Vornholt
#9 *Proud Helios* • Melissa Scott
#10 *Valhalla* • Nathan Archer
#11 *Devil in the Sky* • Greg Cox & John Greggory Betancourt
#12 *The Laertian Gamble* • Robert Sheckley
#13 *Station Rage* • Diane Carey
#14 *The Long Night* • Dean W. Smith & Kristine K. Rusch
#15 *Objective: Bajor* • John Peel
#16 *Invasion #3: Time's Enemy* • L. A. Graf
#17 *The Heart of the Warrior* • John Greggory Betancourt
#18 *Saratoga* • Michael Jan Friedman
#19 *The Tempest* • Susan Wright
#20 *Wrath of the Prophets* • P. David, M. J. Friedman, R. Greenberger
#21 *Trial by Error* • Mark Garland
#22 *Vengeance* • Dafydd ab Hugh

Star Trek®: Voyager™

Flashback • Diane Carey
The Black Shore • Greg Cox
Mosaic • Jeri Taylor

#1 *Caretaker* • L. A. Graf
#2 *The Escape* • Dean W. Smith & Kristine K. Rusch
#3 *Ragnarok* • Nathan Archer
#4 *Violations* • Susan Wright
#5 *Incident at Arbuk* • John Greggory Betancourt
#6 *The Murdered Sun* • Christie Golden
#7 *Ghost of a Chance* • Mark A. Garland & Charles G. McGraw
#8 *Cybersong* • S. N. Lewitt
#9 *Invasion #4: The Final Fury* • Dafydd ab Hugh
#10 *Bless the Beasts* • Karen Haber
#11 *The Garden* • Melissa Scott
#12 *Chrysalis* • David Niall Wilson
#13 *The Black Shore* • Greg Cox
#14 *Marooned* • Christie Golden
#15 *Echoes* • Dean W. Smith & Kristine K. Rusch
#16 *Seven of Nine* • Christie Golden

Star Trek®: New Frontier

#1 *House of Cards* • Peter David
#2 *Into the Void* • Peter David
#3 *The Two-Front War* • Peter David
#4 *End Game* • Peter David
#5 *Martyr* • Peter David
#6 *Fire on High* • Peter David

Star Trek®: Day of Honor

Book One: *Ancient Blood* • Diane Carey
Book Two: *Armageddon Sky* • L. A. Graf
Book Three: *Her Klingon Soul* • Michael Jan Friedman
Book Four: *Treaty's Law* • Dean W. Smith & Kristine K. Rusch

Star Trek®: The Captain's Table

Book One: *War Dragons* • L. A. Graf
Book Two: *Dujonian's Hoard* • Michael Jan Friedman
Book Three: *The Mist* • Dean W. Smith & Kristine K. Rusch
Book Four: *Fire Ship* • Diane Carey
Book Five: *Once Burned* • Peter David
Book Six: *Where Sea Meets Sky* • Jerry Oltion

Star Trek®: The Dominion War

Book 1: *Behind Enemy Lines* • John Vornholt
Book 2: *Call to Arms . . .* • Diane Carey
Book 3: *Tunnel Through the Stars* • John Vornholt
Book 4: *. . . Sacrifice of Angels* • Diane Carey

Star Trek®: My Brother's Keeper

Book One: *Republic* • Michael Jan Friedman
Book Two: *Constitution* • Michael Jan Friedman
Book Three: *Enterprise* • Michael Jan Friedman